The Treasure
of
Pleasant Valley

FRANK YERBY

The Treasure
of
Pleasant Valley

THE DIAL PRESS NEW YORK

The Treasure
of
Pleasant Valley

1

He had this ache in him again—this new ache that rose in him and tore like wild and savage hunger. He had had it a long time now, but he did not know what it was. All he knew was that he had it; and now, finally, the form it took:

I've got to get away, he thought; I've got to go. . . .

He and his brother, David, came out of the sick room where his father lay, and the two of them mounted and rode down to the east section where the Negroes worked, chopping cotton under the sun. They sat on their horses watching the Negroes work, and neither of them said anything—not for a long time.

"Well—" David Harkness said.

"He's going to die," Bruce said flatly.

"Yes," David said.

The Negroes moved down the rows, chopping. And the thing was in Bruce now, stronger than ever. I've got to go—I've got to! Go West. Over the mountain, into the setting sun. Out to California where the gold lies in the stream beds, ready for any man's taking. Gold. He almost laughed aloud as he shaped the word in the darkness of his thought. He wasn't a very complicated man, but he had already gone beyond that. He knew it wasn't gold he was seeking.

"Hell of a thing," David said.

"Pa's old," Bruce said; "still—"

"Still it don't seem right," David finished for him.

"Look, boy—"

"Yes?" Bruce said. "Yes, Davy?"

The ache was very big in him now; the need, the hunger. West to the setting sun. West was where his heart was, and his treasure. He didn't know what his treasure was; but he knew it wasn't gold. What it was, what he was looking for, didn't go into words easily. It was a dark thing that moved before him, getting between him and the light. A fire in him so bright it had the effect of darkness. A hunger that had put the strangeness in him so deep that though he heard and recognized and answered what his brother was saying, he did so with only part of his mind.

"You'n me have always been close," his brother said. "Closer than most brothers ever are. Reckon you know that."

"Yes, Davy," Bruce said again; but his mind had already raced ahead of his brother's heavy plodding. Get on with it! he thought. Speak your piece about the land and why it ought to be all rightfully yours after Pa's dead. Get on with it! Can't you see I've got to go?

"Damned shame to have to talk about it before Pa's dead," David said ponderously; "but in a way we got to. Put things in the clear—better that way. You ain't much more than a kid, but you got a head on your shoulders. And you've changed somehow, got to be more serious. Reckon 'twas the war. What you done in Mexico was fine—mighty fine. Did the family proud. . . ."

"Thanks," Bruce said dryly. "What I did in Mexico was a damned fool trick. I wouldn't do it again. Get on with it, Davy."

His brother stared at him. Then he retreated back in the plodding train of his own thought, ruminating, bovine.

"Trouble is, South Carolina don't have a law of primogeniture. What I mean is, boy, I'm hoping you'll stand by me. Had a law, I'd get it all, and that would be the best thing. Because I'd let you stay on and help me. Hell, I'd insist that you stay. The worst thing you can do with cotton lands is to split 'em up. Small holdings just don't pay. We got to keep the old place together, Bruceboy. The money—heck, we'll divide that fair and square. But not the land, not never the land. . . ."

Bruce closed off his mind from listening. All right, all right, take the damned land! The land is nothing and less than nothing, and hasn't been for a long time. I'm sick of it, Davy. I'm sick of the land, sick of this place, sick of being tied down to a passel of niggers, sick of you, sick even of—he stopped, brought up hard against the incredibility of that thought. But he completed it, examining it in wonder and in awe. For this truly was a new thing.

Yes. Sick even of this thing with Jo. Of wanting her. Of not having her. . . .

He turned to his older brother, and his eyes were peaceful.

"Don't worry about it, Dave," he said. "I don't care about the land. This section is plumb played out. Land doesn't produce a quarter of what it used to. We tried marl, and it richened the soil some. But not enough. Cotton eats land up. Besides, I don't care about planting, anyhow . . ."

Seeing his brother's face, he realized what a blasphemy he had spoken.

"Hell of a thing to say, boy," David growled; "specially since everybody allows that you're one of the best damn' planters in the State . . ."

"Can't help it. I'm sick of it. So take my share off my hands. Pay me whatever you think it's worth. Hell, Davy, I'll give it to you! Take it as a gift, and lend me enough money to get out to California. . . ."

"California, eh?" David said. "So that's what's been on your mind. . . ."

Bruce smiled.

"Reckon it has. Anyhow, anything's better than this. Maybe I have got a hankering to go pick me up a few of those nuggets they've got lying about. . . ."

David looked at his younger brother.

"You're serious, boy?" he said.

"Dead serious. Stay here and what happens? Know how big the old place was in Grandpa's time? Only he had five sons. So what we have now is only one fifth of the old place, big as we may think it is. It's not enough. You've been married a little over three years, and already you've got two boys. We Harkness' run to boys. If I were to get married, it would be the same thing again: split the land up among the sons; split it again among the grandsons until each one can't take two steps without trespassing on his brother's grounds. Maybe out there I'll strike it rich. Folks have, you know. . . ."

"More haven't," David said. "Still, in new country like that, ought to be more than one way of skinning a cat. Don't doubt

you could make a go of it. You always was able. But I sure Lord
would rather you stayed. I—I'll miss you, boy. . . ."

Bruce felt the tug of emotion in his brother's voice. Why, he
means it, he thought; damned if the old cuss doesn't have a heart
after all. But he shook his head, doggedly.

"No," he said; "I've got to go, Davy. Don't ask me why, because
I don't rightly know. I've just go to—that's all. . . ."

David pushed back his hat and stared at him.

"Sure you ain't running away from something, boy?" he said.
"Like Jo Peterson, for instance?"

Bruce looked away from him. Then he looked back again.

"Yes," he said quietly; "reckon maybe I am. . . ."

"That was a hell of a thing," David growled; "you down there
in Mexico getting yourself shot up, and the minute your back is
turned, she ups and marries on you. . . ."

Bruce put out his hand and stroked his horse's neck.

"Wasn't her fault," he said; "not all of it, anyhow. We had words
—mainly about my enlisting. She said it was a tomfool thing. She
was right," he added softly, "it was a tomfool thing. . . ."

"Hardly enough to make her fly off the handle," David said.

"Reckon we both kind of got our danders up," Bruce said. "Anyhow, it ended with her saying that she wouldn't wait for me; and
I said: 'All right then, don't.' Didn't think she would take me seriously . . ."

David peered at his brother's profile. He frowned, cleared his
throat.

"Gathered that she's changed her mind," he said.

Bruce didn't answer him.

"Look, boy," David said; "there's been some talk—And you are
away from home a mighty heap, nights. . . ."

Bruce turned and faced his brother.

"Talk?" he said; "what kind of talk?"

"Now don't go getting riled up at me, Bruce. I only asked you
because I was worried . . . After all, I don't exactly cotton to the
idea of having my only brother shot through the guts in some dam-
fool duel. . . ."

"You mean that folks are saying that Jo and me are . . . ?"
Bruce said. "Yes, I can see how they could be saying that. Jo's
not happy with Ted. Reckon she shows it. And I'm crazy wild

for her—and I reckon that shows, too. But, beyond that, they're wrong. . . ."

He looked at the Negroes, but he didn't see them.

"Don't know why they're wrong," he said softly. "There's no reason for them to be. Except that they are. Except that me'n Jo just aren't that kind of people. . . ."

He looked at his brother and smiled.

"I don't know if I can put it in words, rightly," he said. "Reckon what I really mean is, Dave, that what we had before, Jo and me, was something mighty fine. And it's finished. But we can look back on it—those days before. Now, anything we did, anything at all, would kind of dirty that . . . Funny, but it would be kind of like slinging mud around in a church. . . ."

"I'm damned glad it ain't so," David said, relief moving in his voice; "but you still got to be careful. That Ted Peterson's a hot-tempered boy. And it don't have to be so for him to call you out. It's enough if he even thinks it is. . . ."

"Wouldn't meet him," Bruce said. "Killed the last man I'm ever going to at Chapultepec. Any man who calls me out from now on, I'm going to refuse, on principle. . . ."

"They'll post you as a coward," David growled.

"Words," Bruce said, "add up to a mighty heap of nothing, Davy. . . ."

"Reckon we'd better be getting back to the house," David said.

"Not me. I've got to ride over to the Petersons' and say goodbye to Jo. . . ."

David studied his younger brother.

"Ted'll be home, long about now, boy," he said.

"Want him to be. Going in broad open daylight. Since, as you said, people are talking, that's the best thing, isn't it?"

David sat there, frowning.

"All right," he said; "Just you be careful, boy. . . ."

Ted Peterson sat on the veranda with his wife. He was resting after the noonday meal. His gaze kept straying back to Jo's face. It was white—too white. And she hadn't eaten a thing.

Certain things he had heard, words, phrases, hints—even a quiz-zical look or two as he and Jo had passed on their way to church last Sunday, began to fall into place in his mind. What if it were so? What if she and that Bruce Harkness. . . . ?

But one thing stuck like a burr in his consciousness: when? He had been at home every night since he married Jo—except the nights he had attended the meetings of the Palmetto Regiment, and Bruce Harkness, being a fellow officer, had been there, too—every time.

It just wasn't possible. But the talk went on.

Even if he's only the cause of that indirectly, Ted thought, I should call him out. But then—there are the days. I'm not a big planter. I have to oversee my own hands. And all that young Harkness bastard would have to do would be to jump a few fences. . . .

As if in answer to his thought, he saw the dust cloud rising on the road.

"Somebody," he said to Jo, "is sure Lord in a hurry."

Jo didn't say anything. She was often like that now, falling into silences that went on and on.

The rider burst out of the dust and soared over the fence. The jump was easy, graceful, perfect.

"He's trespassing," Ted growled; "but that's damned fine jumping. I wouldn't risk that fence myself. It's got twelve bars. Still too far away to make out who he is. I wonder. . . ."

"It's Bruce," Jo said; "nobody else in the county can ride like that. Maybe not in the whole state. . . ."

Ted stared at her.

"He comes here while I'm gone?" he said. "Tell me, Jo—does he?"

"No," she said. "This is the first time he's ever come, Ted."

"If you're lying to me . . ." Ted said.

"I don't lie," she said, "not to anybody. Specially not to you. I don't care enough. Do you think that if Bruce Harkness had been here and crooked his little finger, I'd be here now, Ted?"

"Goddamn it, Jo!" he said; but Bruce was there now, reining in the horse, climbing down.

"Howdy, Ted," he said. "Howdy, Jo—"

Ted Peterson stood up. Right then, he wasn't good to look at.

"Bruce," he said; "'pears to me that you'n me have a crow to pick. I been hearing talk. . . ."

"I know," Bruce said quietly, easily. "That's one of the things I came about, Ted. Heard some myself, this morning—for the first time. Reckon it's always like that. Folks most involved in a thing are always the last to hear. . . ."

"Well—" Ted said.

Bruce looked at him.

"I came to apologize," he said, "for any trouble I caused you folks. But it never occurred to me, Ted, that I'd have to tell you it isn't so. I see I do. That surprises me. All right, then, since you seem to have doubts, I'll say it. It isn't so, Ted; not a word of it."

"How do I know that?" Ted said; "what proof have I got?"

Bruce's mouth tightened.

"My word," he said. "The word of a Harkness."

"He doesn't understand that, Bruce," Jo said tartly. "He hasn't the faintest idea of what the word of a gentleman means. . . ."

"That's a mighty unkind thing to say, Jo," Bruce said. "Appears to me you aren't giving Ted the respect that's his due as your husband."

"Respect?" Jo said. "Oh, good God!"

Bruce looked from one of them to the other.

"Looks like I came at the wrong time," he said. "But there's another thing. I came to say goodbye, Jo. I'm going to California. For many reasons. And I'll freely admit that you're one of them. So, Ted—you won't have to worry about the talk any more. Neither the talk—nor me. Appears to me it's the best thing. . . ."

Jo sat there, feeling the knot growing in her throat, choking off her breath. I won't cry, she thought; I won't!

"Yes," she said. "I reckon it is the best thing, Bruce."

"Goodbye, Ted," Bruce said, and put out his hand.

Ted Peterson stood there, staring at his outstretched hand for a long, slow time. Then he took it.

Jo wondered if he had taken Bruce's hand because it didn't matter any more, or because he dared not refuse it. One or the other. Not because he wanted to.

" 'Bye, Jo," Bruce said.

" 'Bye, Bruce." She watched him mount and ride away, his outlines blurred, indistinct. She stood up, walked to the edge of the porch, and leaned against a column, still watching him. She had the feeling that her mouth was going to ache forever for the kiss he hadn't given her in parting.

Then, very quietly without saying anything to her husband at all, she turned and walked back into the house.

2

IT HAD ALL been made easy for him finally, which was a thing a man could ponder over. First, his father had died, exactly two days after his visit to the Petersons, thus putting an end to the contention of the doctors that he would linger on for weeks; and, when his will was read, Bruce found himself in possession of five thousand dollars above and beyond his share in the land. To this, David had added another five thousand, in payment for Bruce's half of the plantation. An entirely normal series of events, when he thought about them objectively; but having within them, to Bruce, something more: a kind of implementing of destiny, his obstacles cleared away, the road before him made smooth.

The buckboard was already drawn up before the house, with his valises loaded on the flatbed behind the seat. He was traveling light, because from all he had heard, a man had precious little need of fine clothes in California. He could see his manservant, Pompey, sitting like a black statue at the reins. He had hurt Pompey's feelings badly by his refusal to take him along. But that was another thing he was running away from: this burdensome business of being an owner of men.

" 'Course," David said slowly, "there's a mighty heap to be done; but one more day wouldn't hurt matters much. I could go down to Charleston with you, boy. . . ."

"No," Bruce said. "No thank you, Davy. Don't much like that business of waving goodbye from the ship. Here—it's different somehow. Like I was just going down to the city for a while. . . ."

"It's going to be years," David said thickly, "if ever. . . ."

"Not as bad as all that," Bruce said. "Be back as soon as I make my first million. . . ."

They were silent, looking at each other.

"Wait here a minute, Dave," Bruce said; "I—I got to go say good-bye to Pa. . . ."

David nodded, unwilling to trust himself to speak.

Bruce walked away from the house, going up the old, familiar path that went through the willow grove to the high ground where the oaks were. They had buried the old man there, in the clearing around which the oaks stood, laying him beside the grave of the mother they had never known; and whose place the first David Harkness had taken, all their lives, with gruff tenderness and silent fortitude.

Way love ought to be, Bruce thought. He spent twenty-seven years alone, because to him she was irreplaceable. A love like that is a kind of glory. Reckon most men settle for less, because they have to. I won't, though. Rather live my life alone like Pa than sneak and steal and make a dirtiness out of living. . . .

He stood beside the headstones, his hat in his hand. And though the sadness was in him bone-deep, he did not cry. It was not a thing to cry over, two headstones, one yellowed by the years and the other white in the wash of sun, in that place of stillness, where the wind talked quietly among the trees, and even the mocking-birds were silent. It was too filled up with—with peace, he reckoned, and anyhow, they were together. . . .

'Bye, Pa, he thought, and you, too, Ma—although I didn't know you. Reckon you've forgiven me for costing you your life in being born. Only thing I can do for you is to promise that I'll never shame you. Not any more. Sure don't know what happens when a body passes on; but, if there is an afterwards, maybe you sort of arranged it so I'd come to my senses about Sue Archer. . . .

He moved over to his father's fresh grave, and knelt beside it. He tried to pray, but the words wouldn't come. So he knelt there a long time in silence. When he got up, the quiet had entered into him. And that, though he didn't know it, was a kind of prayer.

He came down the path to the house and stood beside the buck-board. David came out and stood beside him, blinking his heavy lidded eyes, and making a snorting noise through his nose.

"Well, boy—" David growled.

"Reckon this is goodbye, Davy," Bruce said, and put out his hand.

But David, instead of taking his hand, caught his younger brother to him in a bone-crushing, fierce hug. He held Bruce like that for half a heartbeat. Then he released him and stepped back.

" 'Bye, boy," he said and, turning, marched up the steps like a soldier.

Bruce stood there, looking at him. Then he climbed into the buckboard beside Pompey.

"All right, Pomp," he said; "we'd best be getting on, now. . . ."

The clipper lay in the roads, out from the wharf. Bruce could see her tall masts, with the sails furled on the yardarms, pencilling the sky. And again he felt the excitement working inside him. The launch was already at the wharf. She was sloop rigged, and from the lines of her, very fast.

"Get the stuff out," Bruce said. "Damn it, Pomp, move! They're waiting. . . ."

"Marse Bruce—" Pompey said.

"Look, Pomp, I've told you before. That's rough country out there. I'll have as much as I can do, looking after myself. . . ."

"I know, Suh—it ain't that. Marse Bruce, that lady over there—she sure Lord is alooking at you. Ain't that Miz Peterson?"

Bruce turned. Jo stood there a little apart from the crowd. She had a handkerchief in her hands. He could see her hands moving, twisting it.

"Get the things onto the launch," Bruce said. "Tell them I'll be there directly. . . ."

Then he was gone, walking toward her.

There were people on the wharf whom they both knew. It was always like that when a ship was in. But Bruce Harkness passed them by without a word of greeting, without recognizing them, or knowing they were there.

He stood there before her and was silent. Between her hands the handkerchief gave way, ripping into two halves. She looked at them helplessly, and let them fall. She didn't say anything. Even her lips were white.

Bruce put out his hands and took hers, holding them between his own. They were like ice.

And the people on the wharf nudged each other, the patter of talk dying among them, so that the silence ran from one to another, all of them turning, staring with incredulity, or wrath, or malicious pleasure, according to their natural bents, at this thing that shouldn't have been, couldn't be; but was.

"Jo—" Bruce said.

"Bruce," she whispered. "Oh, Bruce!"

She came up on tiptoe then, surged up, and her mouth on his was wild and sweet and salt from crying. She clung to him, shaking all over. He held her to him, hard.

"Marse Bruce," Pompey said; "Them folks—they's ready, Suh. . . ."

"Directly," Bruce growled, and bending, found her mouth again. Then he stepped back.

"Goodbye, Jo," he said.

She didn't answer him. She took a half step forward, then checked herself. Her hand came up in a sleepwalker's gesture, and strayed along his face as though to memorize his image. Then she turned and moved off, her head bent. The crowd opened and let her through; then closed behind her, staring.

"You better come on, Marse Bruce," Pompey said.

Bruce stood on the deck of the clipper, *Flying Fish*, and watched the shoreline of Carolina sliding past. Aloft, the sailors were cracking on all sail. There was, at that time, nothing that moved, except perhaps the railroads, as fast as a Baltimore built clipper ship; but her very speed saddened him. Within half an hour, they had dropped Charleston astern, and still the mate strode the deck, shouting orders through a megaphone, crowding on more canvas, flying jibs, staysails, skysails, royals, topgallants, tops'ls, mains, everything to the fore and aft trysail at her stern, until she had taken the bone in her teeth, driving southward, leaving a wake as white as milk boiling behind her.

"Lord God!" a voice behind him said, its accents warm, sunny, unmistakably Southern; "Lord God Almighty what a ship! Less than forty hours from Baltimore to Charleston—that's damn near fifteen knots an hour, isn't it?"

Bruce turned. The man was tall, taller by five inches than his own compact five foot nine. His hair was red, and his face was freckled. It was a good face, Bruce saw. A kind, good-humored face; rawboned and ugly and pleasant.

"Reckon so," he said. "Tell the truth, I'm lost with all this sea talk. I know how far a mile is; but a knot—that kind of beats me. . . ."

The man grinned.

"Me, too," he said. "I picked that up from the First Mate. Told me it figured out to fifteen knots. But I'll be dangblasted if I know what a knot is, either. By the way, my handle's Burke—Hailey Burke. And I'm so damned glad to find another Southerner on board I could plumb bust out and holler. . . ."

"Why?" Bruce said.

"There're seventeen Yankees aboard. Nice fellows, mostly. But there's one ringtailed polecat named Rufus King who's been giving me one hard row to hoe. Been threatening to come down to my cabin to see if I got a Nigra wench hid under the bed. By the way, what did you say your name was?"

"I didn't," Bruce said.

Hailey Burke stared at him.

"Why," he said, "that's mighty unfriendly of you, seeing as how we're the only two Southerons aboard. . . ."

"I was ribbing you," Bruce said, and put out his hand. "The name's Bruce Harkness. . . ."

"Mighty proud to make your acquaintance, Mister Harkness. You any kin to the Harkness' of Savannah?"

"Cousins," Bruce said; "their Pa's my uncle. . . ."

"I knew it! Spitting image of the second boy—Alex, his name is, ain't it?"

"Right," Bruce said. "Funny—but I'll bet if there's one Southerner in California, he'll know somebody we're both kin to. . . ."

"Ain't that the truth!" Hailey laughed. "We're damned near all kin. Reckon if you'n me was to go back far enough, we'd find that we had at least one ancestor in common."

"Let's don't," Bruce said. "A body can pick his friends; but kin-folks you're stuck with."

"God's own truth. You sure were looking down in the mouth leaning over that rail. That was why I spoke to you. . . ."

Bruce looked aft. Charleston was a smoke smudge on the horizon.

"Kind of hard, leaving home," he said.

"Not for me. Had a place near Augusta. My wife died three years ago; no kids. It was just too damned lonesome. And by the time I got over Mary Ann's death enough to look around, the only other little filly who interested me at all, had up and married on me. Sweet little critter—blackest hair you ever did see. . . . Wasn't much use in hanging around after that. 'Sides the old place didn't rightly pay. Figure a man can make a new start out west. . . ."

"Reckon so," Bruce said.

"Sorry there aren't more of us aboard. Maybe we'll pick up some re-enforcements in Savannah. That's our next stop. But it appears like the Yankees are going to outnumber us in California, and you know what that means. . . ."

"California will come in as a Free State? Let her. I wouldn't be going out there if I thought there was going to be slavery. . . ."

Hailey stiffened.

"I take it, then, you don't hold with the South's Peculiar Institution, Mr. Harkness?" he said.

Bruce looked at Hailey Burke; then he smiled, very slowly.

"Look, Hailey," he said. "Hope you don't mind if I call you that? I don't believe in standing on ceremony. . . ."

"Not a-tall. All these damyankees are already thicker'n thieves at a lawyer's funeral; so you'n me had better stick together. Your first name's Bruce, isn't it?"

"Yes," Bruce said. "I'll put it to you straight, Hailey. This voyage isn't going to be easy. I got a feeling that in the next three or four months, being cooped up together like this is going to make for some mighty ragged nerves. This slavery question is a touchy business. Be better if we let it die, don't you think? Personally, I don't have any strong feelings about it one way or the other. I just find that having to take care of a passel of niggers is a damned nuisance. When you get right down to it, a case could be made for the idea that it's us who're enslaved. All a nigger has to do is work, breed, and eat. But we have to figure, scheme, take care of them, make them work, make ends meet. Hell, there have been times when I felt like getting out and making my own crop so as not to have the worries. . . ."

Hailey stared at him; then he drew back his head and laughed aloud.

"Damned if you aren't right," he said. "I been keeping my old place going by practicing law. Funny—we've been so heated up defending the South on moral grounds, that we've plumb forgot the practical side. If those abolitionists had sense, they'd talk like you just did, 'stead of getting us riled up over foolishness. Don't know a planter who is out of debt. Do you?"

"No," Bruce said.

"Hard to say if slavery is practical or not; but it doesn't look like it. Say, Bruce! That's him, now. . . ."

"That's who now?" Bruce said.

"Rufus King. The good-looking one with the little black mustache. The other one's John Mead. Heard tell Mead's the richest man in Pennsylvania. Don't know what he's going to California for. . . ."

Bruce glanced over his shoulder at the two men. Rufus King was very handsome. He looked like an actor. The clothes he wore were very fine, perfectly tailored of the most expensive materials. John Mead was much older. He was in his sixties, and he was the kind of a man, Bruce reckoned, you had to be introduced to twenty times before you could remember him. They came toward Bruce and Hailey.

"Ah, Burke," King said; "I see you've found a partner. How many pounds of nigger have you traded thus far? Or don't you sell them by the pound?"

"Don't sell niggers," Hailey snapped. "That's Yankee work. We kind of figure it's beneath us. . . ."

"Really? But not to work them; and even to sleep with them if the number of mulattoes I saw on the dock was any indication. . . ."

"Bred mostly by Yankee overseers," Hailey said; "which is another thing we leave to Northern trash!"

Rufus King looked at him with cool and insolent eyes.

"You amuse me, Burke," he said. "Since you Southern aristocrats are constantly beating a path to our door begging loans, or renewals of the ones we've already granted you, I wouldn't venture to ask why you happened to be in New York the day we sailed. Rather useful trash, aren't we?"

"Damn you, King!" Hailey said. "I got a good mind to. . . ."

Bruce laid a hand on Hailey's arm.

"Easy, boy," he said quietly.

"And you, my friend," King said, "are not a fire-eater? How strange! Didn't know there was such a thing as a peaceable Southerner. . . ."

"Reckon there're a good many things you don't know," Bruce said. "But maybe you'll learn 'em, given time. That is, if you have any time, which isn't likely if you go around baiting hot-tempered folks. . . ."

"Are you threatening me, Sir?" King snapped.

Bruce shook his head.

"No," he said; "I never threaten. What needs to be done, I do—without wasting words. But fighting and killing aren't things I hold needful. . . ."

"Very intelligent. You'll live a long time that way, Mister—"

"Harkness. Bruce Harkness. I aim to. But that's not the reason I'm against fighting and such like. . . ."

"This is interesting," John Mead said suddenly. "Why are you, Mister Harkness?"

"They don't prove anything," Bruce said. "Mister Burke and your friend here have been exchanging words ever since they came aboard. Suppose they fought and one of 'em won, maybe even killed the other. What would it prove?"

"I'll bite," Mead said. "What?"

"Only that the one who won was stronger, or a better shot. Not that he was right. Reckon violence never really settles anything. . . ."

"Ah, but you're wrong," King said. "It does, sometimes, Harkness. 'To the victor belongs the spoils', as Old Hickory used to say. It has settled the fact that you can go to California without the permission of the Mexican Government—or ranch in Texas; or hunt bison in Arizona, or dwell in Colorado or Utah, if you so desire. . . ."

"Reckon you've got a point there," Bruce said; "but hardly a new point, King. Folks have always known that a strong thief can keep what he stole, which don't make the whole thing a mite more honorable to my way of thinking. . . ."

"Honorable?" King said. "That's the wrong word, Harkness. Practical is better. Besides, you seem to be rather free with your criticisms of our country."

"Did you ever see Mexico?" Bruce said quietly. "The New York Rifles were one damn' fine bunch of fighting men. Were you with them?"

"No," King said; "but—"

"I was there. Captain, South Carolina Palmettos. Wounded at Churubusco. That wasn't much. Wounded again at Chapultepec —on top of those walls, King. Six months in a Mexican hospital, being cared for by Mexican nuns. Damned wonderful women. I'll never forget them. Mind you, I'm not bragging. I just happen to think that unquestioning patriotism is stupid. And I venture that I've earned the right to criticize. . . ."

"And I," John Mead said, "think you're absolutely right, Mister Harkness. First man I've met abroad who talks sense. Maybe you and I could get together for a little chat in a day or two. What do you say?"

"Be glad to," Bruce said.

"Good," John Mead said. "Come along, King—and try not to be so unnecessarily tiresome. . . ."

"Lord God!" Hailey laughed after they had gone; "Lord God, but you sure pinned his ears back for fair! And Mead sided with you! Who would have thought it?"

"Strange," Bruce said; "but King talks mighty low before Mead. That's not natural for a fellow like him. Wonder why? Fast talker like him. . . ."

"Probably trying to pry Mead loose from some of his money. They share a cabin, and I heard one of the crew blabbing that Mead's got a suitcase full of bank notes. Crisp, new ones. Seems the cabin boy went down to make the bunks, and stumbled upon him counting 'em. The cabin boy thought they were both out. It's all over the ship by now. . . ."

"Wouldn't be a thing I wanted known," Bruce said. "Come on, let's take a turn around the deck. . . ."

"Right, get stiff hanging here in this breeze," Hailey said.

It was apparent, from the outset, that the Captain meant to break all existing records for the voyage, even that miraculous passage by the clipper *Sea Witch*, of ninety-seven days from New York to California, around the Horn. He, as the crew put it, hung out everything including the cook's shirt. They scudded southward with the wind three-quarters astern, clocking three days in a row at speeds approaching twenty knots. The *Flying Fish* heeled over hard, her mainsail yards almost, it seemed to Bruce, touching the sea, the lower third of her jibs, staysails, and dolphin strikers actually wet from the spray of her passage.

Bruce had four miserable days in the Caribbean, green with seasickness, which was a thing he could have predicted, because the same thing had happened to him on the voyage to Vera Cruz, two years before. And it was no help to his state of mind that Hailey was laughingly, profanely immune, while Rufus King strode the heaving decks like a man who had spent all his life at sea.

But off South America, it was better. He recovered his health and his appetite, and was able to spend the long days, and worse, the nights blazing with tropic stars bigger and brighter than any he had seen before, dreaming of Jo. He became morose and sad, so that Hailey, who had fine, instinctive sympathies, learned soon there were times when it was better to let Bruce be.

They were off Rio de Janeiro, now, flying South. The tension aboard mounted with every knot that foamed behind them. There were sudden, bitter quarrels. Twice the mate had to break up fist fights. So it was that when, that afternoon, a new uproar broke out on deck, neither Bruce nor Hailey paid it much attention. But, suddenly, Hailey caught Bruce's arm.

"Lord God!" he said; "it's Mead! And is he riled! Never saw him in a temper before. . . ."

Bruce turned. Mead was waving his arms and shouting. The mate had the cabin boy by his shirt front and was shaking him until his bones rattled.

"Blast and dammme!" the mate roared. "Speak English, you little bastard! You can, I know that! Tell me what in the name of hell-fire were you doing in this man's cabin—again?"

Bruce strolled over, moving without apparent haste.

"Maybe I can help," he said quietly. He turned to the boy. "What passes, Chico?" he said; "is there something in the cabin of el Señor Mead which you have envy to possess?"

"Lord God," Hailey said. "Spanish, too! How in the world. . . ."

"Tell him to tell the truth," the mate growled; "or it will go hard with him. Then tell me what the lying beggar says, Mr. Harkness. . . ."

"No, Señor!" the boy wept; "I have not entered the cabin of the very gentlemanly Señor Mead with intent to steal. I went because the other one, the Señor King, said to me I was to come at three hours to make a small service for him. . . ."

"He says," Bruce said to Mead, "that King told him to come down there at three o'clock."

"Nonsense!" Mead snorted. "He knows very well that King is always out of the cabin in the afternoon. He's a thief, and I want him put in irons!"

"Easy, Mead," Bruce said; then he turned back to the boy. "You know the habits of Señor King," he said. "Is he usually in his cabin at this hour?"

"No, never," the boy said quickly. "It was this that surprised me. I asked him again to be sure I had heard correctly the hour, but he repeated it. And that, Señores, I swear it—is why I came. . . ."

"He's not lying," Bruce said. "King told him to come. Reckon you'd better ask him about it, Mead. . . ."

"I will," Mead said; "but all the same. . . ."

"Tell me one thing, Mead," Bruce said; "is anything missing?"

"No," Mead said slowly; "still, I don't like his butting in. . . ."

"Look," Bruce said. "You can't put the boy in irons on account of that. It's his job to come into the cabins and attend to things. If you went around punishing folks for what's on their minds, every man with a good-looking wife would have to shoot half the men in town. . . ."

The mate grinned and turned the boy loose.

"You're a reasonable man, Mr. Harkness," he said. "Seems to me, Mister Mead, that you've got a touch of nerves. . . ."

"Could be that I have," Mead said slowly. "But it does seem to me that the boy is unnecessarily zealous. . . ."

"Got a suggestion if you want to listen to it, Mead," Hailey said. "If you have any money or valuables in that cabin, you'd be a damned sight smarter if you turned them over to the Captain for safekeeping. Sleep easier that way, 'pears to me. . . ."

Mead shook his head.

"I couldn't do that," he muttered. "No, no—it's quite impossible. . . ."

"Then," Bruce said, "I'm going to tell this boy not to enter your cabin until he has checked with both you and King. If one of you tells him to do something, he has to look for the other party and clear it with him. It'll slow things down; but it'll stop this. . . ."

He turned to the boy.

"Can read English, Chico?" he said.

"No, Señor," the boy said sadly. "I can speak it, a little; but read it—unfortunately—no. . . ."

Bruce put his hand in his pocket and brought out his wallet. From it, he took a visiting card.

"Got a pencil, Hailey?" he said.

"Sure," Hailey said and passed it over.

Bruce wrote on the back of the card and gave it to John Mead.

"Here," he said. "You copy this in big letters, Mr. Mead. When you don't want the boy to come in, hang it on the doorknob outside. That will fix everything, I think."

Mead looked at the card.

"*Occupado*," he read; "*Se prohibe entrar*. Why it's very much like English, isn't it? I can understand this. Thank you very kindly, Mister Harkness. . . ."

"Then it's all settled?" the mate asked.

"Yes," John Mead said; "thanks to Mr. Harkness. I'm glad we have one cool head aboard. . . ."

"Get back to work, you!" the mate said to the boy.

"Si, Señor," the boy said; then to Bruce: "*Muchissimas gracias, Caballero!*"

"For nothing," Bruce said.

"You must have spent a long time in Mexico," Hailey said, "in order to palaver Spanish like that. . . ."

"Over a year. But it was the six months in the hospital that did it. Had to speak it, there. Besides, it's plumb down right easy, once you put your mind to it. . . ."

"Will you teach me to speak it?" Hailey asked. "Might come in handy in California. And it'll give us something to do to pass away the time. . . ."

"Sure, why not?" Bruce said.

They fled southward, seldom falling below seventeen knots. They were well ahead of the *Sea Witch's* record. The crew talked confidently of ninety-five days, if the waters around Cape Horn were good. But the older seamen shook their heads. The seas off the Horn were never good, they warned. They spoke of ships that had lost a week trying to round that narrow point of land. Or, more ominously, of men swept overboard by the mountainous seas, longboats smashed to kindling, vessels demasted, driven onto the rocks and slowly pounded to bits by the breakers.

And already, as though to give point to the old salts' warnings, in that stretch of sea between the Falklands and the bleak and lonely coast of Tierra del Fuego, the seas began to whiten. The *Flying Fish* rolled sickeningly, wallowing in the long troughs of slate-grey sea. The wind shrieked in the rigging; but Captain Winters would not furl a sail. The speed climbed above twenty knots. She was pitching now; the bow rising skyward, then crashing down into the crest of a mountainous wave, ploughing through it, shuddering, while tons of white water swept the forward deck. Above them, the sea birds scudded: man o'war, and grey gull, and tern and ominous albatross. In the lulls between the gusts, they could hear them crying.

Bruce had gotten his sea legs now. He strode the deck like a seafarer, rolling with the ship.

They reached the Horn at night. The mate stood by the barometer, his face tight with worry. He kept casting his eyes aloft, gazing at the skysails and royals. At ten o'clock, one of the topgallants went with a noise like crackling thunder. The mate went down and told the Captain.

"All right, Mister Lodge," the Captain said. "I don't mean to lose my ship for a record. You can reef sails." Then he turned and got back into his bunk. "Better keep the jibs and staysails up," he said. "Got to keep her pointing, you know. . . ."

"Yes sir," the mate said, and went back on deck.

They were tacking in the teeth of the wind now, under almost bare poles. The fore-and-aft-rigged triangular jibs and staysails and the little schooner-like trysail at her stern, which were better than the square sails for the zigzag course of tacking, held her pointing accurately enough; but were dangerously insufficient for clawing off a lee shore. Every time Bruce looked, the breakers on the rocky point of the Horn showed whiter. The mate was no fool. He bawled orders and the big mainsails were unfurled, held down by double guys.

The *Flying Fish* began to hold her own again; then the stretch of white water between them and the knife-edged rocks began to widen, inch by painful inch. Bruce sighed.

Reckon I'll go below now, he thought. Damned little difference between drowning awake or asleep; but it looks like we're going to make it. . . .

He went down, settled himself in his bunk fully clothed, and started going over the old, aching business of Jo.

Damnfool thing to kiss her before everybody. Ted's sure to have heard about it. Hope to God he hasn't given her too hard a time. . . .

The door opened, and Hailey came in.

"Glad you're awake," he said; I'm too damned scared to sleep. . . ."

"Me, too," Bruce said. "Sit down, boy. There're some stogies in that box. Have one, then pass them to me. . . ."

They sat there, smoking, bracing themselves against the roll and pitch.

"Got a wee snort o' bourbon left in my cabin," Hailey said. "And if there ever was a night for bourbon, this is it! You'll join me, won't you? I'll go fetch the bottle. . . ."

"Don't mind if I do," Bruce said.

Hailey got up, and putting his hand against the bulkheads to steady himself, made his way to the door. Then he stepped out into the passageway and stopped dead.

"Now, what the hell?" Bruce heard him say. Bruce got up and went to the door. The Captain and the mate came along the passageway. With them was Rufus King. He had on a great coat, soaking wet, and under it, only a nightshirt. His feet were thrust into unlaced boots. His face was very white, so that his foppish little mustache stood out in a dark line.

"Sorry to disturb you gentlemen," Captain Winters said heavily; "but we're making a search. It appears that Mr. Mead is—missing. Have either of you—?"

Slowly they both shook their heads.

"He's gone overboard, I tell you!" King said, his voice taut with near hysteria. "He told me he was going up for some air. I warned him it was dangerous, but he wouldn't listen—"

"How long was he gone before you started searching for him?" the mate asked.

"More than an hour. I've searched the whole deck. A wave must have washed him over. He wasn't very strong. . . . Good God! I never should have let him go. . . ."

Bruce looked at Hailey.

Hailey nodded.

"Damned fine acting," he said quietly.

"What the hell do you mean, Burke?" Rufus King said.

"Now that depends," Hailey said. "You're damned sure that Mead is over the side, King. Nobody else is as sure as you are—yet. Except me. I think he's gone, too. And I think that if the Cap'n orders your cabin searched, he'll find that a valise full of bank notes is missing along with him. . . ."

The Captain and mate both turned, staring at King.

"You bastard!" King said. "Just because you've a grudge against me, you don't have to accuse me of—"

"Murder and robbery? I'm not. As a lawyer I know better than to make such an accusation. All I'm saying is that it would be mighty interesting to see if that valise is still there. . . ."

"What valise?" King shouted. "I've shared a cabin with Mead all these weeks, and I assure you I have never seen such a valise! Maybe you, Attorney Burke, should tell the Captain where you got your information from!"

Bruce spoke quickly, trying to head Hailey off.

"Remember that incident with the cabin boy?" he said to the mate. "Doesn't it strike you a mite curious how heated up Mead was over that boy's butting in? Mild-mannered kind of a person, it appeared to me. But that got him plenty riled. . . ."

But Captain Winters was not to be diverted.

"You might tell us how you knew about the valise, Mister Burke," he said quietly.

"Overheard a member of the crew talking. Said the kid stumbled in while Mead was counting—oh, damn! Didn't mean to drag that poor kid into this. . . ."

"He's in it already, Mister Burke," the mate said.

"Exactly!" King said. "Since he knew about it, and I didn't! If Mead had such a valise, he kept its contents carefully hidden from me. It seems to me if there has been murder done, your cabin boy would bear investigation. Search his quarters. All right, search mine, too! I assure you, you'll find nothing there. And a whole suit case full of bank notes would be rather difficult to hide. . . ."

The Captain looked at Bruce and Hailey.

"I think you'd better come along, both of you," he said.

The cabin boy was asleep. But his uniform, his socks, his shoes, were all dry, which Bruce was quick to point out to the two officers. A search of his bunk and foot-locker produced nothing. They marched him up to King's and Mead's cabin, and searched it thoroughly. In Mead's effects they found three thousand dollars.

"What a clever bastard!" Hailey whispered to Bruce; "he had sense enough to leave that. . . ."

The Captain questioned the cabin boy. As always, when frightened, the boy retreated into Spanish. Bruce interpreted for them.

"This is of the valise of bank notes," he said to the boy; "is it true that you have seen it?"

The boy's face was grey with terror.

"I am not sure," he whispered; "not securely. I saw the old one counting something. But the light was dim, you understand, Señor, and I left in haste as the Señor was much annoyed. . . ."

"*La familia santissima!*" Bruce said. "Why don't you speak the truth, Chico? I give you my word, boy—that nothing will happen to you. . . ."

"I have fear," the boy whispered. "What is to prevent him from killing me also?"

Bruce turned to the others.

"He says he is not sure that it was money he saw," he said. "Under those circumstances we haven't any proof. But, Captain, if you don't mind my suggesting it, maybe you'd better transfer that boy to another section. He seems terribly afraid of King."

"He has no reason to be," King said quickly. "I submit in the first place that this suitcase existed only in his imagination. Or perhaps he saw John Mead counting the money that we found here. But it appears to me you owe me an apology, Burke—"

"All right," Hailey said. "I apologize—under protest, and with serious reservations. Can't prove you shoved John Mead over the side; but I believe you're capable of having done it. And that's a belief I won't apologize for. . . ."

"Mr. Burke," Captain Winters said, "as Master of this vessel, I'm the highest authority here—and that includes passengers as well as crew. I'm ordering you, formally, to cease and desist from making public accusations against Mr. King. Your opinions are your own, and you're entitled to them; but, damn it, man, keep them to yourself!"

"And I'm ordering both of you to stay away from each other. Any trouble between you two, and I'll clap you both in irons. Is that well understood?"

"Yes, sir," Hailey said.

"I'll go along with that," King said.

"All right," the Captain said. "You'd best go back to your cabins and stay there, gentlemen, until the search is over. But in the absence of proof of foul play, I don't want suspicions raised among the other passengers. Have I your promise that this will go no further?"

They all nodded in agreement. Bruce and Hailey went back to the cabin.

"Goddamnit!" Hailey swore. "I've been practicing law these ten years, Bruce Harkness, and I know men. That murdering bastard is as guilty as hell!"

"Don't doubt it," Bruce said.

3

Bruce leaned over the rail of the *Flying Fish*, watching the shore line of California creep backward through the haze. And the ache in him that had brought him here was very small and quiet, and did not tear at him with the old urgency. Some time in those ninety-nine days of sailing, only two over the record for the voyage, it had lessened in him. There had been times on the Northward passage, broiling along with a fair wind and the Humboldt Current, when he thought it was dead. But then Hailey would come and talk eagerly, excitedly, of California and he would feel it stir again. But faintly, still; with nothing like its old force.

Every man has his California, he thought now, looking at it; but he can't map it. Do that, he'd have a chart of the inside of his soul. . . .

Then he saw Hailey coming toward him, picking his way among the dozens of passengers sleeping on the deck, blanket-wrapped against the December cold. They had come aboard at Panama City, fighting with animal ferocity to gain a place even on the open deck. There were hundreds of them who had chosen the terrible Isthmus crossing, in the mistaken belief that they would save time. But the green hell of the jungle, the slopes of the Culebra Mountains, and the gorges of the wild Chagres River held the unhallowed bones of many who had dropped from heat prostration, or tropic fevers, or died of snake bites. And in Panama City they had had to wait an average of three months for passage on a northbound vessel.

Seeing their desperation, the Captain had charged them all the traffic would bear: more, in most instances, than the original passengers had paid for the entire voyage. But they had come aboard anyhow, accommodations or not. The vessel was packed with them. Most staterooms, by virtue of partial refunds Captain Winters had granted to the men who had engaged them in New York, Baltimore, Charleston, and Savannah, now sheltered five men; a condition Bruce had flatly refused to countenance, compromising only so far as to share his with Hailey Burke, thus freeing Burke's cabin for the newcomers.

December, 'forty-nine, he mused now, watching his friend's tortuous passage. Half a century gone. Wonder what the next half is going to be like?

Hailey was smiling.

"End of the line, Bruce!" he said. "We'll sight Frisco in an hour. Got it straight from the horse's mouth. Cap'n told me himself."

Bruce looked at Hailey, peacefully.

"Reckon you're glad," he said.

"Glad!" Hailey said. "When I see the Golden Gate I'm going to let out a whoop'n a holler so damned loud that—"

He stopped and looked at Bruce, hard.

"Aren't you?" he said.

"So—so," Bruce drawled. "I don't excite easy, Hailey. Besides, if there's any sure thing in the world, it's that things never turn out the way a body expects them to. . . ."

"Aw, don't be so down in the mouth! Bet you we both end up rich!"

"Could be," Bruce said. "If you aim to get rich, reckon you will, Hailey, come hell or high water. You're that kind of a fellow. Even think I could too—that is, if I really want to. . . ."

Hailey stared at him.

"Name of God!" he said; "you mean you don't want to?"

"Didn't say that. If being rich will guarantee the kind of life I want—fine. If not, to heck with it."

Hailey stood there, studying him.

"Tell me, Bruce," he said; "what kind of a life do you want?"

Bruce smiled. He had a good smile, slow and easy and calm.

"Appears to me," he said, "the kind of life I want shouldn't interest you much, Hailey. You're going to be mighty busy, rallying around high, wide, and handsome, arranging your own. . . ."

"It does though. You're a curious cuss, Bruce. Never met a

man quite like you before. Go on, tell me—what do you want
out of life?"

"Nothing much," Bruce said slowly. "Hard to say it, though.
Never was real handy with words. Things I want are kind of
simple, Hailey: just plain, ordinary things like health and happiness and contentment. Like to live peaceably with my neigh-
bors; play fair with everybody; stay out of debt. Reckon that's
about all—except maybe to live the rest of my days with one good
woman, and bring up kids I can be proud of. . . ."

"Nothing in that money will hinder," Hailey said. "You got that
one good woman picked yet, Bruce?" Then he saw his friend's
face change. "Sorry," he said; "didn't mean to touch you in a sore
spot, boy. . . ."

"It's all right," Bruce said. "Happens to a lot of men, I reckon.
Had her picked, marched off to Mexico; and when I came back—"

"She'd married the little storekeeper who didn't know the muzzle from the breech?"

"Yes. Something like that," Bruce said.

"Too bad. But a flighty little filly like that wouldn't of—"

"She wasn't," Bruce said. "She had her reasons. Damned good
reasons, too; now that I've had time to think about them. . . ."

"You'll find another one. Fine, good-looking young feller like
you. . . ."

"Thanks, Hailey," Bruce said. "Now put down that trowel."

"I ain't laying it on! Damn it all, Bruce, you get a body plumb
downright aggrievated!"

"Sorry," Bruce said. "I'll bet that a fine, good-looking young fellow like you will find yourself not one filly, but half a dozen. . . ."

"Sure Lord aim to," Hailey grinned. "Say, Bruce, there's another
thing I been meaning to ask you. I know you don't hold with
fighting and killing; but don't you even own a gun?"

"No," Bruce said.

"How come? You're the first Southerner I ever did see who
didn't feel downright undressed without a handgun. Put 'em on
before we put on our pants. You know you're the only unarmed
man on this boat?"

"So?" Bruce said quietly. "I don't like the idea of killing folks;
and what the hell else is a handgun for?"

"Hell, Bruce, a handgun ain't necessarily for killing! It's mostly for keeping other folks from killing you. You better rush right out soon as we dock and—"

"No thanks, boy. I carried a gun from Vera Cruz to the walls of Chapultepec. That was enough. Ever see a gutshot man die, Hail?"

"Yep—once. It ain't a pretty thing."

"'Specially not when it was you who pulled the trigger. Reckon won't many situations come up I can't handle without a gun. . . ."

"But there just might be one, boy—just one is enough, you know —when a Colt will be the only thing standing 'twixt you and eternity. Like poor Mead. What about a thing like that?"

"Don't think King could have shoved me overboard gun or no gun," Bruce said. "If a thing comes up I can't handle that will be just too damned bad. . . ."

"Noble," Hailey said; "but downright impractical—'specially in Frisco . . . But, speaking of Mead, I wonder just where that damned, murdering blackguard hid that money?"

"Reckon we might have been wrong about that, boy," Bruce said; "better drop it, Hailey. . . ."

They leaned over the rail not talking any more. They had reached that now—that ease with one another that could fall into silence without embarrassment. It was, Bruce thought, a thing that was curiously fine. He had a dislike for useless talk. A man you could be friendly with in peace and quiet was a good friend, the best.

Funny. That business about the gun, now. That was Bible truth, and yet it wasn't the whole truth. But it wasn't a thing he could talk about. It was bound up too close with Jo. Jo, now, Jo—just to think her name hurt. . . .

Maybe the way I met her was unlucky, he thought; too bound up in hate'n violence . . . He went back then, out of time, the slow creeping shore line fading out, the sea, the sky, gone, changed into the then, the long ago, the achingly unforgotten; back to that wild, heady summer of 'forty-five, the one he had spent in dangerous dalliance with Sue Archer, risking the addition of his blood to that of all those which had stained the old dueling ground for the privilege of initiating Henry Archer, Sue's husband, into the Right Ancient and Dishonorable Society of Cuckolds, under the sign of the Horns crossed, on a night-black field.

There had been, actually, such an order, for he and his friends had founded it. He had been certain sure of eventual success in his intent, up until that day that—

That they had come up to the Rogers' House, bearing Sloan Rogers between them, his teeth set into his lower lip until they drew blood, to prevent any moan, any cry from escaping him. Barry Poindexter, who had done this thing, talked on, wildly, unceasingly. He seemed to have a need to talk.

"Didn't mean to hit him. You know that, Bruce. Meant to throw close to him and scare the living daylights out of him. But the way he looked at me unnerved me. That's what it was—the way he looked . . . Lord God, if I'd meant to hit him, would I have gutshot him like that? You've seen me shoot—you've all seen me shoot. Hell, I can drop pigeons from horseback with a handgun! Meant to kill him, I'd have done it clean!"

"Shut up, Barry," Bruce said.

"Lord God, Bruce, lemme talk! I wronged him—I had to meet him; I was honor bound to. But you don't shoot a man after you've pleasured yourself with his wife, you don't. . . ."

"Barry," Bruce said, "there're things a man don't talk about. Even if he's done 'em, he keeps his trap shut. I'm asking you to be quiet, Barry. I'm asking you mighty kindly. . . ."

"You mean you'll call me out? I wouldn't meet you. I'm never going to fight again, so help me God! Anybody can post me for a coward who wants to—but I won't—"

"Tom," Bruce said to Barry's second, "you'd better take him back now. We're most to the house. Better if he doesn't come in. . . ."

Tom had led young Poindexter away, still babbling.

And on the veranda, Josephine Rogers had met them.

It was the first time Bruce had seen her since she had come back from Mistress Anne's Academy for Young Ladies, in Richmond. Before that, she had been only one of the many young girls he knew, all teeth and freckles and flying hair. But now—

He almost stopped breathing, looking at her. She stood there, swaying a little, her face white, all color gone from it, and looked at her brother. Then she said, very quietly:

"You can bring him in here. . . ."

Bruce had come back again, each one of those eighteen days it

took Sloan Rogers to die, lying there, through the breathless heat
of the hottest August in twenty years, without a moan or a murmur or a whispered complaint, dying of the meanest gunshot
wound any man can take with patience and dignity and lonely
honor. But not for one instant did that look that Barry Poindexter
had talked about leave his face.

It got to Bruce, that look. Before the duel, he had been typical
of his class and his times, holding, in the Carolina of the 1830's
and forties, where duels were a daily occurrence, it was better
to die over a woman than a gambling row or even the color of a
man's waistcoat, which were things he had seen men shoot each
other about, with all the formality and circumspection of their
archaic code.

But after that day, he never saw his Sue Archer again, never
accomplished the overt act whose edges the two of them had
been skirting all summer; more from fear that he might some day
put that same look into Henry Archer's eyes than from any fear
of the consequences; arriving through his self-imposed ordeal of
watching his friend die, at the bone-deep conviction that no man
has the right to make another suffer like that, not only the physical
pain, which could be borne, as Sloan was bearing it now, but the
spiritual destruction, that intolerable, unquenchable anguish in
the soul of a man who has built his life around a woman, and has
been betrayed.

More, he came away from Sloan's funeral with the beginning
of the belief stirring in him that Churubusco, Chapultepec, and
Mexico City were to crystallize into a certainty: that there is nothing on earth or under high heaven that justifies killing a man. Not
anything. Ever.

But those eighteen days were the beginning of something else,
too. Jo had hated him at first for his part in it; for not deterring
her brother from challenging his wife's lover. But she had seen
that Sloan, dying, accepted Bruce still; she saw that what brought
Bruce back day after day was more than sympathy, more than
even friendship. It was suffering and shared guilt, and expiation.

So, in the end, she had come to love him. But not sadly, for
what he was; rather for what he was in the process of becoming.
Racing ahead of him, she saw as already completed the slow
emergence of the angel from the ape. And when he fell back

again, as he had to, into his age, his class, his milieu, she was
shocked and disappointed. For the day came when she found a
rival in his lust after glory; his desire to go and play the hero
above a shot-torn field. She tried, as women have always tried in
all ages, to show him the essential childishness of his dream of
martial valor. She failed, as women have always failed; but
wounded and angered, she rejected him.

To her sorrow. For he had in him, even then, the beginnings
of a man. And that, Ted Peterson, whom she afterwards married
out of loneliness and pique, for all his strength and vainglory
would never be.

Bruce shook his head, bringing the California coast into focus
again.

"Well," Hailey began; then they saw Rufus King coming toward
them, his even, perfect teeth, flashing in a smile beneath his trim
mustache.

"Since the voyage is over," he said, "I want you to know I have
no hard feelings against either of you. I suppose I gave you
grounds for suspicion with my talk. I guess I am a cynic; but not
a very active one. Let's bury the ax, shall we?"

He put out his hand.

Slowly Bruce took it.

"Won't condemn any man without proof," he said. "I'm not God.
Good luck to you, King. . . ."

Hailey shook hands with him, too.

"If," he growled, "you know in your heart you didn't do it, my
apologies are as sincere as your innocence, King. That's the best
I can manage. I liked John Mead. . . ."

"A pity," King said softly; "he was a fine man. Incidentally,
when I'm open for business, you're both welcome. . . ."

"Business?" Hailey said.

"You didn't imagine I came out here to swing a pick, did you,
Burke?" King laughed. "There's gold to be had all right, but I prefer to have it delivered to me—in comfort. No, within two or three
weeks, I'm going to open the Blue Diamond—the most luxurious
gambling establishment the West has ever seen. There'll be re-
freshments, of course, and entertainment. But I'll be only too

happy to pry you two loose from any gold you might find. . . ."

"I'll drop in for a drink and the entertainment," Bruce said slowly; "but gambling's a thing I gave up a long time ago. . . ."

"I'll drop in for a drink and the entertainment," Hailey drawled; "just long enough to see that your wheels aren't crooked. . . ."

"They won't be," King said easily; then: "By God, I believe that's Frisco!"

Somewhere near the bow of the *Flying Fish* a man started shouting, then another one took it up, and another and another, until they were all shouting it:

"Frisco! Frisco! Frisco, by God!"

The men who had been sleeping on the decks got up, hurling their blankets out and away from them, rushing to the rail, peering toward the dimly seen shore, toward the hundreds of vessels lying rotting at anchor for lack of crews to man them, the sailors gone, fled to the hills, to the goldfields—gazing toward the slowly growing cluster of tents, unpainted shacks, and rough-hewn hotels. They said it again, whispering the words like an invocation or a prayer:

"Frisco! Frisco, by God!"

Bruce and Hailey did not move. They stood there watching the passengers running to the staterooms, gathering up their duffle-bags, valises, shouting for the trunks which had been stored in the hold.

Hailey looked at Bruce and grinned.

"Gold fever's got 'em," he said. "Looks like they're taken right pert bad!"

"Pack of foolishness," Bruce said dryly. "It'll take better'n hour to dock from here. Even after that you can count on another hour or so before they get the stuff off. Where's the fire? No matter how they rush, they can't get off any faster. . . ."

"I can understand them," Hailey said. "All that gold out there—waiting. Got to be first, before somebody else gets it. Hell, Bruce, it's like a race! They're straining at the post. Out there, beyond those hills, lies the stuff that dreams are made of: No more hard work, the finest cigars to smoke, the best likker, pure silk shirts, broadcloth suits, handmade boots; the finest rig that money can buy with a matched, five-gaited pair of thoroughbreds to pull

it; the biggest house on top of the highest hill, the prettiest
women. . . ."

"That," Bruce said, "is a mighty puny dream, Hailey—"

"Puny!" Hailey exploded. "That's the dream of ninety-five percent of all the folks alive! Don't sneer at it, Bruce-boy, because
it's what made this country great. We're a pushy folk, Bruce Harkness, and the one thing you can't say about us is that anything we
do or say or dream or think is puny!"

"All right," Bruce said, "not puny. Childish. Crude. Maybe even
—wrong. You pick the one that fits it, Hailey. They all do, kind
of, to my way of thinking. . . ."

"Childish! Crude! Wrong! Name o' God, Bruce, it's a good thing
I like you! You're about the craziest, wrongest-headed cuss—"

Bruce smiled.

"I know," he said; "so I've been told. . . ."

"Aw hell," Hailey said; "a body just can't stay mad at you, can
they? You remind me of an old piebald nag I used to have.
Dumbest critter you ever did see. Did everything wrong. But he
was just so dadblamed nice and gentle I kept him till he died
of old age. . . ."

He looked at Bruce.

"Tell me, boy," he said; "if it's wrong to want the biggest and
the finest and the best, what is right?"

Bruce looked away from him, over the rail, at the young city.

"The question of Pilate," he said quietly, "or nearly. How the
heck do I know, Hailey? Finding out what's right for any man,
personally—I mean what is specially right for him, not for the
world in general, is a lifetime job. I just started working at it
since I got back from Mexico. Haven't found out all the answers
yet—not even most of 'em. Maybe I never will. But I aim to
try. . . ."

He had that feeling again. Not of lying exactly, but of skirting
the edges of the truth, kind of. It wasn't a good feeling. He knew,
or was beginning to know, what was right for him.

A little place, down in the valley of a river, where a body could
look up and see the mountains, and feel his soul grow tall with
them. A place of sun and talking waters, where things grew under
a man's hand. Not things like cotton, eating up the good earth,
and drawing men on and on to turn it into cash, into money.

Strange—there was a thing about money that seemed pretty near always to dirty a man's insides. But things that put bone and blood into a young'un, and the quietude into his soul . . . a strand of trees, maybe with the wind in them, whispering. Cows belling in a far field. A little house with a veranda, where a man could sit and look up into the everlasting hills from whence came his strength, when a good day's work was done. And a good, quiet woman beside him, sitting there, making baby things. The kind of plain, solid woman who had quietness and ease inside her, undriven and peaceful. Maybe some old hound dogs bugling as they quartered a field. Peace—the kind the Good Book said passeth all understanding. That, yes, that. . . .

But why hadn't he said these things to Hailey? Why couldn't he? He turned the question over in his mind, twisting it this way and that, tugging at it like a wire-haired terrier with a rat. And when he had it, finally, he said it:

"Reckon that ain't rightly so, Hail. Reckon I do kind o' know what I want, what's good for me. But I can't say it. Lies a mite too deep to be dredged up into words. Funny. There're some feelings a man has, he doesn't like to put tongue to—that speaking out would cheapen—like the kind of things that get all tarnished by light. Know that doesn't make much sense to you; but that's the way it is. . . ."

Hailey laid an affectionate hand on his shoulder.

"Know what, old hoss?" he said, "I don't understand you; but you're right. Don't even know how I know; but you are. I feel it in my bones."

"Thanks, Hailey," Bruce said.

It took them even longer than Bruce had thought it would. By the time they got ashore, finally, it was late afternoon. Hailey looked worried.

"We'd better look for lodgings right away, Bruce," he said. "I have a cousin who's been here since last February. From what he wrote me back, that's one of the main troubles, getting a place to sleep. . . ."

"He still here?" Bruce said. "Maybe we'd better look him up. . . ."

"No, worse luck. He's up around Sacramento way, panning gold. Never did write that he found any, though. . . ."

They moved through the gullies and the wagon-rutted paths that served as streets. The mud was ankle deep anywhere; but in the middle there were places where it came up to a man's knees. They went over the muddy, uneven streets that seemed to always go uphill, never down. They stopped now and again, to look around them.

They stood on a corner, staring at the men, nearly all of them wearing the red shirts which, by some curious quirk of fashion, had come to be almost a uniform for the goldseekers. All of them, without notable exception, were heavily bearded. That wasn't too surprising, for even back home, men were beginning to let their beards grow again, after nearly a hundred years of being clean shaven. Bruce wondered why—from the very beginning Americans had been a clean shaven folk, except for an occasional mustache. And now in the late forties you suddenly started to see beards everywhere. But nowhere else like here in California. . . .

The men rushed by, bearded, roaring, laughing, drunken. An old Chinese came by running. Behind him a burly miner came, waving a bowie knife and roaring with laughter.

"Pigtail!" he guffawed; "gonna cut me a nice long pigtail!"

The others watched, grinning, until both runners had rounded a corner out of sight.

"My cousin wrote me about that," Hailey said. "Told me cutting off the Chinks' pigtails was the miners' favorite sport. . . ."

They stood there, trying to decide which of the various gullies and washouts that served San Francisco as streets to take. Hailey touched Bruce's arm, and pointed to a sign.

The sign read: "This street ain't passable. Not even jackassable!"

Bruce smiled. "At least," he said, "they're truthful in this town. Now, where do we go from here?"

Across the street, a man stood, staring at them. He was a tall, heavy set man in his middle fifties, with a big Western hat pushed far back on his bald head. He started toward them, slowly, zigzagging around the mudholes. When he was close enough, he spoke to them.

"You boys Southerners?" he said.

"Yep," Hailey said at once; "how did you know?"

"Damned if I can figure it out, but I never miss. It's in the blood, I reckon. I'm a Mississippi man myself. Natchez. Where you boys from?"

"Augusta, Georgia," Hailey said; "and my friend's from Charleston. Might I be so bold as to ask your name, Sir?"

"Nathan Johnson," the man said, and put out his hand. "I run the gen'l store up Marysville way. And I'm mighty proud to make your acquaintance, gentlemen. California is fair overrun with damyankees. By the way, you ain't told me your names yet. . . ."

They introduced themselves. The man, Bruce decided, had a good face. A red, rugged kind of a face that looked good on a man.

"Yessir," Nathan Johnson went on, "mighty proud. And if there's any little thing I can do for you, just you name it, that's all. . . ."

"So happens there is," Hailey said. "Could you recommend a good hotel, Mr. Johnson?"

"Ain't no sich animal. They range from bad to God awful. Crown Inn, where I'm staying, is a little better than most. Come on, and I'll take you there. By the way, I'd esteem it as a favor if you called me Brother Nate. Folks most in generally does, hereabouts. . . ."

They started out, through the non-jackassable street. Before they had gone half a block, they saw a crowd of men, silently staring over a board fence into the yard of a house. The expressions on their faces were reverent and sad.

"What are they looking at, Brother Nate?" Bruce said.

"Come see," Brother Nate said; and his voice, speaking, had a curious timbre to it. Bruce and Hailey came up to the board fence. In the yard three children were playing. They were happily making mudpies under the benevolent gaze of a black-bearded miner who looked like he might have just stepped ashore off a buccaneering vessel.

"I don't see anything," Hailey said; "just some kids playing in the mud. . . ."

"By God, you *are* new!" Nate said. "Them there is pure-bred white, American kids. Men come from all over town just to look at 'em. Cap'n Ellis had to put up that fence 'cause the miners was always getting 'em sick, giving 'em sweets. . . ."

"I still don't see—" Hailey said.

"I do," Bruce said. "Know how many decent white women there are in this town, Hailey?"

"I can answer that," Nate said. "Thirty-nine. And twenty-five thousand men. 'Course there's about three hundred whores, mostly Chinks and Chilenos. . . ."

"Chilenos?" Bruce said; "from Chile?"

"Naw. Mostly Mex. But the first bunch come from Chile so we sort of got into the habit of calling all Spanish speaking folks Chilenos. Look at them kids! Know how rare a sight that is? Does your heart good just to look at 'em. . . ."

"Children are so rare in California," Hailey said softly, mostly to himself, "that men come from miles around to watch them play . . . That's goddamned sad, come to think of it. . . ."

"It is that. 'Minds them of the families they left behind. Some of these boys been here since the fall of 'forty-eight. Never will forget the day Cap'n Ellis got off the boat with Mrs. Ellis and them there kids. Three minutes after they stepped ashore, there was five hundred men following that little family through the streets, more'n half of 'em crying without shame. Had to put a guard around them—not that anybody meant them any harm, mind you; but them rough miners kept reaching out their filthy paws to touch a child. . . ."

"And it's been like this ever since?" Bruce said.

"Yep. Damnedest thing you ever saw. Cap'n went off to the gold fields and made a pretty good strike. But when he come back, them kids had twice as much gold dust as he did. Miners kept dropping by, giving it to 'em. And Miz Ellis—as pretty a li'l' yaller-headed filly as you ever did see—never had a thing to worry about; men took turns guarding the house to keep them Sydney ducks out . . ."

"Sydney ducks?" Hailey said.

"Rough necks, escaped convicts and such like from Sydney, Australia. Teamed up with another bunch of Five Point and Bowery hoodlums from New York who call themselves the Regulators. Nine-tenths of all crime in Frisco can be attributed to one or the other of them. Come along, now. It ain't far . . . What was I saying before?"

"That the miners guarded Captain Ellis' house," Bruce said.

"Sure Lord did. Never an hour went by when there wasn't an armed man patrolling up and down. Big rough miners with whiskers a yard long took turns minding the baby, doing Miz Ellis' wash—did it damn fine, too—cutting wood, running errands; and wouldn't take a cent or even a drink of likker for doing it. Just wanted to talk to a decent white woman, and see some clean, white, American kids. . . ."

"Kind-hearted lot, aren't they?" Hailey said.

"Wish I could say yes to that," Nate said slowly; "but I honestly can't. All their goodness is reserved for their own kind. We don't treat a dog nor a nigger back home the way they treat a Chink or a Chileno—Well, here we are. . . ."

The Crown Inn, as Brother Nate had said, was a little better than some of the other hotels. That is, the management only put four men in one room, by which term the proprietor of that august hostelry meant a tiny cubicle made of partitions of unbleached muslin tacked up from wall to wall.

"Yes," the owner said, "I guess I can find sleeping space for these boys, seeing as how they be friends of yours, Brother Nate. The price will be ten dollars a night. . . ."

"Good God!" Hailey said.

"Ain't bad," Nate whispered. "Most places gits twenty. An' steals the blankets off you once you're asleep, to rent over again to newcomers at three dollars the blanket. 'Nother thing, notice they ain't no signs about rats? They keep 'em out of here. But in them other places they post signs, 'Beware of Rats, The Management Ain't responsible for Damage Inflicted by Rodents;' and even so, many a man's woke up to find the tip of his ears or his nose chewed off by them big rats, damn near the size of a month-old puppy, that come in on the first ships. . . ."

"Reckon we'd better take it," Bruce said.

"Be wise to leave your valises with Honest John, here—he almost deserves that name—while we go out and get something to eat, and a wee snort alongside of it. My treat, since you're strangers. . . ."

"Why, that's mighty white of you, Brother Nate," Hailey said.

Following Nate's suggestion, they ordered sirloin steaks and potatoes, which were both fairly cheap, by California standards, and good. Any green vegetable at all would have cost them five dollars a plate despite the fabulous crops grown just outside of town. Afterwards, Nate showed them the town, talking all the while.

"Naturally you're going prospecting?" he said.

"I'm not sure about that," Bruce said. "I'd kind of like to invest in a decent spread of good farming land somewhere hereabouts. . . ."

"You mean you ain't going placer mining? Put her there, Mister Harkness! Does me good to meet a real smart man!"

"Didn't say that," Bruce said; "I mean to take a little whack at it. But unless I strike it rich enough to make it interesting within a month or two, I'm going to quit. Doesn't tempt me too much—beyond the fact that I'd like to have enough cash to stock whatever place I buy. . . ."

"Go to it, boy!" Johnson said. "Maybe you'll be lucky. Leastwise you got sensible ambitions. 'Sides you look like a man who can take disappointment in his stride. . . ."

"Then mining is disappointing?" Hailey asked.

"Yes—and no. Most everybody most in generally finds some gold. Put it this way, young feller: You can stand in icy water fourteen hours a day, pan five to ten tons of dirt, and come out ten or twelve dollars richer at the end of the day. Considering the way you break your back, that's damn poor pay. . . ."

"I'll say it is," Hailey said.

"Figure the percentages, son. There're over a hundred thousand men digging the bottom out of California. Four or five hundred have struck it rich. Five hundred out of a hundred thousand. That's what your chances are. And the ones who made a good strike don't always have it so good. Take Cap'n Sutter, the man on whose place they found the first gold. . . ."

"What happened to him?" Bruce said.

"Same as happens to any man who ain't quick with a gun, and mighty handy with his fists. Claim jumpers overrun his place, destroyed his crops, pulled up the vegetables in his garden looking for gold stuck to their roots. Lost everything, even his land. Marshall, the man who actually found the yellow stuff, got run out of the district because them claim jumpers thought he was holding out on 'em about where more gold was to be found. I tell you, son—I mean Mr. Harkness—gold is an evil thing!"

"Don't mind what you call me," Bruce said. "But even at ten dollars a day, a man ought to be able to live pretty fair. . . ."

"Pretty fair? Lord God, boy! For ten dollars a day, you can't eat in California! See that man over there selling apples? Go over and ask him how much one costs—go on, ask him!"

Bruce went over to the apple seller. The apples were magnificient; bigger and redder than any he had ever seen before. He picked up a huge one.

"I'll take this one," he said; "how much?"

"Five dollars," the man said calmly.

Bruce put the apple back.

"I got cheaper ones," the man said. "These here is three dollars apiece. And them over there is my cheapest—one dollar."

Bruce looked at the dollar apples. At home, in Carolina, he would have fed them to the pigs.

"No thanks," he said; "from now on, I'm off apples." He went back to the others.

"You see," Johnson said, "that's the way it is with everything. Laundry, twenty dollars a dozen pieces—and it takes a month to get your shirts back. And they ain't laundrymen any more. They're 'Clothing Refreshers' and don't forget it! Notice I had to call that damn' sloppy waiter in that joint where we ate, 'Mister Steward'? Wouldn't of waited on us if I hadn't. Folks out here is stark, raving crazy—and it's gold what's done it all. . . ."

"Lord God, Bruce," Hailey said. "What are we going to do about laundry? I can't afford those prices—and I don't have enough shirts to wait a month!"

"Folks," Nate said, "what has enough extras, sends their shirts out to Hawaii by clipper to get 'em done. That takes eight weeks, but it's a hell of a lot cheaper, and your duds come back looking real nice—which is more than you can say for these 'Refreshers' who most in generally ruins 'em. Thing to do is to buy some red mining shirts and do 'em yourself. Wear 'em roughdry. Considering the number of wimmin in town, you ain't got no call to try to look pretty. . . ."

"Everything is like that, Brother Nate?" Bruce said.

"Every living thing. A shovel'll cost you twenty-five dollars.

Miner's pan, five—made out of the cheapest kind of tin. Five dollars a pound for coffee, thirty dollars for a butcher knife, and a pound of nails is worth exactly their weight in gold. Tacks, too. Figured that out once—when I needed some tacks to hang up a partition in my store. It comes to one hundred and ninety-two dollars for one measly pound o' carpet tacks!"

"Then how in God's name can a man live?" Hailey said.

"Keep a store—that's what I do—and charge all the traffic will bear. Go into real estate: build a shanty hotel on a vacant lot, and rake in fifty thousand dollars a year 'til it falls down, on a total investment of less than five thousand dollars. Practice medicine: ten dollars per pill, a hundred even to write a prescription. Law: stir up a wee doubt about the validity of land titles—hell, son, there ain't a valid land title in the whole of California—and you'll die a millionaire!"

Bruce smiled.

"All of those things strike me as being a mite too close to stealing," he said.

"They are stealing. I get down on my knees every night and ask the Good Lord to forgive me for the prices I charge. Then I get up the next morning and raise them another notch. As I said, gold's an evil thing. It gets you, even indirectly. . . ."

He looked at Bruce.

"By the way, son, speaking of land, maybe I'd better introduce you to Preacher Rowe. He's got a little farm up in Pleasant Valley —right close to Marysville. Prettiest spread of land you ever did see. Only he neglects it right smart, because of the crazy ideas he's got that God's done called him personally to preach the Gospel to sinners. Damn' fool thing, 'cause these Frisco hellions ain't ready for nobody's word—not even God's. The pity is, he's one damn fine farmer, too. . . ."

"I'd be mighty proud," Bruce said.

"He'll be glad to meet you boys," Nate said. "Fill you full of Scriptures, then give you the biggest feed that ever bust a waistcoat. Him'n me come down together. . . ."

He stopped and looked at them, grinning.

"Talking about that—how would you boys like to ride up to Marysville with me'n the Preacher tomorrow? I got a big wagon— a real prairie schooner, still sound in spite of the fact I drove it here all the way from Independence, Missouri—took nigh onto five months, and was it hell! An' won't be nothing in it but me'n the Preacher and a few things I bought. . . ."

"I think," Bruce said, "you've done enough for us, Brother Nate. We'll be glad to pay you for the trip. . . ."

"Hell, boy! Don't insult me like that! It's a pleasure. Lord God, I ain't heard no good old Southern talk in so damn' long . . . 'Sides it's the wisest thing for you to do. First off, you can see the Preacher's place. Then I can supply you with miner's outfits—at cost, and you can pay me when you git around to it, so's you don't git robbed by these here pirates in Frisco. And I can steer you clear of the usual greenhorns' pitfalls. Come on, boys, what do you say?"

"Delighted!" Hailey laughed, before Bruce could open his mouth.

"Good. C'mon now. We'll find the Preacher right around that corner. . . ."

They turned the corner and saw him. He stood on the steps of an adobe building, holding a Bible in his hand. His hair was long and white.

He looks, Bruce thought, like a prophet. Or a saint, maybe.

"The way of the Transgressor is hard!" the Preacher said. "Repent! Oh, Brothers, why risk hellfire?"

There were a crowd of miners around him. They were nearly all drunk. They stood there listening to the Preacher and grinning.

"Beware of the Scarlet Woman!" the Preacher went on. "He who consorts with harlots is in danger of everlasting torment!"

"Well now, Rev," one of the miners called out, "if we don't consort with harlots, who th' hell is we gonna consort with?"

The others laughed then; the sound of it bullthroated, ugly.

"I tell you, by that path you go down to destruction! Her lips drippeth honey—"

Their laughter drowned the old man's words.

"Wait a minute, Rev," one of them yelled; "I'm gonna bring you sumpin' to preach about. Do better with what you're talking 'bout in front of you. . . ."

He dashed off. Minutes later he was back, dragging a woman behind him. The woman's dress was strange. She wore long black gloves, and a black hat with plumes. The top of her dress fitted her like a second skin—what there was of it, which wasn't much. A goodly proportion of her bulged out above it. Her skirt was modest enough. It was ankle length and very full.

"C'mon, Suzette!" the miner yelled. "Show the Rev what he's been a talking about. C'mon, baby-doll, give him an eyeful!"

He started clapping then, making a rhythmical sound. The others took it up, one after another, until they were all clapping.

The girl smiled, a slow, lazy smile. Then she started to dance. The dance was mostly kicking. She could kick higher than anybody Bruce had ever seen. She came toward the Preacher, kicking. She had on black stockings with sequins woven into them. There were fake jewels in the garters which held them up. Her underthings were lace. Black lace.

"Can-can," Nathan Johnson said. "Poor ol' Preacher!"

The miners roared. They hugged each other, tears streaming down their faces. They kicked too, imitating Suzette.

The girl was so close to the Preacher now, that her high heels almost touched his face. He shrank back, paling.

"That," Bruce growled, "is a mighty ugly thing, Nate—"

"Damned right it is," Johnson said; "but you can't break it up. Start a riot sure'n hell. . . ."

"You think so?" Bruce said, and started forward; but, before he was halfway across the street, it happened. By accident, or design, the girl's toe caught the big Bible and sent it spinning from the Preacher's hand. It landed in a mudhole, and sank out of sight.

The miners stopped laughing. They looked at each other.

"Damn it, Sue!" the man who had brought her said. "You hadn't oughta of done that!"

"Don't hold with playing with the Good Book," another said. "That there's the worst kind o' bad luck. . . ."

"Damn right it is. Wait a minute, Rev. I'll go fish it out—"

"Naw," the man with the dancer said. "It were my fault. I brung this here wench out here. You git, Sue! Dagnap it, git afore I really gits mad!"

The girl started back toward the saloon, with a slow, insolent saunter. The man swung his arm back and brought his open hand down across her bottom, hard. She jumped straight up, and came down running.

The miner waded into the mudhole. It came up to his thighs.

He reached down, feeling for the Bible. Finally he found it and straightened up, holding it. He stood in the midst of the mudhole, looking at it. Then he waded out, still staring at it.

Bruce could feel the silence in the street. It crawled along a man's nerves.

The man approached the Preacher. He took his hat off.

"Reckon it's ruint, Rev," he said. "I'm mighty sorry . . ." He fished in his pocket and came out with a little bag. "Here," he said, "take this an' buy yourself another, Rev . . . A real fine one with red leather bindings and gold letters. And the first time you preach outen it, I'm going to come listen to you. Real quiet like, by God!"

"Me, too!" the others chorused.

The old man stood there, the tears pencilling his cheeks until the last of them had gone.

"God moves in a mysterious way," he whispered, "His wonders to perform!"

Then Brother Nate came up to him and touched his arm.

"Brother Nate," the Preacher said; "you saw that? The day of miracles is not yet over. . . ."

"I'll say it ain't," Nate said. "Reverend, I want you to meet two brand new friends of mine. This here red-haired beanpole is Mr. Hailey Burke, from Georgia; and this kind of sawed off, square-built young feller here, strong as a mule, I'll bet—is Mr. Bruce Harkness from South Carolina. . . ."

"Pleased to meet you both, I'm sure," Preacher Rowe said. "Have you gentleman been saved?"

"Now, now, Reverend. You gonna have lots of time to save their souls. They're riding up with us tomorrow. Mr. Harkness is kind of interested in buying a farm. Reckon you could put him up whilst he looks around."

"Delighted," Preacher Rowe said; "in fact, I'll help him look. Number of deserted farms we got in the valley now, he ought to be able to take his pick. . . ."

"Deserted?" Bruce said. "Thought you said that was good farming country, Brother Nate?"

"The best. But gold fever got 'em. C'mon now, boys, we'd best be starting back. Frisco ain't no town to be out in after dark, 'less you're plumb hankering after trouble. Lord God, I'm tired!"

"So'm I," Hailey said; "come to think of it. . . ."

Bruce didn't say anything. He didn't hear them. There was the sound of laughing waters in his ears; a talking wind stirring the plane trees. Before his eyes, the wheat bowed a little to the wind, and the yellow corn tossed its tassels.

Hailey Burke stared at him.

"What ails you, Bruce?" he said.

"Oh?" Bruce said. "Reckon I was dreaming, kind of, Hailey. . . ."

All four of them started back up the street together.

Honest John, the owner of the Crown Inn, came out from behind his desk.

"Mr. Harkness," he said; "there was a Chileno kid here looking for you. Said it was important. . . ."

"Where is he?" Bruce said.

"I sent him away. Good God, Mister Harkness, I can't have no damn Chilenos hanging around my place—give the Inn a bad name. I must say you got some mighty peculiar friends. . . ."

Bruce looked at him. His eyes were level and still.

"Did the kid leave any message?" he said quietly.

"Matter of fact, he did. Lemme see—Yep. Here it is, right here. . . ."

Bruce took the little scrap of paper and held it a long moment, still staring at the manager.

"Anybody who comes looking for me in the future," he said; "Chink, Chileno, or Nigger—you let him wait. Understand me, Honest John?"

His voice speaking, was flat, calm, without emphasis, or emotion. But hearing it, seeing his eyes, Honest John took a backward step.

"Yessir," he said; "didn't mean no harm, sir. . . ."

But Bruce was already reading the note. He straightened up after a moment and met Hailey Burke's eyes.

"It was in the lifeboat, hid in the boxes of emergency rations," he said. "He must have heaved the grub over the side, then hid the money there. Then he got rid of the valise the same way. He waited behind until everybody was gone ashore. The crew was too busy, trying to figure out a way to jump ship. Probably waited until the wind swung her around 'til that particular lifeboat was on the seaward side, and all those beggars had gone over to the other side to gaze at San Francisco. Then he took it out. But the kid was watching him—I'd tipped him off to. . . ."

"And they searched the lifeboats," Hailey whispered.

"But not the ration boxes. They were looking for a valise, remember. . . ."

"And I shook hands with that dirty, murdering bastard!" Hailey said. "And the worst part about it, Bruce, is we'll never be able to prove it now. . . ."

Slowly Bruce shook his head.

"Wasn't the first time for him," he said quietly. "The job was too expert. And it won't be the last. . . ."

"What do you mean, Bruce?"

"That we'll just have to wait 'til he tries it again," Bruce Harkness said.

4

They crossed the bay in the *Pioneer*, the little shallow draft steamer that was already beginning to ply between San Francisco and Sacramento. And all the way across the bay, until they reached the mouth of the Sacramento River, where he had left the wagon, Nathan Johnson talked.

Bruce didn't much mind the talk, because he recognized it for what it was: Nate's stored up loneliness for his own kind of people. But there was something else in it, too: that garrulity which is one of the signs of the coming on of old age, that curious total recall that remembers everything except the fact that the same story has been told more than once, guarding this one avenue of forgetfulness sometimes up to the twentieth telling.

"You said that before, Nate," the Preacher said dryly.

"Did I now? Beats me—reckon I'm a gitting old. . . ."

But Hailey egged Nate on, the questions he put to the storekeeper having more than a little of the shrewdness, the hidden probing of the cross-questioning lawyer, pumping him dry, and pondering over his answers. Bruce pondered over them too, but differently. Hailey's plain intent was to find out how to do things, where to look for gold, what to avoid, all the downright practical things that came to him, but Bruce's mind didn't work like that.

He was, he realized now, more concerned with the "why" of things than the how. He was content to be that way. Sometime during the long voyage back from Vera Cruz, after the War was over, sometime in the bitter darkness when he fought against accepting his loss of Jo, he had come face to face with himself and made his peace with what he was. He had too much humility to realize what a fine thing that was, or even how rarely it happened. Since talking, 'dredging up a thing in words' as he put it, was a thing that came hard with him, he was shut off from knowing that this feat of growing up, of becoming a man was one of the rarest things in life. Most men are worn down, dragged down into defeat, into death, learning to their rebellious sorrow that the things they wanted out of life are not to be; but carrying, even so, to the very grave their adolescent dreams in all their pristine puerility. But most men never learn that their dreams are about things that don't exist, fantasies born of boredom and discontent reaching into the child world of what never was except in the half bright vale of dreaming.

Not that Bruce had ceased to dream. But his dreams themselves were of the stuff of reality. Even his nice stretch of farmland carried with it in his imagination the ache of tired muscles after a day of ploughing, the search for a strayed cow, pulling her out of the mire at the last, the mending of broken fences, a well gone dry, a hail storm flattening the wheat, a crop failure. He even looked forward to these difficulties, knowing they were a part of it, the bitter condiments that gave spice to living. And even in the curiously mild hope he had of someday finding a woman who suited him, lay the recognition that he must accept as the price of the qualities he held most desirable in a woman, easefulness and tranquility, a certain dullness, even perhaps, a kind of stupidity. He was aware that in many ways, Jo wouldn't have suited him at all; he had known that she was flame and fury, a hard driving woman with an edge to her tongue and the flash of sudden lightnings in her eyes; but he had accepted that, knowing that love was not a sensible emotion. At bottom, mingled with his sorrow, but not displacing it, was a certain sense of relief. And this he accepted, too, without surprise or anger or shame, as he had come to accept all things, realizing how little any one thing, in the long stretch of a man's years, really mattered. . . .

But in the wagon, now, going up the trail that followed the river northward, the talk had changed. The jolting prairie schooner took Nate back to the crossing of the plains in the wagon train, five months of slow plodding out of Missouri until they had rolled down the last slopes into the green world of California, dragging back against the wagons to keep them from overrunning the oxen.

Nate remembered it all, every detail; and he told it with the un-
imaginative man's total honesty.

He made them see it: the oxen staggering along in the breathless heat as they crossed the Humboldt Desert of Nevada, the
men forcing draughts of vinegar down their throats to save them
from the alkali dust which rose and choked them; people doubling
up in the wagons as the last of a friend's team dropped and died,
or dividing among them the passengers of the two wagons whose
owners had been foolish enough to buy mules, and who had had
their teams stolen in the night by the Indians who came like ghosts
and drove the animals off without the guards even hearing them.
The leather boots they made for the oxen's feet to protect them
from the sharp stones and the burning, alkaline sands. The young
wife, four months pregnant, who died of snake bite on the prairie
where she had gone to gather buffalo chips to cook her husband's
supper; and he, looking at her, saying: "Tried to leave her behind
'til I could get set. She could of come round the Horn by ship, later.
But she wouldn't hear of it—She wouldn't. . . ."

. . . The taste of prairie dog broth which was the only fresh
meat they had for weeks, except for the rare occasions they could
trade with the Indians for new-killed buffalo. For though they
saw hundreds of the great, shaggy beasts, being Easterners and
mostly city men they lacked the skill in stalking that it took to get
close enough to shoot. . . .

The wagons overturned, crossing a stream. The intrigue and
bickering in the selection of a leader. The mistakes and stupidi-
ties which forced them to depose him finally, and elect another—
no better—whose mistakes they endured, realizing now, that not
a man among them knew enough to do the thing right. . . .

The wagons they met coming back, the people in them de-
feated, saying: "We've seen the elephant!" A phrase, Nate explained, they took as a catch word, arising out of Barnum's
exhibition of the first such beast ever seen in America, but coming
to mean among them: "We've had enough. We're licked. . . ."

The piles of stuff abandoned on the prairie to lighten the wagons, most of it deliberately rendered useless: flour scattered about,
turpentine poured over the sugar; mattresses, clothing, blankets
ripped, torn, partially burned to keep those who came behind
from gaining any use or comfort from them.

"Damn!" Hailey said. "Wouldn't have thought folks could be so blamed mean. . . ."

"They was though, and we was beginning to run out of grub by then," Nate said. "Could of used some of that stuff if they had let it be. Not everybody was like that, though; once or twicet we found stuff piled up real neat with a little sign on it saying, 'Help Yourself.' There's always goodfolks, Hailey. . . ."

"What about Indian attacks?" Hailey said.

"Told you before: we hardly ever even seen an Injun. And the ones we saw was mostly peaceable. 'Course we corralled the wagons every night; but Injuns don't attack a train of fifty wagons. They most in generally waits for little teams of five or six. 'Sides they prefer to come at night and steal anyhow, without having to risk a scrap. . . ."

"Doggone it, Nate!" Hailey said half seriously. "You're taking all the romance out of it. I'd almost decided to come that way so I could brag to my grandchildren about shooting buffalo and fighting off redskins. . . ."

"That's the way it were," Nate said stubbornly. "Even so, we was lucky to get here, considering how green we was. . . ."

Bruce turned it over in his mind; all of it: the malice which had destroyed supplies that might have saved a newcomer's life; the weariness, the boredom, the small, pitiful tragedies. Yes, he thought, reckon that's the way it was all right 'cause that's the way things generally are. If a thing ain't flashy and exciting, we can't see the bigness in it. But that was big; hell, it was great. They didn't know it, but what they did, the muddling through, the going on, making their mistakes and paying for them; but keeping it up, tired, hot, sick, hungry, moving on, enduring—is the real stuff of greatness. Takes people a long time afterwards to forget how it truly was and to write in the flash, the fire, the excitement. Got to be heroes, then—only they don't know what the word means. Most men can be brave for ten minutes, an hour, two hours; but to be brave for five months at a stretch, when it's tiresome, when there ain't no apparent glory in it, takes some doing. Heck, they were heroes—real honest to God heroes; the kind that count, that move, and build, and endure. Reckon I got my belly full of quick, useless bravery in Mexico. That kind was better. . . .

"No," he said to Nate, "you weren't lucky. You would have made it, come hell or high water. Reckon you had it in you to make it. Funny, Brother Nate, but it's greater the way you tell it—like true things are always greater than lies. . . ."

They plodded on, up the river bank, behind the mules that had replaced Brother Nate's oxen. Mules were faster than oxen, but more difficult to manage. Still even with mules, it seemed to take forever.

About halfway, on the fourth day of the eight it took them to get from San Francisco to Marysville, Nate pulled the mules up with a hard jerk, a grin splitting his face.

"Pepe!" he roared.

Bruce looked at the man who had drawn his horse to a stop. He was a Mexican and he was something to see. Taller than Bruce, almost as tall as Hailey, he was a type of Mexican that Bruce knew was extremely rare. That is, he was nearly all Spanish, fair-skinned, aquiline of feature, handsomer even than Rufus King, who was one of the best looking men Bruce had ever seen. Because of his service in the Mexican War, Bruce knew that the Mexicans were one of the purest strains, racially speaking, in all Spanish America. There never were more than a handful of Spaniards in Mexico. And though they had done their lusty best to produce a mestizo race, it was the Indian strain that predominated, even in such mixtures. But most Mexicans were not mixed at all; remaining Aztec, Tarascan, or Oaxacan, with a scattering of other tribes among them.

He looked at the man called Pepe with interest. Pepe was very fine from his snowy sombrero to the heels of his magnificent boots, capped with tremendous silver spurs. He had a multicolored *serape* over his shoulder, and his tight pants were ornamented with silver coins. Even the cord which held his sombrero on, riding high on his chin instead of beneath it, was carried through a silver ring. His revolver had a hammered silver handle, and his saddle was of tooled leather, inlaid with silver fillagree.

I'll bet, Bruce thought, he hasn't a *real* in his pockets—all on his back, like most of that type. But he's upper class, an *haciendado,* if I ever saw one. Wonder what the hell he's doing here?

"Boy, oh boy!" Hailey whispered. "Look at that!"

And then, for the first time, Bruce saw the woman.

She rode behind the Mexican on a burro. She was very simply dressed in the style of a peon woman, without jewels or ornaments of any kind. She seemed at first to Bruce to be all Indian; but then he remembered what the Indians of Mexico looked like. Flat faces, impassive eyes as slanted as those of an Oriental, broad features—all of them, to the Anglo-Saxon taste, as ugly as homemade sin. The woman was as dark as an Azteca; but her features were as fine, as sharply chiseled as her husband's—if he were her husband. She, for all her simplicity of dress, was finer than the man. She came, Bruce guessed, of a race older than the white man, and from the very best of that race. Everything about her was regal. He did not know, could not decide if she were beautiful or not. It required an adjustment difficult for him to make to see beauty in a woman darker than many of the mulattoes on his father's plantation; but she was striking. Nobody was going to forget a woman like that in a hurry, he reckoned.

The man rode up to the wagon now, smiling.

"*Que tal, Amigo?*" he said to Nate. "You 'ave taken all the gold of all the poor miners of Frisco? Seguro it is so!"

His English was fluent and good, if heavily accented. But Bruce was curious to find out about him, his incessant urge to know the "why" of things, tugging at his mind.

"Nope," Nate laughed. "Can't beat those bandits, Pepe. Man who can outsmart them ain't been born. . . ."

"*Buenas dias, Padre,*" Pepe said to Reverend Rowe. "The saving of the souls of the *malos* goes well?"

"Don't call me *Padre!*" the Preacher snapped. "How many times do I have to tell you I'm not a priest, Pepe?"

Pepe shrugged, his face filled with mirth and good humor.

"*Padre*—Reverend," he laughed; "this makes the small difference, does it not, in the eyes of God? Permit me to call you *Padre*. It is hard to break old habits, and are you not truly *el Padre mio* in the spirit?"

"I try hard," Reverend Rowe said dryly; "but you're hopeless, Pepe. If even Juana can't keep you straight, reckon I can't, either. Call me *Padre* if you like; it doesn't make much difference. . . ."

"*Muchas gracias, Padre,*" Pepe said. "Ah, Señor Nate, I see that you have friends. Is it permitted that I make their acquaintance?"

"Why sure," Nate said. "This here is Mister Burke—and this is Mister Harkness. . . ."

"Pleased to meet you, Pepe," Hailey said; but Bruce took the Mexican's hand and said quietly:

"*Mucho gusto, Señor—*"

Pepe's dark eyes lighted.

"Ah!" he said; "you speak our language? That is very rare, Señor. . . ."

"Rare," Bruce said; "but of much necessity if all men are to be friends. I have remained for many months in your so beautiful country, which I entered as a soldier, a thing for which I have now much regret. But the Little Sisters of Mercy saved my life, so afterwards—"

"You have felt differently about the poor 'Greasers' eh, Señor Harkness?"

"*Si,*" Bruce said. "So differently that I like not that word. . . ."

"Ah, *bueno!*" Pepe said. "It is good to have friends among *los Americanos.* I have not many such."

"Your name of family is?" Bruce asked.

"Córdoba. Pepe Luis Miguel Hernando de Córdoba—Vallejo, your secure servitor, Señor! You go to search for gold?"

"Perhaps," Bruce said; "but chiefly to buy a rancho. I have much envy to become a ranchero. The miner's life does not appeal to me. . . ."

"It is hard," Pepe sighed; "but it has its fascinations. Still, Señor, if you ever have need of a good peon to help you with your rancho, bear me in mind. . . ."

Bruce laughed aloud.

"A peon?" he said. "You? Do not forget I know *Mexicanos,* Pepe."

"Still it is a peon that I have become. Since I met Juana. My father, who is one *gran haciendado,* you comprehend, indicated to me the door of the *hacienda* when he found out about it. . . ."

"Why?" Bruce said.

"Clearly because she was a peon on the little ranch of my uncle. My father, you understand, is very strict."

"This," Bruce said, "is a very rare thing. That a daughter who had disgraced herself with a peon might very well be shown the door of the *hacienda,* I believe; but a son, no. That would be a very small thing over which your father would surely have laughed, and said: 'Ah, but he is very manly, my son!'"

"*Si*. You are right. But not when this son is so ill advised as to make a marriage in church before the *Padre* with the daughter of peons. That is, you comprehend, another thing, and even more rare. . . ."

"But comprehensible, also. She is very attractive, your wife. . . ."

"Attractive?" Hailey said, glad of this chance to prove how well he had profited from his shipboard lessons. "Hell, Bruce, that there girl ain't just attractive; she's one of the damned most beautiful women I've seen in my whole blamed life!"

And looking at her now, Bruce saw that it was so.

"Clearly," he said to Pepe, "your Uncle did not share your father's prejudice against peons. . . ."

"My father," Pepe grinned, "had no prejudice against them—only against marrying them. And my uncle doubtless was of the same opinion. I think that Juana is my cousin, or she would have a face like a soup platter like all the rest of the Aztecas. Perhaps this is why we make a warfare in the blood and cannot make children," he added sadly.

"Still," and Bruce smiled, "it is a kind of work that one does not find difficult to continue—and always there is hope. . . ."

He saw the dull red flush under Juana's coppery skin.

"Pardon me, *Señora*," he said; "I meant no offense. . . ."

"For nothing," Juana said, and her voice, speaking, was like a golden gong, deep and rich and vibrant.

Nor her voice, Bruce thought. A man, hearing it, would never forget that, either. . . .

"Ah," Pepe said, squinting at the sun, "we must go. But do not forget, *Señor*, if you should have need of help. . . ."

"I shall call upon you," Bruce said; "though it is to be doubted that the son of an *haciendado* knows too much about the actual work of planting. . . ."

"You wrong me," Pepe said. Then, in English, to Reverend Rowe: "Am I not a good farmer? Tell the *Señor* it is so. . . ."

"The best," Reverend Rowe said. "Used to work for Murphy, on the farm next to mine—before Murphy got gold fever, and ran off, leaving the place. Pepe's got a touch of that disease himself. Had any luck, Pepe?"

"Various. I have found gold, but only a little. And each discovery called for a celebration, at the termination of which the gold was gone in payment for the wine. I think that God knows what He is doing to put only a little gold in each place, or else we should all be dead of the sickness induced by drunkenness. *Hastas la vista, Señores. . . .*"

"*Vaya con Dios,* Pepe," Bruce said. "Go with God. . . ."

They moved on, up the trail. Bruce looked back, seeing the man riding the blooded stallion as though he had been born on a horse, and after him the woman plodding along on the little burro, sitting tall and erect like a queen. He continued to look at her for a long time. Then, at the very last moment when it was possible for him to see such a thing, she turned and looked at him. Hailey was looking at her, too; but Bruce was sure it was not Hailey she looked at. Her eyes were night black, deeper than night, as full of concealment. They rested on his face a long time, without movement, without any discernible emotion; deep and calm and sure. He felt hot, somehow. He cursed under his breath.

If a mulatto wench looked at me like that, he thought, I'd be insulted. That type isn't much better. Precious little difference between a mestiza and a mulatto, anyhow. . . .

But Hailey spoke then, unconsciously driving a knife into the very heart of his thought:

"Funny," Hailey said; "but I always did have a lot of respect for Indians. And that's what she is, mostly. I kind of cotton to anything that's proud. Can't read or write her name, I'll bet; but gawddamnit, that one's a queen!"

"A queen?" Bruce said; "you got a mighty heap of imagination, Hailey—making a queen of a mestiza wench. . . ."

"No," Hailey said; "doesn't take too much imagination, Bruce. Remember the stories you told me about the Conquistadores, and what they came up against when they met the Aztecs? Hadn't been for the Spaniards, that one would have been a queen amongst her own people. The lines are there, and the carriage. All right, you can hitch a blooded mare to a plough, and break her wind and spirit. But nobody, even after she's been broken, will ever mistake her for a ploughhorse—not nobody who's any judge of horseflesh. What was that you called her?"

"Mestiza. Means a breed. Half Spanish, half Indian. . . ."

"So? When you cover a Morgan mare with an Arab stallion, you get a bad foal? Do you now, Bruce?"

"No. Reckon you're right, Hailey. But that wasn't an Aztec mixture. Something else—something older. The race that built those temples in the jungles of Chiapas maybe—I don't know. But not Aztec. They were Johnny come latelys who took over a civilization already there. And debased it with their cruelty. Whatever she is beside Spanish, she's not Aztec. She's much too fine. . . ."

"I understand how Pepe felt," Hailey said. "He wanted to keep that one—get sons on her that weren't just bastards, but his own, in legitimate line. His old man was a fool!"

"Mighty heap of heat, Hailey," Bruce said mildly, "over something that doesn't rightly concern either of us. . . ."

"Right," Hailey said. "Still I wouldn't like to be in Pepe's shoes, being married to that one in a country where women-folks are scarcer'n hen's teeth. . . ."

"Me either," Bruce said.

They spent the fifth night of their journey in Sacramento, a village which managed to seem as noisy and as wild as San Francisco, despite its much smaller size. Closer to the gold fields, it had a character subtly different from California's new metropolis, as their first hour in it proved to them once and for all.

"Lord God, Nate!" Hailey said. "Look at that! Don't tell me that's gold he's leaving there. . . ."

Bruce turned and saw the leather pouch of no mean size the bearded miner had left atop the hitching post to which he had tied his donkey.

"Yep," Nate said. "It is. There's two reasons for that. First he don't aim to be gone long. And second, nobody'll dast touch it, since he left it there like that in the presence of witnesses. Come along and I'll show you why. . . ."

They followed him along the muddy streets for a few yards until they came to a little square, lined with trees. From a stout limb of one of the trees, a man was hanging. He hadn't been up there very long. Bruce had seen enough dead men in his time to tell that. Not more than a day. And Nate and the Preacher hadn't been in Sacramento in over two weeks.

"How'd you know he'd be there?" he said.

"Always is one," Nate said dryly. "Some of these greenhorns never learn. . . ."

"Greenhorn?" Hailey said. "What makes you so sure he's a greenhorn?"

"Would of known better'n to try to steal if he was an old timer," Nate said. "C'mon now. Big Pete's a friend of mine, but even his place gets overcrowded at times. . . ."

"One other question, Nate," Hailey said. "How did you know it was stealing he was hung for? Couldn't it have been murder?"

"Naw," Nate said. "Not unless he killed somebody real well known. Folks most in generally don't git hung for killings out here. You see, nearly everybody is a stranger to everybody else. Couple of boys gits real riled and shoots it out. After it's over, some of the miners drags the dead man off and buries him. And that's that. . . ."

"You mean to say," Bruce said, "that they hold thievery a greater crime than killing?"

"Yes, son," Preacher Rowe said; "they do. Out here, gold is everything, and a human life is nothing—or nearly. Two strangers start a shooting scrape, and one kills the other. And the bystanders shrug their shoulders. 'Didn't know either of 'em,' they say. 'They shot it out over something we didn't know about either. Anyhow, it's none of our business . . .' Their sympathies don't extend that far. Or their imagination. But they can imagine what it's like to have that evil yellow dust stolen—or a horse. They know how hard it is to pan a few ounces of gold. And a man afoot is at the mercy of Indians, wolves, and the elements. If that miner you saw came back and found that gold dust stolen, he'd have the whole town at his back, helping to find the thief, even though they don't even know the miner's name. Gold is a thing they understand, but human life is beyond them, not unless it's their own. . . ."

"Know what, Rev," Bruce said dryly, "I'm beginning to like California less by the minute. . . ."

"California," the old Preacher said, "is a garden spot—a true paradise. So was Eden. It's only when you bring mankind into a para-

dise with all his lusts and hungers and natural cussedness that
things get spoiled, kind of. That's why I've got to preach. Somebody, sometime, has to straighten out this mess, has to bring these
erring souls to their Maker. . . ."

"From what I've seen," Nate said, "a rope does the job a lot
quicker and more effective-like than a sermon. Wait 'til the gold's
all gone, Reverend, and folks settles down to more normal living.
Then they'll listen to you; but not now. . . ."

"I'm afraid you're right, Brother Nate," the Preacher said.

They had one more night of camping along the trail, which,
on the whole they found preferable to the hotels, reaching Marysville the evening of the second day out of Sacramento. Nate's
store was something to see. It was stoutly built of logs, with a roof
of rushes, and boasted real glass windows, the only edifice in town
which did. The rest of them had blankets hung over the openings,
or the universal red calico, which made their interiors take on a
certain appropriately hellish aspect when the sun shone through.
And nearly every house was roofed with canvas.

"Had a canvas roof myself," Nate said; "but the rain spoiled all
my flour, sugar, and such like. So I built this roof. Now folks come
in here just to get dry. And most in generally they's 'shamed to
leave without buying something. . . ."

Bruce looked about the store. Every possible inch of it was
crowded with merchandise. Harnesses, single trees, double trees,
saddles, bridles, whips and spurs hung from the ceiling, along
with smoked hams and cured haunches of mountain goat. On
the shelves were bolts of calico—all red. Barrels of flour, sugar,
gunpowder, lard, and rice stood on the floor. Guns, pistols, bowie
knives, lariats, and various other kinds of rope and cord hung
around the walls. Jars of preserves stood on other shelves. Ready-
made red shirts, slouch hats, boots and pants filled the others.
There was even a row of books which included Shakespeare and
the Bible, and hogsheads of molasses, vinegar and coarse salt.
There were miners' pans, rockers, cradles, picks, shovels, pack-
saddles, for mules and burros, divining rods and gold meters guar-
anteed to locate the precious metal beneath the earth's surface;
testing outfits with balances and vials of acid to distinguish gold

from pyrite. Medicine for snake bite. Fishing poles, hooks, lines, sinkers. Snow shoes. Sides of bacon. Bins of nails and tacks. Hammers, saws, axes.

"Quarters is above the store," Nate said, pointing to a ladder which led upward through a trap door. "I'll sling some of these hammocks for you boys. Tell you what, Bruce—how about you taking my wagon, and driving the Preacher up to his place tomorrow? Don't need the wagon 'til I have to make another trip for supplies. Looks like I won't have to be going to Frisco much longer, the way Sacramento's booming. When you're ready to start gold seeking, you can bring it back, and I'll outfit you. But this way, you can spy out the lay of the land up in the valley. . . ."

"Thanks, Nate," Bruce said. "Coming along, Hailey?"

"No. Reckon I'll hang out here with Nate 'til you get set. I'll buy us both an outfit, so we won't lose any time when you get back. Meantime I'm going to rally round and listen to talk. That way I aim to know a right smart lot about mining by the time we start. . . ."

"Good idea," Nate said. "Well, let's rustle up some grub." Nate sent a boy to a neighbor's for fresh eggs; then he hooked a ham down from the ceiling with a long pole. Bruce and Hailey made a fire in the fireplace, and all of them dined royally on ham and eggs, both of which were still worth their weight in gold in California.

They were dog tired, and anyhow Bruce reckoned that every man, except maybe the Preacher, had already had his say. So one by one they climbed the ladder and stretched out in the hammocks. After the board beds of Frisco and Sacramento, they were a miracle of comfort, especially since Nate piled on enough blankets to suffocate a man.

Bruce could hear the others snoring. But he couldn't sleep right off. Jo, he thought, Lord, Jo—And that was a strange thing; for her face didn't come readily to mind. Something kept getting in the way. He fell asleep, finally, trying to call up her image, which up until now had been printed on his brain as sharp and as clear as a daguerreotype; but after he was asleep, he managed it. Jo was there before him, her blue eyes filled with light and love and tenderness; but he couldn't make out what she was saying. He leaned forward, listening; but the persistent little shadow that hovered near one corner of her face rose and darkened and blotted out her image.

"Damn it all!" he said. "Get out of the way; it's Jo I want to see, not you. . . ."

But the night black eyes rested upon him imperturbably, and the full, wine-red lips shaped themselves into a smile. She moved, shaking out hair that was darkness itself above a face of duskrose and translucent copper, and when she spoke, the words were, naturally enough, in Spanish. And he understood every one of them, perfectly.

But, in the morning, when he awoke, with the echo of her voice singing in his heart like the tones of a far away, long struck golden gong, he couldn't remember what she had said. He tried hard, but he couldn't remember.

He lay there in the hammock, blinking his eyes against the light.

Loco, he thought, dreaming of a woman you've seen just once, like some moonstruck kid. Reckon this place gets you. It's just too damned big and lonesome. . . .

Then he swung down from the hammock, found his boots, and began to make the fire.

5

HE HADN'T REALIZED when Nate said Pleasant Valley was right close to Marysville, that it was with the Westerner's conception of distances that the Mississippian had spoken. Actually the journey took them a leisurely two days, for the valley itself was a little over thirty miles northeast of Marysville; and fifteen miles a day was a good stint over those roads in a wagon. It didn't bother Bruce, though, because even in midwinter, the country wasn't very cold. What did strike him as strange was the fact that a little way out, along the Yuba River, the road began to climb. Marysville itself, at the junction of the Yuba and the Feather, lay in the upper end of the two hundred and fifty mile-long by seventy mile-wide Sacramento Valley, in the midst of some of the finest farming country Bruce had ever seen. Even as far north as Ophir City, thirty odd miles further on, the land was still all flat or gently rolling.

But now, sitting beside the silent, brooding old man, he was following a trail that wound up into what were obviously the foothills of the high Sierras. Bruce had never seen mountains before his service in Mexico; and though, while there, he had come to love them with something approaching passion, he couldn't imagine a man choosing mountains as a place to locate a farm. He turned to put the question to the old man; but the Preacher had retreated so far out of time, withdrawn so deep into some private sanctuary of the spirit, that Bruce closed his mouth again, shutting off the words unsaid.

So they wound upward, and still upward, going along the trail that the woman who had given Marysville its name, Mary Murphy

Covillaud, had taken that terrible winter of 'forty-six, when forty-five people out of the eighty-one who had started out from Ohio came down from the snows of the Sierras, after having eaten the fallen bodies of their companions. There were forests of pine, spruce, fir, balsam, and here and there a lonely oak; cascades foaming white as they thundered into the gorges, and under the shade of some of the trees, patches of snow. The air had a bite to it; and the glistening snowpeaks of the Sierra Nevadas were visibly closer.

Then, toward evening, they came out into the valley itself. And before Bruce, as though his imagination had created it out of the stuff of his dreams, lay the sweep of gently rolling fields, the waist-high grasses brown and sere now with winter, hiding here and there a little snow; but so exactly the thing he had wished for that his chief emotion was one of recognition.

Home, he thought; I've come home. . . .

It had been beyond his imagination to picture a perfect farm-land lying in a valley whose very floor was more than two thousand feet above sea level; but beyond that, this high valley lying between the Yuba and the American rivers, reaching out to touch the mining camps—which within a year or two at most, would grow into the towns of Grass Valley, so named from the emigrants' first sight of the waving grasses of the valley itself—Nevada City and Dutch Flat had it all: the rim of snow-capped mountains, the cold dry air, the brooding darkness of pine forests a little way up the slopes, water—everything.

"Why'd you come here, Reverend?" he asked. " 'Pears to me that any man seeing the Sacramento Valley first would have stopped there—fine as this is. . . ."

The Preacher smiled.

"Hard to explain," he said. "Reasons practical and impractical. First off, in the big valley you have to irrigate—so the bigger your holdings, the better off you are. Here, you don't. There's water in God's own plenty. And all I wanted was a small place that I could attend to with as little help as possible. Second place, I wanted peace. Never dreamed that they'd find gold near here, too. Even so, it's still peaceful here. It's a Godly place, son. 'The mountains declare the Glory of God, and the firmament showeth His handi-work . . .' Not too many folks about. In fact, I'm alone here now. The Murphys and the Tildens have both gone. . . ."

"But how did you find it?" Bruce said.

"Sean Murphy. He came out here in 'forty-three, Oregon bound. His party decided for California, and watered and fed their stock here. I met him down in Sacramento, in the fall of 'forty-eight, after a whole summer in the gold fields. He'd made a fair strike, blown it all on liquor, and was sick and repentant when I met him. Swore he'd had enough. No more placer mining for him. He told me about this place, and he and Rad Tilden, a friend of his, and I came up here and started farming. Both Sean and Rad had their wives and children along, because, unlike the Forty-Niners, the first immigrants were settlers, come to stay. Pleasant Valley seemed likely to them, too. So we farmed the Valley. What can be grown here has to be seen to be believed. . . ."

"And yet they left it," Bruce said. "Strange. . . ."

"No, son, it's not. Farming's hard work, even on good lands. So's mining; but that gives a man the hope of getting rich. Gold fever got them again—both of them. Tilden struck it rich, right off, and took his family back East. But Murphy didn't have much luck. Panned a good bit of gold, but kept on moving, looking for a richer claim. Lost his wife and both his kids when cholera broke out in a mining camp. For all I know, he's still at it . . . Look, boy, there's the house now. . . ."

It was a log cabin, neat and tight, with a stone chimney. A Mexican boy came running out of the barn and caught the bridles.

"'Allo!" he called. "You 'ave come back, eh *Padre?*"

"Given up trying to stop them from calling me *Padre,*" the Preacher said. "Yes, Jaime, I'm back . . ." Then, to Bruce: "Come along now, it's getting cold. I'll have Josefina rustle up some grub. . . ."

"Pretty far North for Mex, isn't it?" Bruce said.

"Brought them with me from down in Santa Clara. Knew them before. You see, son, I've been in California since 'forty-three. . . ."

Bruce climbed down from the wagon. It was colder than he had thought. The Preacher pointed toward the mountains.

"Sometimes, when the wind blows down through Emigrant Gap —that's the route the Donner Party took, you know—we have snow storms. But not often. Mostly the mountains are a protection. Never go into them in the winter, though. Only man I've ever seen who could do that and get away with it was Pepe. . . ."

"You mean that Pepe—and Juana were up here, too?"

"Worked for the Murphys. Pepe and Sean were good friends. And when Sean decided to come up here, Pepe, who'd lost his last cent gambling as usual, begged to come with him. Best thing that ever happened. Pepe is a good farmer. Says some old peon on his father's place taught him. And he'd go out in the worst weather and come back with mountain goat or antelope. He's got a cave he generally keeps stocked with rations and firewood where he holes up when the weather gets too bad. It's almost to the snow line even in midsummer—more than seven thousand feet. Calls it Bear Cave because he swears he routed a grizzly out of it. But then Pepe's the biggest liar who ever drew breath. . . ."

"I liked him," Bruce said.

"Everybody does. Which is why he's alive, considering what usually happens to his kind in California. Funny thing, Pepe can ride his horse up to the mouth of that cave. I don't see how he does it. That trail is too much for a bighorn. But, beyond that, even he has to go on foot. He's used to mountains though. His father's *rancheria* lay in a mountain valley, and he's been climbing all his life. . . ."

Bruce was helping the boy take the Preacher's goods out of the wagon. But a Mexican who was clearly the boy's father came out of the barn and stopped him.

"This, Señor, is work for our hands," he said.

Bruce looked at the Preacher.

"Don't you ever get lonesome up here?" he said.

"No," the Preacher said serenely, "never. I have my hills for company, and God's Word to read. Besides, I'm an old man, son. My fires are banked. I don't have many of the needs that drive a man to seek the company of his fellows . . ." He turned to the boy.

"Jaime," he said, "go tell your mother we have company. Tell her to prepare something good. . . ."

"*Si, mi Padre!*" the boy said, and scampered off.

That night, after supper, they sat before the fireplace and talked. There was hardly a thing a man could think of that the Preacher hadn't done or been at one time or another, Bruce reckoned. Keelboating on the Mississippi, fur trapping, Mountain Man, plains country guide to the wagon trains bound for Oregon back

in 'forty-three, farming, preaching . . . He had wandered over all
of California, from Oregon to the Mexican border. Part he liked
best, he allowed, was the South with orange groves showing golden
beneath the snow-capped mountains, and great ranches spread-
ing out beyond the rim of the world, with herds of cattle and
horses so vast as to be beyond a man's counting. Life was gracious
down there in the Santa Clara region where he had found Jesus
and his family. . . .

Jesus' face lighted with memory as the Preacher spoke of that.
His hands, moving, gesticulating, made pictures a man could
read: the old days, the good life, before the *Americanos* came;
and after that the wave, the avalanche of them washing over the
old, good time, destroying it. The barbarities heaped upon his
people, the cruelties—with only Joaquin Murieta, bandit and
killer, but also, you comprehend, *Señor*, the savior of his race,
the avenger, to meet barbarity with barbarity, cruelty with
cruelty. . . .

"Without him," Jesus said, "what would we do, *Señor?* There are
not many such like our *Padre* here; and being beaten, robbed,
and hanged becomes wearisome . . ." He stood up.

"*Bastante,*" he said; "enough of talk. I am tired. Come my son,
and my woman, let us go. *Buenas noches, Caballeros—*"

After they had gone, the Preacher turned to Bruce.

"We'd better talk over your situation," he said. "Maybe I can
make a few suggestions. . . ."

"Glad you brought it up," Bruce said; "because I was going to.
Got any idea where I should locate?"

"All this end of the valley is taken," the Preacher said. " 'Course
you could squat on the Tilden place because it is abandoned.
But folks have a way of coming back to California. Might make
trouble in the future. What's more, there's no house on it; Tilden
used a lean-to and tent combination. If there were any way to get
in touch with him, I'd say go ahead, because he'd probably sell
for little or nothing . . . But there isn't any way. I don't even know
where he went. So that leaves the Murphy place. . . ."

"What's wrong with the Eastern end of the valley?" Bruce said.

"Gold."

"Gold?" Bruce echoed. "Can't see what that's got to do—"

"Everything," the Preacher snapped. "Want to see your streams turned into sluices, your crops trampled under foot, your best land dug up; and hundreds of bearded villains squatting on your property? That's what happens where gold is found. . . ."

"I see," Bruce said. "Like Sutter, eh?"

"Exactly. I pray God every night that no one ever stumbles upon it down here. After that, to keep what's yours, you'd have to fight —and kill. From what your partner says, I take it that you're dead set against such unchristian ways. . . ."

"I am," Bruce said. "So the thing to do is to dicker with Murphy, in your opinion?"

"Yes. That shouldn't be hard. Main trouble will be to find him. He's always on the go, looking for a real strike. Funny part about it is, if he'd stayed put and worked some of the claims he's already found, he'd be comfortably off by now. But he's always on the move. I think it's his loss that drives him. With all his devilish ways, Sean was devoted to Bridget. . . ."

"Any idea where I should look?"

"Not the faintest. Tell you what though. You go find Pepe. He'll know right off where to find Sean—"

Bruce frowned.

"Appears to me," he said, "that's just swapping one problem for another. . . ."

"No. Finding Pepe is easier. First off, you know which way he's heading. Then, don't know whether you noticed it or not, but Pepe is—well, kind of striking. Easy man to ask after, because folks notice him. And then, of course, there's Juana—"

"Yes," Bruce said; "there's Juana—"

The Preacher turned his face away from the fire and looked at Bruce.

"Don't think you'n me mean the same thing, son, when we say: 'There's Juana,'" he said mildly. "But without delving too deep into what you do mean, I expect I ought to tell you a few things about her—"

"I," Bruce began, "have no interest at all in—" He stopped suddenly, and his eyes, staring into the fire, had the look of wonder. "No," he said, "that's not so, Reverend. I am curious about her. Go on, tell me. . . ."

"Like your honesty, son. Wouldn't be natural for a healthy young fellow like you not to be interested in Juana. Nearly every man who has ever seen her, has been. Like your partner for in-stance. . . ."

He paused, gazing into the fire. Bruce did not prod him to continue his thought. He was aware by now that the Preacher's mind wandered from subject to subject without apparent con-nection. But whatever he touched, he illuminated.

He turned back to Bruce, his old, curiously saintly face softening into a smile.

"Would it shock you," he said, "if I told you my honest opinion—that neither one of you, as a man, is fit to tie Juana's shoes—as a woman?"

Bruce looked at the Preacher. Slowly, he smiled.

"Is Pepe?" he said.

"No," Reverend Rowe said; "but, maybe better than either of you. Pepe, in some ways is a child, a fool, a clown. But in other ways, he's a man. Man enough to marry Juana before God's Priest, in the church, when nothing in his country, or his society would have censured him for degrading her. Man enough to make friends with me and Brother Nate and Sean despite the fact that we're Americans—"

Bruce shot him a startled glance.

"I know. I know," the Preacher said. "That surprises you. But it does require manhood to find and know the exceptions among the race of your persecutors. Especially when you're a cultivated, educated gentleman, it requires something big not to give way to your fury at the insults and mistreatment at the hands of hairy, filthy, ignorant, quarrelsome louts, who above all believe them-selves superior to you. That's what I admire in Pepe. He has a kind of—of sweetness of soul. He is without hate. And he is full of laughter. As an old man—a mite too serious, that pleases me. I like Pepe. . . ."

"So do I," Bruce said.

"Good. And Juana adores him. Yep—I'm saying that as a warn-ing; because I can see you're tempted. More than that, Juana is a genuinely good woman. I honestly believe that she'd kill herself before she'd betray Pepe. She's everything to him. She bears with him, humors him, mothers him—smiles through his tempers, his black moods. In fact, she's one of the rarest things on this earth—a wife."

"Rare?" Bruce said.

"Yes, rare. Because it's the hardest job in the world. I was bitter once, when I was a young man. Reason I came West, became a Mountain Man was over trouble with my wife. But the mountains cured my bitterness. You can't stay small in the mountains, because in the high Sierras small men—die. Plenty time for thinking around a campfire, under the stars. Dawned on me finally that Rachel wasn't rightly to blame. Life asks a mighty heap of a woman. . . ."

Bruce waited.

"Bring forth children in pain and sorrow. Remain mated to a creature who, in his essence, is half devil, and half child. Hold her tongue, because, tied up in a man, part, maybe, of the maleness of him, is a mule stubbornness that resents both advice and help. Settle down to dullness, when in her heart of hearts, every woman needs a little changefulness, excitement, glamor. Accept indifference and sometimes even brutality instead of tenderness and romance. Even in the relationship which to a woman is a kind of glory, the expression of, and the culmination of love, she finds haste, the wolfish satisfaction of a mere physical appetite in her husband. God knows there must be times when a woman wonders if men really do have souls. . . ."

"You give us some hard lines, Reverend," Bruce said.

"Because I like you, son. You've got possibilities. Appears to me that steered right, you could develop into something kind of fine. . . ."

"Thanks," Bruce said.

"Think you've got another rare thing: the ability to learn. Most folks don't, can't, or won't learn—ever. But I think you can."

"Hope so," Bruce said.

In the morning, they saddled two of the Preacher's horses and rode over to Murphy's place. Just looking at it set Bruce's heart a-singing. The house was built with craft, tight against the wind and cold, fashioned with loving hands. The barn could stand some repairs, but he looked forward to that. The one apparent drawback he could see to the whole layout was that the only source of water was a creek, a tributary of the Yuba River, more than a half mile from the house.

Have to sink a well, right off, he thought.

" 'Course you could just stay here," the Preacher said, "and take your chances of Murphy stopping by in the Spring. Then you could talk business with him. Only it will make him mad. He might not even want to discuss the matter with a squatter. Or, if you were a different type, you could just squat. All this land is Mexican government grants from before the War. And in the eyes of the Forty-Niners, they're all questionable. You could go down to Sacramento, file a claim for the whole thing with the territorial authorities, and there wouldn't be a thing that Murphy could do. Except shoot you, maybe. Because those folks in Sacramento would uphold your claim merely because it was made to them in the first place and supports their policy of superseding Mexican claims whenever and wherever possible. I'm just telling you that to test you. If you're the kind who can do such a thing, I'd like to know it now, before I put too much hope in you. . . ."

"No," Bruce said. "Got my faults, Reverend, but I reckon dishonesty ain't one of them. . . ."

"Yep, reckon I know that, else I wouldn't take up so much time with you. Sorry I jawed at you so heavy, last night. . . ."

"It was—interesting," Bruce said. "Made me think about things I never thought about before. Gather that foreigners have a hard time in California. . . ."

"Foreigners?" the Preacher said. "Like the Indians who have been here since the dawn of time? The Chinamen, I grant you, but the Spanish speaking folk? They have been here for hundreds of years—and this land was theirs . . . 'Pears to me that we're the foreigners in California. . . ."

He pushed back his hat, and sat there peering at distances beyond the mountains; beyond perhaps, even the stars. . . .

"Well," he said. "Have you made your mind up yet?"

"Yes," Bruce said. "I'll go back to Marysville tomorrow and pick up Hailey. Then we'll look for Pepe, and through him, Murphy. When and if I close the deal; I'll come back here. . . ."

"No point in that. Nothing you can do in the winter time here, not unless you're already stocked up, and in operation. Even the mines shut down—thank God. Miners head southward like sparrows. And Sean's sure to drive a hard bargain. You got enough money for stock and such like after you've bought the place?"

"No," Bruce said.

"Stay South, then. Pan gold—work at it hard, staying in one place 'til that runs out, and by Spring you'll have enough to start in style. Better that way. Team up with Pepe, if possible, long enough to learn the ropes. But when he gets the miner's itch to move on, don't follow him. Ninety-nine percent of the trouble with prospectors is that they can't stand to work a small paying claim. They want hundred-dollar pans, if there is such a thing. Never saw one myself, and every time I ran down the story of one, it turned out to be hearsay. You can expect ten dollars a day. Up to fifty, if you're lucky. But don't give up a good claim looking for motherlodes, or pans that turn up nuggets the size of hen eggs every time you swish 'em—"

Again Bruce smiled.

"Thanks—*Padre*," he said.

They moved out of Marysville on foot, leading the two burros loaded with their mining gear. They had both been dead set upon buying horses, but Nate had talked them out of it.

"Look, boys," he said: "Whatever money you got left, you'd better hang onto. I've known men to go six months without making a strike. Heck, there's folks who was already here in 'forty-eight, when Marshall found the first gold, who ain't never seen flour shining in their pans. Another thing, any time you need a grub stake, don't be too proud to come to me. All right I let you pay for your gear right off because you're grown men and you've got your pride. But don't carry it too far—"

"You sold us the stuff at cost," Bruce pointed out.

"Hell, son, that wasn't nothing. Glad to do it. You being home folks makes it different. But you be tightfisted, daggum it! You never know. . . ."

"Tightfisted and sorefooted!" Hailey laughed. "Damn it, Nate, I haven't walked a mile since I was big enough to climb a fence and jump off of it onto my Pa's old piebald gelding. . . ."

"Better get used to using shank's mare, boy. First place, hosses cost a damn sight more'n they're worth up here. Second, stands to reason you're going to have a fling at some quartz mining. . . ."

"Quartz?" Bruce said; "I thought—"

"Gold-bearing rock, Bruce," Hailey said quickly. "I've been

doing a mighty heap of learning since you've been gone. Two ways to hunt gold: wash, or dig. Every big stake in California has been made by digging. Stands to reason. Gold in the streams has been washed there by the water. Naturally the big lodes are in the rocks, where the water washed the little stuff from in the first place. What we want to do is to find a vein twice as big around as your arm and a mile long!"

"Panning's surer," Nate said. "Most in generally always find dust in streams running through gold-bearing country. Veins is pure luck. Ever hear of Sailor's Hill?"

"No," Bruce said.

"Sailor came into the saloon down the street. Says to the miners, there: 'Boys, where's a good place to look for gold in these parts?' So for a joke they sent him up to the top of the hill just outside of town—"

"But, Nate," Hailey protested, "there ain't no hill just outside of town. . . ."

"Used to be. That sailor's the reason it ain't there now. This salt ain't never heard tell that nobody ain't ever found gold at the top of a hill. Always on the slope, or down in the valley. So he goes up there and in two hours takes out seven thousand, five hundred dollars worth of nuggets. Comes back and shows 'em to the boys—"

"And they tore the hill down?" Hailey laughed.

"Exactly. Week later, warn't nothing there but a field."

"How much they take out?" Bruce said.

"Nary an ounce. That there sailor'd got it all!"

"That a true story, Nate?" Bruce said. "You wouldn't be pulling the long bow on us, would you?"

"Not a word of it," Nate grinned. "Leastways it didn't happen here. Bet you every time you stop, somebody'll tell you that story. Only it'll be Nigger Hill, Dutchman's Hill, Chileno Hill, or Frenchman's Hill. Heck—it could of happened. Just got kind of changed in the telling . . . What was I asaying afore we climbed up on Sailor's Hill?"

"About why we don't need horses," Hailey said.

"Hoss ain't surefooted enough for some of them mountain trails. A hoss is more delicate and harder to feed. Can't stand the weather like a jack. Can't pack half the weight without dropping under you. And he's a natural, living temptation to thieves. Down south, where they got herds of 'em running wild, it's different. But you ain't going that far south. . . ."

"Depends upon where we find Pepe," Bruce said.

"First gambling tent you come to in Sacramento," Nate said. "That is, if his luck's holding good. Would of been a fandango dive, but Juana put a stop to that. One thing she won't tolerate is other women. She lets him gamble, because that keeps him in good humor, and that's the way she likes him to be. . . ."

"Gal like Juana," Hailey said, "wouldn't have to worry about nobody else, if I was in Pepe's shoes. She could keep me so damn busy I wouldn't have time. . . ."

"But you aren't in Pepe's shoes," Bruce pointed out; "and strange as it may sound to your horny ears, I'm getting mighty damn' sick of the subject of Juana. C'mon now, let's get started. . . ."

Walking wasn't half as bad as Hailey had thought. For one thing, Nate had chosen their boots with care, and heavy wool socks to go inside them. They felt good on a man's feet. Bruce was used to walking, having done his share of it in Mexico; and even Hailey, being himself a countryman, had walked more than he liked to admit. They made better time afoot, leading the burros, than they could have in a wagon. And they reached Sacramento without even one blister between them.

"Here's a gambling tent," Bruce said. "Might as well start asking after Pepe—"

"Lord God, Bruce!" Hailey groaned. "My backbone's asking my belly if my throat's been cut! Let's eat first, then ask after him. I'm damn near hungry enough to take a bite out of one of them critters. . . ."

"Wouldn't try it," Bruce said. "Heard tell that old boots make better eating. All right, come on. . . ."

They went up the street, sloshing through the ankle-deep mud. It had rained every day since long before they had left Marysville, so that the rain had come to be a thing they didn't talk about or even think about very much. It was still raining, a slow, sullen drizzle that chilled a man to the marrow of his bones. Below them, they could see the masts of vessels tied up along what had been the bank of the river. Only there wasn't a bank any longer. The whole lower third of the city was under water. They stopped before a shack marked simply, "Eats."

Looking at the menu which was tacked to a board outside the shack, they saw for the first time what it meant to be north of San Francisco in January. The only meats listed were jerked beef, ham, and pork. Besides that, they could have salt mackerel, tinned sardines, or oysters—also from a can. In addition to these, the menu listed flapjacks, griddle cakes, shortcakes and atole, a cornmeal porridge. The only drink was coffee. No vegetables were listed.

Hailey stared at the menu, dubiously.

"Not much choice, is there?" he said.

"Rest of the places will be no better," Bruce said. "Food's a problem in winter. Come on."

The restaurant was greasy, evil smelling. Bearded miners sat before redwood planks set on saw horses, wolfing down their food.

Through the half door that led to the kitchen, they could see the owner-cook. He was a Mexican, villainous looking enough to have qualified for membership in Murieta's band. They looked around at what the miners were eating. The jerked beef was revolting. The mackerel had been preserved in black salt. The flapjacks, griddle cakes, shortcakes, and atole were either burned or undercooked. None of this bothered the miners even slightly. Next to them, a huge miner whose iron-grey beard could have been used to stuff a mattress, was eating raw onions chopped up in vinegar, and canned sardines. His methods of disposing of his food were beautifully effective: he scooped up the onions with a soup spoon, dipping huge chunks of bread into the vinegar, so that red trickles of it ran down into his beard. Then he picked the sardines out of the can by their tails, lifted his head, opened his mouth and swallowed them, whole.

"I don't feel so hungry any more," Hailey groaned.

"Leave it to me," Bruce said. "I'll fix it." He called through the half door to the cook, speaking very rapidly in Spanish:

"*Ay*, Chico—know you how to make enchiladas?"

The cook's face split in a huge grin.

"*Si, Señor!*" he said; "if you will wait, I will send the Niño to my woman for the tortillas. For the filling I have only some bacon. How does *el Señor* prefer the sauce—red or green?"

"Green," Bruce said, "and as hot as the *Infierno* to which you consign all gringos. But *pronto*, Chico; we have hunger of the canine variety. . . ."

The miners stopped eating and stared at Bruce. Many of them had acquired a smattering of Spanish since they had come to California; but they had never before heard it spoken like that except by the Mexicans themselves. The big man put down the plate he had been holding to his mouth to drain the rest of the vinegar, and stared at Bruce.

"Mister," he said; "you ain't no 'Greaser' are you?"

Bruce looked at him.

"And if I were?" he said.

"Throw you out of here so damn fast it would make your head spin. But I see you ain't. You look like a white man. You talk like a white man, and you're dressed like one, too. But damn me deep and bury me in a gopher's hole if you don't habla spik just like a 'Greaser'! Never heard no white man speak it so good before. . . ."

"Throwing me out just might be a trifle strenuous," Bruce said mildly. "So I reckon it's lucky for all concerned that I'm not Mex. As for the language; if you're going to do a thing, might as well do it right, I always say."

"You got a mighty unfriendly way of talking, partner," the big man growled.

"Have I? Sorry. Didn't mean it that way. There's enough needful trouble in the world without looking for what isn't exactly necessary. If I were Mex, you'd throw me out—you say; and I say that would take some doing. But since I'm not, I don't see why either one of us is called upon to prove it, one way or the other. So let's let it drop, shall we?"

The miner looked at him, his face frowning and puzzled.

"You're a curious cuss," he said. "What you say sounds like fighting talk, and yet the way you say it sounds downright peaceful. Damned if I can make you out, nohow, Mister. . . ."

"He's my brother," Hailey said, his freckled face twisted into an impish grin. "When he was real little he got kicked in the head by a horse. . . ."

"You mean he's loco?" the big miner said.

"Didn't say that. Far as I can see, it had no apparent effect on him. But it broke the hoss's leg. Pa had to shoot him. . . ."

All the miners roared with laughter, even the big fellow. Mingled with their laughter, Hailey could see, was relief from a kind

of—fear. Funny, he thought, there ain't one of 'em what wouldn't
take on a grizzly barehanded; but they're plumb scairt of Bruce
—mainly because they don't understand him. Reckon that's the
strongest kind of fear: being afraid of the unknown. . . .

The cook came in with the steaming platter of enchiladas.

"This what you order?" Hailey asked. "Damn, but they look
good!"

"They sure Lord do," the big miner said. "Damn it, Angel, you
been holding out on us!"

"But, *Señor*," the cook protested; "this *señor* is the first to ever
ask for them. They are unknown outside of my country. . . ."

"Bring me a plate of them, pronto!" the miner said.

"Wait," Bruce said. "You'd better taste one of these first. They're
as hot as hell. Pass me your plate."

Wonderingly the miner passed his plate over. Clearly, Bruce
was outside of all his conceptions of humanity.

He took the enchilada, stared at it. All the others gathered
around him, watching with all the anticipation with which they
would have watched a hanging.

He bit into the sandwich-like arrangement of a flat pancake
made of cornmeal and water, called a tortilla, wrapped around
pieces of bacon and a thick green sauce. Tears came to his eyes.
He opened his mouth, gasping. He yanked off his slouch hat and
started fanning himself with it.

"Water!" he bellowed; "Lord God, Water!"

Somebody gave him a canteen. He drank deeply, sloshing the
water into his huge beard in his haste.

"Now," he spluttered, "now I know what the devil serves up for
grub in hell!"

All the others were laughing. But the big miner stood there,
watching Bruce quietly eating the enchiladas, with the green sauce
that the Mexicans call *mole verde*. He looked back at his own
unfinished enchilada. Then, very slowly, he sat down and cut it
into small pieces, and began to eat it, keeping his canteen beside
him.

A wide grin stole over his face.

"Damned if it ain't good," he said; "if you don't take on too
much of it at a throw. Thanks, partner. . . ."

"You're welcome," Bruce said.

"Bring me that plate, Angel," the miner said.

"Me, too!" another roared; "I'm game!"

Then they were all ordering the enchiladas.

"I think, Señor," Angel said, "you have made my fortune. *Mil gracias!*"

The big miner pushed away the empty platter.

"Partner," he said. "Don't know whether or not you know it, but you got yourself a pal—and here's my hand on it. The name's Bill Watkins—from Kansas. . . ."

"Bruce Harkness," Bruce said. "And this is Hailey Burke. . . ."

"Knowed all the time you warn't brothers," Bill Watkins said. "But I'm glad to know ye both. Tell me, Mister Harkness, how come you know so much about 'Greasers'? Their palaver and their cooking, I mean?"

"The war," Bruce said. "Besides, I kind of like them."

"Oh, there's some good ones," Bill Watkins said. "Like that young feller I was playing poker with last week. Spoke good English and looked just like a white man. Wasn't for his mustache and the way he was dressed, I would of thought he was Eyetalian or French maybe. . . ."

"Could of been Spanish, Bill," one of the others pointed out. "It's only the ones who come over here what's mixed with Injun. . . ."

"Could be. Anyhow, he damn near cleaned me. Did clean me, in fact; but I got part of it back before we quit. Heard he went down the line, and won every place he went. Good-looking young feller. . . ."

Bruce and Hailey both looked at each other.

"Pepe!" they said at the same time.

" 'Pears to me his name was something like that," Bill Watkins said.

"Know where he went?" Bruce asked.

"Damned if I know. You can ask in the gambling places. Somebody in one of 'em might have heard him say. What's the matter; he stole something of your'n?"

"No. I'm not looking for him so much as I am for a fellow he knows—name of Sean Murphy. So I have to find Pepe in order to find Murphy. You know him?"

"Nope," the big man said. "Know lots of Murphys, but none whose handle is Sean. . . ."

They left the restaurant and made the rounds of the gambling places. And here, at once, they had luck: every proprietor knew Pepe well. But they had to try three of them before they picked up his trail.

"Gone South," the owner said. "Heard him say he was going to do some placer mining down around Mokelumne Hill. Don't know why; the way he cleaned this town was a caution. . . ."

"Thanks, partner," Hailey said.

Mokelumne Hill lay forty-odd miles southeast of Sacramento. They reached it the night of the second day out, and made camp to wait for morning. But while they were eating the last of their hardtack and bacon, they heard the uproar.

A stream of miners came pounding down the hillside, passing in sight of their campfire. One of them stopped.

"Coming boys?" he said. "Fellows done caught a 'Greaser' loaded down with dust. Richest strike ever seen in this district. They're aiming to make him tell where he found it. . . ."

Hailey looked at Bruce. Bruce stood up.

"Yep," he said. "I'm coming."

"Me, too," Hailey said.

They hurried along after the others.

"Think it could be Pepe?" Hailey whispered.

"Practically sure it is," Bruce said. "The question is, how the devil are we going to get him out of this? Not to mention keeping those goats off of Juana. . . ."

He saw Hailey's hand go to the butt of his heavy Colt.

"No," he said; "this is a prime example of how useless a gun is, when you get right down to cases. You got six shots in that cannon. Say you drop six men. Then what the hell are you going to do? Stand up, bow politely, and say: 'Just a few minutes, boys, while I reload?'"

"Damned if you ain't right," Hailey said. "Then what—?"

"Stay back and keep me covered. I'm going in there and get that poor devil out, be it Pepe or not—"

But it was Pepe. The miners had him tied to a tree. They had a noose already set, dangling a foot above his head.

"Damn it, 'Greaser'!" the man who was acting as interrogator roared: "Where'd you find the stuff? You got ten minutes. After that we gonna stretch your greasy neck. . . ."

Pepe smiled.

"But I have told you," he said. "I won it, variously. At poker, roulette, faro, monte. . . ."

The miner brought his hand back and smashed his fist into Pepe's face. A thin trickle started down from the corner of Pepe's mouth, black in the glare of the campfire.

"Damn it! Tell us!" the miner said.

Bruce came out of the crowd.

"That's enough," he said; and though he did not raise his voice, it cut through the miner's bluster like a knife. "Release him," he added quietly.

The miner stared at him.

"Who the devil do you think you are?" he said.

"Don't see where that matters," Bruce said; "but I'll tell you, anyhow. The name's Bruce Harkness. Now that you know that, either cut this boy loose, or stand back while I do it. . . ."

"Why I'll be double damned and buried in the motherlode!" the miner said. "You mean to tell me that you, a white man, are going to stand up for a lousy 'Greaser'?"

"Yep," Bruce said. "I mean exactly that. Or to put it right, partner, I'm going to stand up for justice. He's telling the truth. He won that dust in Sacramento."

"Can you prove it?" one of the others called.

"Sure. But it'll take a little time. Anybody willing to ride back to Sacramento and ask in any gambling tent if a fellow named Pepe Córdoba didn't have the damndest run of luck ever seen sometime last week?"

"Naw!" a miner growled; "hang the bastid! Hang this nosy fool with him!"

"Right," the man who had been questioning Pepe spat. "Hang the both of 'em!"

"Wait, Señores!" Pepe called. "I will give you freely all the gold, if you will spare the life of my friend. . . ."

Bruce looked at him, seeing the high and shining pride that

would not bargain for his own life, but only for that of another. It was a thing curiously fine, come to think of it. You, he thought, are a man, Pepe Córdoba. . . .

"Hardly a bargain, 'Greaser'," the questioner said, "since we already got the dust. And we can keep it, after you're hung—both of you!"

Bruce looked at the miner, his own eyes level and still. He didn't know exactly when it was that he had moved out beyond fear. But sometime during the fighting at Churubusco, he had escaped it, so that although, being human, he felt it still, it had no longer any influence on his actions. What he had to do, what was right for him, he did, leaving the consequences to arrange themselves; holding them of less account finally than the necessity of having to live with himself, knowing with bone-deep conviction that this was a thing no man can do lacking the saving grace of honor and of pride.

"If," he said, "I can prove he won that dust without anybody's having to budge from this spot, will you turn him loose?"

"That's fair enough, Terry," one of the others called. "Providing we keep the gold!"

"The gold is yours," Pepe laughed. "With my compliments, *Caballeros*. A few bags of yellow dirt are scarcely worth dying over. . . ."

"All right," the miner growled. "Prove it!"

"The sacks the dust is in. Got marks on 'em haven't they?"

"Yep. Sacks is always marked."

"If they're his, there won't be but one mark. Probably P.C. for Pepe Córdoba. That right, Pepe?"

"*Seguro, Señor!*" Pepe said.

"All right. Look at them. I'm betting my neck you'll find several different marks. Another thing. Anybody here know a Bill Watkins?"

"Why shore," several of the miners called. "Great big fellow, rough as they make 'em. . . ." •

"Yes. Over six foot, with a pepper'n salt beard. Comes from down Kansas way. . . ."

"That's him all right!"

"You'll find several sacks marked B.W. or whatever brand he uses. Because Bill Watkins told me, himself, in a Sacramento eating shack, run by a Mex called Angel, that Pepe won them from him. . . ."

"Look at the sacks, Joe," the leader said.

The man called Joe picked up the heavy little chamois sacks one by one.

"Yep," he said, "they're all different. Here's one with B.W. on it, by God! And here's another . . . Two more. Hell, Terry, looks like the 'Greaser' warn't lying after all. . . ."

Terry stood there, frowning. Then, very slowly he took out his bowie knife and cut the ropes that held Pepe to the tree.

"Now, git, both of you!" he spat.

Bruce stood there, looking him in the face, a long, slow time.

"What the hell you looking at?" the man growled.

"Just fixing how you look in mind," Bruce said, his voice quiet, peaceful, still. "So the next time I meet you, I'll know. Come along, Pepe. . . ."

Then the two of them walked through the crowd of miners without haste, to where Hailey waited, holding the gun.

Hailey's face was white. His hands were shaking.

"Damn it, Bruce!" he said. "Goddamnit, boy! Damn it all to hell!"

"Let's get back to camp, Hail," Bruce said.

"I think," Pepe laughed, "that in the interest of our health, and also having a great envy to become an old man and have my grandchildren play about my knees, we should strike camp at once and proceed in the direction of Stockton. . . ."

"Why Stockton?" Bruce said.

"Because it is to Stockton that I sent Juana with the horse and my pistol. I am very fond of my horse, and the pistol, also, has *un gran valor*. . . ."

"Damn!" Hailey exploded. "So Juana doesn't count, eh, Pepe? Only the pistol and the horse. You should have let those brigands hang him, Bruce!"

"I make *una broma*—a joke, *Señor* Burke. At a time like this, one can only jest, which is a thing superior to crying, no?"

"You're all right, Pepe," Bruce said.

"And thou likewise, *hermano mio*—my brother. From now on, my life is thine. Come, let us go. . . ."

"Why did you send Juana to Stockton?" Hailey asked.

"There was this very small chance that she might find *los Tres Dedos* in time," Pepe said.

"The three fingers?" Bruce said; "what do you mean, Pepe?"

"Manuel Garcia, who has but three fingers upon his right hand. *Los Americanos* call him 'Three Fingered Jack.' He is the lieutenant of Joaquin Murieta. It is not pleasant to die, especially when one is young and the señoritas still flash their eyes at one; but if Joaquin could not come in time, it would have robbed the dying of half its bitterness to know that he would avenge me. . . ."

"Who is this Joaquin?" Hailey said.

"Mex. Outlaw. Or protector of his people," Bruce said. "Depends on your point of view. Heard about him from the Preacher's hired hands. Came into California with a circus. Found gold in Stanislaus county last spring. Americans jumped the claim, beat him, raped his wife. When he came back on a horse to get what was left of his things, they accused him of being a horse thief. Mind you, he was only seventeen years old. He led them to his brother's *rancho*. So they hung his brother, ran off his stock, and beat the kid into insensibility. That was the end of Joaquin Carillo. After that he was Joaquin Murieta, the man who lassoes people he doesn't cotton to, and drags 'em down mountain trails behind his horse 'til the rocks cut them to pieces. The story has it that he's killed every man who raped his wife. . . ."

"Good!" Hailey said. "Don't blame him a bit!"

"I understand his reasons," Bruce said. "But I don't hold with killing. . . ."

"No," Pepe said. "Only with walking unarmed into a camp of murderers and sticking your head into a noose to save a man you had encountered but once before. This is a thing of total incomprehensibility; but also a thing enormously fine. I shall never forget it, *Señor*. And from this day forth, I put my hands in thine, and call you, Patron. . . ."

"No," Bruce said. "*Compadre*. It is better so. . . ."

"*Si*. Or brother; for you do not seem to hold yourself above me as do most *Americanos*."

"To hold myself above such a man as you, Pepe," Bruce said, "would be damned hard. . . ."

They met Juana at midmorning, galloping up the trail. She

pulled up the stallion, and rolled out of the saddle, landing on her feet, like a cat.

"Pepe!" she wept; "Pepe! Ay-yee! Oh, my heart, thou livest! Soul of my soul, now I can live also."

Hailey looked at Bruce.

"God what a way of talking," he said. "Goddamn it, but that's fine!"

But Pepe was talking to her, after he had kissed her, telling her the story, the Spanish rolling out in music and thunder, the words winged and flying, bright with imagery.

Juana turned and looked at Bruce. Very slowly, she came up to him.

"*Permisso, Señor?*" she whispered; and going up on tiptoe, kissed his mouth.

"*Gracias, Señor*," she said. "For the rest of this life and all of the next, I rest in your debt. . . ."

Bruce stood there, looking at her. And nothing about him moved; neither his eyes, nor his breath, nor even his heart.

Then very slowly, he turned, and walked back to where Hailey stood.

"That," Hailey grinned, "was worth 'most getting hung for! Boy, I could fair hear your toes curling inside your boots!"

"Aw, shut up, Hailey," Bruce growled. "Come on you all, we'd best be moving on. . . ."

6

THEY CAME DOWN the hillside, hunched over in the face of the rain. Below them, the streams boiled white, and they could hear the water crying. They hadn't seen another human being in four days now, because ever since they had left the fairly permanent camp on the Mokelumne River, they had been crossing claims abandoned by their owners gone to winter in Sacramento or San Francisco. It wasn't hard to understand why. To work the diggings during the rainy season, a man needed a shack that was both tight and dry, and practically nobody had the time or the patience to build. They had already found out what it was like to try to camp under tents. Every one of them had a cold except Juana.

"Damn it, Bruce," Hailey said. "If we don't find this Irishman soon, I vote we go back to Sacramento or Marysville and hole up for the winter. Man half dead of flu is going to make a mighty poor miner. . . ."

"Remember Sacramento?" Bruce said. "Third of the city, the whole river front section, was under water when we passed through. If we have to hole up, I reckon Marysville is better. It was raining there, too; but all you had to contend with was mud, not water up to your waist. . . ."

"Lord God, ain't it ever going to stop?" Hailey said.

"Not until spring, *Señor*," Pepe told him. "You must get accustomed to it, that's all—"

"Hate like hell to hole up," Bruce said. "What it'll cost us to live two or three months, I won't have enough left to buy the farm. . . ."

"That's the truth," Hailey said; "still. . . ."

"Ah! *Finalamente!*" Pepe said. "There he is!"

They saw the lonely figure squatting by the rocker at the edge of the river. He was yanking at the handle, while the stream of dirt and water poured out of the hopper over the ripple bars set in the bottom of the cradle. The rain dripped off the brim of his slouch hat, already sodden and shapeless, and a steady trickle of water came out of his red beard. He saw Pepe and came toward them, sloshing through the mud.

"Pepe!" he said; "'tis thinking I was that someone had put a bullet through your worthless carcass by now, and made off with Juana. But you must be part Irish, from your luck—"

"And you, my friend," Pepe grinned; "part 'Greaser' from yours!"

"True words, lad. This claim would break the back of a jackass. Good day to you, gentlemen—which is a form of greeting, and not a reference to the weather. . . ."

Pepe made the introductions. "This *gran caballero* is seeking you, *especialmente, amigo;* though he did delay himself long enough to risk his life to save mine—"

Sean Murphy put out his hand again.

"Thanks, lad," he said simply. "This world would be a sadder place without Pepe in it. How did it happen?"

Pepe told him, though Bruce wondered if the young Mexican was talking about the thing he had taken part in. Pepe colored the story, adding many details to it that hadn't happened at all but which made it much more exciting than it actually had been.

"Good God!" Sean Murphy said. "Why the ditch-delivered sons of sluttish mithers! 'Tis a pity you could not have blasted a few of them. . . ."

"They were many," Pepe laughed; "and we were few. It is good to be able to turn my neck without rope scraping it. Besides, the gold came even more easily than it went, and for this reason, it does not trouble me. . . ."

Sean turned to Bruce.

"Might I ask why you were looking for me?" he said.

"Your farm," Bruce said. "I want to buy it, if you'll sell. . . ."

Sean looked at him for a long, slow time.

"How much money have you?" he said.

Bruce hesitated. But lying was a thing he didn't hold with. The

Preacher had said that Sean would drive a hard bargain. Still, he had to have that farm.

"Seven thousand dollars," he said. "Keeping back three hundred to live on a while. . . ."

"I will take that for it," Sean said. "It's worth all of that and more, lad. And because of what you did for Pepe, I'll throw in this claim, too. It's not bad as claims go. I average about fifteen dollars a day, here. . . ."

"What will you do," Bruce asked. "Move on?"

"No. With the money for the farm, I'll take the first steamer East. I've been working since Bridget and the children died, to get enough for that. But every other claim I've had played out in a few days—and all the wandering about, buying food for myself and fodder for the beasties, always left me without enough. This is the first claim I've had that might eventually have given me enough to go back to Boston. . . ."

"Then you don't think much of California, Mr. Murphy?" Hailey said.

"No, it isn't that, lad. To me every rock, every stream here, is filled with hard memories. California is a land of opportunity—to those who have sense enough to let gold alone. . . ."

"You're contradicting yourself in a way," Bruce pointed out. "You don't hold with placer mining, yet you throw in your claim along with the farm. . . ."

"You're going to need stock, supplies, seed, equipment," Sean said. "I think you can take enough out of this claim to get a start. And you put your finger on it when you used the word placer. Within two years, three at most, there won't be enough gold left in the streams, or in surface pockets to earn a man his bread from a day's labor. No—you'll have to go up those banks there, tunnel beneath those hills. Then you will make your fortune, but only after having invested a small fortune in the machinery and labor it will take to do the work. The future of gold mining lies in large corporations, with hundreds of thousands of dollars' invested capital. Mark my words, lads, before 1855, there won't be a prospector left in this whole territory. . . ."

Bruce stared at the primitive mining gear Sean had been working.

"We were sort of aiming to stay together," he said; "but fifteen dollars a day sure Lord won't feed four. . . ."

"There's more than that there," Sean said. "You've got to develop the claim. Put some money into it. Borrow it if you have to. Build a dam there—" he pointed upstream. "Lead the water down here through sluices into a long Tom instead of a rocker. I take out fifteen dollars because I'm alone, and can't afford what I need to take out more. But work this claim right, and it should pay you twenty dollars a day per man. . . ."

"That's better," Hailey said. "That's a hell of a lot better. . . ."

"Another thing. Build yourselves a couple of cabins on that flat there. Take your time and build them tight. Working this claim will give you rheumatism enough without having to sleep in a tent. That way, you can work the claim the year round. The dam will keep the water level high enough in summer so that you can wash gold through most of the dry season. Science, lads. That's the answer. Besides you'll have the advantage of having Juana to cook for you. And she's one helluva fine cook. Aren't you, *Chicita?*"

Juana smiled.

"So-so," she said in Spanish. "Neither good nor bad. . . ."

Bruce looked at her, for the first time realizing she understood English. He wondered if she spoke it, too. It was hard to tell about Juana. She seldom spoke at all, even in Spanish.

"This," Pepe said, "is but modesty, *Querissima;* your cooking is not just so-so, and much more good than bad. . . ."

"Look, Bruce—and you, Mr. Murphy," Hailey said. "As a lawyer, I want to suggest something to you both. For the protection of both your interests, we ought to go down to Sacramento and register this sale. There's been some trouble already over Mexican land grants; and, unless I'm way off the mark, there's going to be more. Just in case anybody ever finds so much as a flake of gold on any of the land in your district, you oughtn't to leave the slightest loophole open to give these claim jumping bastards a chance to question the validity of your deed. Because they would question it, you know. Gold and legal trickery seem to go together in this territory. . . ."

"All right by me," Bruce said. "What do you say, Mr. Murphy?"

"I will go with you, of course," Sean Murphy said.

"We will have also," Pepe pointed out, "the opportunity to purchase a cart, and load it with lumber to haul to this spot. I will gladly share in the expense—if you will allow me a few nights at the gaming tables, and a stake to start with. . . ."

"No," Juana said quickly. "This of the gambling is finished, my love. I have no envy of becoming a widow. You must borrow the money from these *señores* and pay them by working. . . ."

"She's right, Pepe," Bruce said.

"Additionally, there is this of Mercedes. You promised me, Pepe. . . ."

"Mercedes?" Bruce said; "who is Mercedes, Juana?"

"My little sister. My parents are dead now, and she has not anyone to look after her. Pepe promised me long ago he would send for her; but always he loses the money at gambling. She—she is a little wild, my sister, and I have fear that a disgrace will fall upon her. . . ."

"Is she—like you?" Bruce said.

"No," Juana said seriously. "Mercedes is very pretty, *Señor* . . ."

"And you're not?" Hailey hooted. "Lord God, Pepe, she is modest!"

"Too much so," Pepe said; "but she has right. Mercedes is prettier than she is. Unfortunately, a man is not permitted to have two wives in California. . . ."

"Don't preoccupy yourself with your sister," Bruce said to Juana. "It will be arranged . . ." He turned back to Sean. "You'll come with us to Sacramento?" he said.

"Gladly. Only we may need a boat. Last time I was there—on the eighth of January—the whole city was flooded. I shall be only too happy to leave these diggings. . . ."

"Then what are we waiting for?" Hailey growled. "Lord God, but it'll be good to have a roof over my head!"

This time, at least as far as the weather was concerned, they had better luck. The rains held off, though the clouds hung just above the tree tops like bolls of dirty cotton, sullen and threatening. Part of Sacramento was still under water; but from the mud traces on the sides of the houses, they could see how high it had been. They plodded up the dismal street towards the District Court, passing, as they did so, several buildings in various stages of construction. Sacramento was a mushroom city, determined to make good her citizens' boast that she would "—beat Frisco, by God!" One of the new buildings caught their attention, because it was built of brick, probably, they guessed, from Sutter's kiln. It was an imposing structure, three stories high, already finished except for the roofers who were busily engaged in putting what seemed to be the last coat of tar on the roof.

"I don't remember that one," Hailey said. "Reckon they started that since we been gone? Lord, Bruce, if they did that's some kind of a record. . . ."

"About two weeks," Bruce mused. "They must have begun it before, boy. So much building going on, we didn't pay it any special notice . . . Even so, they've built it damned fast. . . ."

"Here's the court," Sean Murphy said.

It took them a little over two hours, during which time both Bruce and Pepe read the entire original Alvarez grant to the Judge, translating it into English as they read. The official translation, as a quick comparison of its first page with that of the original showed, was worse than useless. Any title based upon it, Bruce pointed out dryly, wasn't worth the paper it was written on.

"Whoever wrote this," Pepe said politely, "had very small knowledge of Spanish, your worship. . . ."

"Thought so," the Judge grumbled. Then his eyes kindled. "Wait a minute! Hold on there, boys! I'm going to call in the clerk. If you'll translate that grant over again to him, this here session won't cost you nothing. Heck, this way I'll be able to save the town's leading citizens a bushel'n a peck of money. Yep, sure will, the way land's booming hereabouts—and don't think they won't be grateful. . . ."

Bruce could see the territorial governorship, or that of the state, when the wrangling in Washington could be gotten over with, gleaming in the Judge's eye. He smiled.

"Be glad to, Your Honor," he said.

The clerk bustled in, an ink-stained, fat little man, with a grotesque turf of grey hair surrounding the glistening baldness of his head. He seated himself, rowed out his pens, uncorked the inkwell, and Bruce began the reading. When he tired, Pepe took it up, while the clerk's pen flew. Thus alternating, they read it all, and the clerk looked at the Judge in triumph.

"Your Honor," he squeaked. "Bet you we got the first honest to God, true'n valid translation of a Mexican land grant in the history of Californy!"

"You're right, Josiah," the Judge said; "but it's going to cause a peck of trouble. New surveys, first off; then adjustments. Appears to me we ought to get a binding agreement between all holders of city lots to abide by present boundaries, or to make additional payments if the discrepancies are too great—at a fixed rate, of course. That should fix it. . . ."

"Right, Your Honor. Another thing, Sir: we ought to get these gentlemen's John Hancocks to this translation, above a duly notarized statement that they've done it fairly, honestly, and correctly, to the best of their abilities . . . You gentlemen agree to that?"

"Why sure," Bruce said.

"*Si, Señor*," Pepe said; "providing no one will shoot us if it is found that we have—well—rearranged the borders of their lands. . . ."

"No danger of that," the Judge said. "I'll vouch for you. Besides, I've accepted it and that makes it legal. Write out the statement, Josiah, then swear these gentlemen to it, and notarize their signatures. Then you'n I'll sign it as presiding officials, and these other two gentlemen as witnesses. That'll make it ironclad. . . ."

The rest of it took barely a half hour. The deed that Hailey drew up was recognized as valid and final; signatures and the court seal were affixed. Bruce passed over the money to Sean Murphy, and received the deed and a receipt declaring the sale free and clear.

"Young fellow," the Judge said to Hailey. "You want a job? We could use a county recorder with your knowledge of land law. You could practice on the side, too. Heck, boy, inside of a year you'd be twenty times richer than you'll ever get in the gold fields. . . ."

Hailey smiled.

"Tell you what, Judge," he said. "Hold that job open 'til spring. If I haven't made a million by then, I'm your man!"

"You be here April first," the Judge said. "I'm not worried about that million. Never seen anybody make any big money out of placer mining yet—and fewer'n that who could keep what they did make. Good luck to you all, gentlemen. And my respects to your Missus, *Señor*. She don't speak English, does she?"

"No," Pepe laughed. "Which is one language at least in which she must hold her tongue!"

Outside on the sidewalk, Hailey turned to Bruce with a wide grin.

"Now about my fee—" he said impishly.

Bruce stared at him.

"All right," he said. "How much, you pirate?"

"Pepe," Hailey said; "how much will it cost to bring Mercedes to California?"

"Five hundred dollars—to San Francisco. And I, of course, will meet her there. . . ."

"Then my fee is two fifty," Hailey said; "to which I add two fifty more. C'mon, you tightwad, give Pepe the money."

Bruce looked at him, hard.

"You realize you're damn near cleaning me?" he growled.

"Sure," Hailey said cheerfully. "Don't worry about it, boy—your credit's good with both me'n Nate. . . ."

"Look, Hailey," Bruce said. "I know women are scarce in California; but I won't be a party to any funny business. If Mercedes is anything like Juana, she's not the type for you to. . . ."

Hailey stopped grinning.

"I'll put it to you, square, Bruce," he said, "and to you, Pepe. I've been lonesome long enough. If Mercedes looks anything like Juana, she'll suit me. I was very happy with my wife, and I know from experience that butting around from pillar to post don't pay. Reckon what I'm trying to say is, that if Mercedes is one half as pretty as Juana, I'll marry her so damn' fast it'll make your head swim—that is, if she'll have me. Think she would, honey?"

"I don't know," Juana said in Spanish. "Who can read the heart of a woman, *Señor?*"

"Well," Hailey said; "I'm a born gambler, *Chicita*—specially when half the money I'm gambling with belongs to somebody else. Here, Pepe—take it. All I'm asking is that I meet her first, before this sawed-off polecat!"

"With this," Juana said, "you have no cause for preoccupation— at least as far as *el Señor* Harkness is concerned. . . ."

Bruce stared at her.

"What do you mean by that, Juana?" he said.

Juana smiled.

"Nothing, *Señor*," she said. "Or everything. It is as the *Señor* wills it. . . ."

Bruce looked from her to Pepe.

Pepe shrugged.

"It is a thing she has," he said; "this making of riddles. The answers are of no importance—if there are any answers. . . ."

They went back up the street, toward the hotel. But this time, as they approached the new building, there were men standing in front of it. Even before he could see their faces, Bruce was sure he knew all three of them. One of them turned. He was a tall, powerful man, bearded to the eyes.

I know that face, Bruce thought. Or at least I knew it once, before he hid it under that brush. Now who the devil . . . ?

The man stiffened, his eyes opening wide, staring at Bruce. Then he turned and walked off down the street.

But of the other two men, there could be no question: one of them was the man called Terry, who had officiated at Pepe's would-be hanging; and the other was Rufus King. He was as dapper, clean-shaven, handsome as ever. His clothes were as fine.

"Goddamnit, Bruce!" Hailey got out. "That's that murdering son of a two-bit whore, sure as shooting! Now what the hell . . . ?"

"Easy boy," Bruce said. "Don't let on. Shake hands with him if necessary. He finds out we know, he'll cover his tracks real good. We've got to give him rope, lot's of rope. He'll do it again. I'm sure of that. . . ."

"Why, Bruce? Why are you so all-fired certain-sure?"

"Because he kills in cold blood. Man who kills out of anger generally does it just once. But people like King have a kind of contempt for ordinary folks. They think they're smarter. Sometimes they are, at that, for a long time. But, because they've got no respect for anybody else's thinking power, they get careless. That's what we've got to wait for: the first mistake that King makes. C'mon now. . . ."

He saw Pepe's hand steal toward the butt of his revolver.

"None of that, Pepe," he said sharply. "I'm handling this."

"*Si, Señor!*" Pepe sighed. "Still it would give me an immense pleasure to perforate the hide of that coyote. . . ."

"Immense enough to balance out being hung as a murdering 'Greaser'?" Bruce said quietly; "and leaving Juana to be passed down the line among all those attending the ceremonies?"

"That, no," Pepe said. "Thou hast right, *Amigo!*"

"What's this all about?" Sean Murphy said.

"We know positively," Hailey said; "that that good-looking fellow with the mustache murdered a man in cold blood. But we can't prove it. And that big hulk there is the skunk who tried to hang Pepe. . . ."

"Let me at him!" Sean exulted. "I'll kick his backside so hard his front teeth will come out!"

"No," Bruce said. "No fighting, Sean. The stake's too big to show our hands this early. Look, I'll bet you whatever amount you care to name that that building belongs to King. And I'll lay you odds, on top of that, he aims to own this town before the year is out. . . ."

"And he will, too, unless we stop him," Hailey said.

"Best reason to keep a tight rein, Hailey," Bruce said. "Come on now, we look a mite foolish, standing here. They know by now it's them we're talking about. . . ."

They came on toward the two men. When they were ten yards off, the man called Terry moved. The draw was so clean and fast that Bruce knew that the man had to be an authentic gunslinger in order to be able to do it like that. He shook his head admiringly.

"Stay where you are, boys," he said quietly. "And for God's sake don't draw. A gun battle is the last thing we want, now. Let me handle this. . . ."

Then, very slowly and peacefully, like a man taking an afternoon stroll, he started toward the two men. As he walked, he unbuttoned his coat, starting from the top button.

"You could miss from there," he said. "Which would be a pity. 'Cause, if you have got a hankering to get yourself hung for shooting an unarmed man, you might as well make sure you got me. . . ."

"Unarmed?" Terry spat. "Who th' hell you think you're fooling, Mister?"

Bruce opened his coat wide.

"See for yourself," he said. "I never carry a gun."

He stood there, like that, holding his coat open, a yard from the gun muzzle.

"Howdy, King," he said peacefully. "Didn't expect to see you in this neck of the woods. . . ."

Rufus King threw back his head and laughed aloud.

"Damn my soul, Harkness!" he said. "I like your nerve! I truly do. Put up that artillery, Casey. Mr. Harkness is a friend of mine. . . ."

"Mighty queer friends you got," Terry Casey growled. "The next thing I know you'll be hanging out with 'Greasers', like this critter does. . . ."

"Why not?" King said easily. "Wouldn't be at all difficult if they all looked like that wench there . . . Friends of yours, Harkness?"

"Yep," Bruce drawled. "The girl's Pepe's wife—"

Terry put the gun back in the holster.

"Now I know we should of hung the 'Greaser'," he said.

Bruce looked at him.

"Pepe," he said quietly, "is a friend of mine. So's his wife."

"What the devil do you mean by that, Harkness?" Casey said.

"Oh—nothing much. Just that I don't take kindly to folks hanging my friends—or otherwise abusing them. Keep that in mind, Casey. Might save you a sight of trouble. . . ."

Casey's big hand went to his coat, tearing at the buttons.

"You little sawed-off, son of a bastid!" he roared. "Reckon I better learn you; and I don't need no gun, neither!"

"Cut it out, Casey," King said. "I won't have this. Neither Mr. Harkness nor any of his friends is to be molested in any way. You'd better pass the word around to the rest of the boys."

"All right—Boss," Casey said; "but damn if it ain't hard to take. . . ."

He turned and moved off down the street.

"Call your friends over, Bruce," Rufus King said. "Have a drink on me in my new emporium. . . ."

"So this is the Blue Diamond?" Bruce said. "Funny. Thought you were going to set it up down Frisco way. . . ."

"I intended to, at first. But after I got the lay of the land down there, I decided the already established competition was too much to buck. So I took a look at Sacramento. It has certain advantages.

For one thing, it's closer to the gold fields, so I can head off the miners before they get down to Frisco. For another, Sacramento's booming. It's going to be *the* city of California. It's got Frisco beat —central location, deep enough river channel for fair-sized sea-going vessels to come up the river. Mark my words, Frisco is going to be a mere port for Sacramento—"

"Could be," Bruce said; then, raising his voice: "Come on over folks, the war's over. . . ."

"I've invited you all for a friendly drink," Rufus King said. "My lieutenant, Casey, was being a little overzealous. He didn't realize we were old friends. The lady's welcome, too—that is if we have something light enough to suit her taste. . . ."

"You 'ave wine, no?" Pepe said.

"Yes, as a matter of fact, we do. Come on in. I'll set up a glass of the best for your lady. . . ."

"Many thanks, *Señor*," Pepe said.

They went up to the semicircular bar.

"What you going to call your bar, King?" Hailey asked. "The John Mead Bar?"

King stared at him.

"Why do you suggest that, Burke?" he said.

"Oh—no reason. Just thought it would be a nice tribute, seeing as how you'n him was such friends—"

"It hadn't occurred to me," King said softly. "But, actually, Burke, it's not a good idea. One could hardly display one's respect for a departed friend by naming a bar after him. Poor Mead. He was a fine man. . . ."

"He was that," Hailey said. "By the way, what's that you've got covered up there—a picture?"

"Yes. I'd show it to you; but—with a lady present, I'm afraid that—"

"Oh, Juana won't mind," Pepe laughed. "And I have a great envy to see if American girls are made as other women are, *Señor!*"

"Your permission, *Señora?*" King said smoothly.

"*Si, Señor*," Juana said; "it makes nothing. . . ."

King drew the curtain away.

"Ah!" Pepe laughed delightedly; "but they are different! Look, *Chicita!*"

Bruce looked at the fat, pink nude. Then he turned and saw Juana's eyes.

"Better cover her up, King," he said; "or we will have a war. . . ."

King smiled and did so.

"Poor devil of an artist I met in Frisco did that for me," he said. "He was starving. I thought he was going to kiss me when I gave him a hundred dollars for that fat obscenity. But it's worth it. It'll draw the miners like flies. . . ."

"Do better," Hailey said, "if you had some real, live gals about, King. . . ."

"Oh, I've arranged that, already. Friend of mine in Marseilles, one Marcel Laurier, to give his latest alias, is shipping me a boatload of the French demi-mondaines . . . And you know the French, boys—they have a certain talent in that direction. . . ."

"If," Juana said flatly, in English, "you ever enter thees place again, I weel keel you, Pepe!"

"So!" Bruce said. "You do speak English, Juana! You've been holding out on us. . . ."

"Two words, *Señor*," Juana said. "No more. . . ."

"She lies, as usual," Pepe sighed. "She speaks many more than two words. But I have had to forbid her to speak them. Because, you see, *Señores*, she comprehends neither the meaning nor the gravity of these words. I taught them to her as a joke, a thing which I have many times been sorry for when she becomes angry at me. . . ."

"I," Hailey Burke said, "was under the impression that she didn't talk very much. . . ."

"She doesn't," Sean Murphy said, "which is a rare and excellent thing in a woman. But what she does say, she says beautifully. Strange, but 'tis only in Ireland and the Spanish speaking countries that even the peasants are poets. Never met a Mexican, for instance, who wasn't full of lovely-sounding words. And when they're said in a voice like Juana's—it fair shivers the soul within ye! Why is that, Pepe? Have you a Blarney stone in Mexico?"

"This rock of eloquence that you Irish kiss? No, we have not that. We have many little streams that run through the bottoms of the river beds, and talk to us at night with magic voices. We have the winds of the deserts, whipping the sands to fury, and

speaking dark thunder into our hearts. We have the little birds
who sit on the cactii above the canyons, and tell us secrets, and
the great solemn music of the Mass to make poems in our souls.
And the blue sky of Mexico to give us clarity, and the bright sun
of Mexico to burn the beauty into our hearts so deep that the
words awake in us like birds, already winged and flying . . . Ai-
yi-ee! So it is! What gran' nonsense I talk, *Caballeros!*"

"Wish I could understand this lingo," Rufus King said ruefully.
"It sounds deuced interesting. . . ."

"It is," Juana said suddenly, startlingly. "It is—*bastante*—How
do you say *bastante* in English, my soul?"

"Enough," Pepe said.

"It is enough," Juana struggled with the words, "that you understand naked women above bars. And to sell wines, and whiskey.
And this of chance. For if—" she made a hopeless grimace,
and gave it up, lapsing into Spanish: "If you could comprehend, *Señor,* the beauty of life, nevermore could you do these
things. . . ."

"What the devil is she saying, Harkness?" King demanded.

"That if you understood the beauty of life, you couldn't hang
fat blondes in the raw on the walls, sell whiskey and run a gambling den," Bruce said.

"Quite a little blue stocking, isn't she?" King laughed. "But a
deuced pretty one for my money. To your health, gentlemen. . . ."

They came out into the muddy street.

"I'll be taking my leave of you, now," Sean Murphy said. "The
next steamer for Frisco is due to leave in an hour. I mean to be
on it. Likewise the next steamer for Panama—then home. I'm going to open a little saloon in Boston—perhaps even marry again.
A man alone, is but half a man. . . ."

"God's truth," Hailey said quietly. "I lost my Missus, too—about
three years back. . . ."

"She was a good woman," Sean said. "I can tell by the sadness
with which you speak of her. Why is it that the good ones—die?"

"Reckon God needed a replacement in the Corps of Angels,"
Hailey said, "'cause my Mary Ann was a true angel on this earth.
. . . Never did know but one other girl anywheres near as sweet,

and she was already married soon after Mary Ann died. Still, reckon I can't complain, having had Mary Ann for ten good years. . . ."

"Then you were fortunate," Rufus King said. "There aren't many such. . . ."

"Reckon not," Bruce said. "Say, King, I just remembered something. Who was that fellow who hightailed it away from here so fast when he saw us coming?"

Rufus King smiled.

"I'm not at liberty to divulge his identity," King said. "As a matter of fact, he's an old friend of yours, Harkness. But it seems times have changed. The first time I casually mentioned knowing you, he specifically asked me not to tell you he was here. Until he releases me from that promise, I'm honor bound. . . ."

"Have it your own way," Bruce said. But he walked away from there with his forehead knitted with thought. I know him. That build. That walk—that walk! He turned back to King.

"Peterson!" he said. "Ted Peterson! But it couldn't be—I left him in Carolina, and we damn near broke the record, coming here. . . ."

Rufus King smiled.

"Perhaps you're mistaken, Harkness," he said.

7

BRUCE POKED UP the fire in the fireplace, and hung the kettle over it. Then he sat on the edge of his bunk, waiting for the water to heat. He looked at his face in the bottom of a frying pan scoured with fine sand until it was bright enough to reflect an image—and passed his hand over the coarse stubble of his beard.

His image stared back at him stonily: a square-cut face with grave dark eyes. He tried to smile; but his mouth wouldn't respond to his will, remaining tight-lipped and a little grim. He had lost weight from all those weeks of crippling labor. There were hollows in his cheeks and his eyes were sunken. After five months of placer mining, he knew the limits, the boundaries of his strength. He had the feeling that he was riding hard on the final edge now—like a lone horseman pounding the canyon's rim.

Goddamnit! he thought. Goddamnit, why doesn't Pepe come?

He took the little daguerreotype that Jo had given him, out of his pocket and looked at it. Her face smiled up at him, its pastel coloring translated into various shades of grey. His mind made the effort, reconverting them back into silver blond and wintery blue and shell pink and snow. His mind. There was no quickening within him, no anguish knotting in his breath. Only the anguish of knowing no anguish, the drift of dead leaves down an empty sky.

He stood up, the motion stiff, jerky, without grace, and crossed to the mantel. He propped the little picture up there, and stepped back, looking at it. It was a good likeness, a very good likeness, the kind people called "a speaking image." But it didn't speak to him any more.

Outside, the river gorge was a jagged bowl filled with sun. It was already hot, now that the rains had gone. He could hear the diminishing laughter of the water, and through it, Juana's singing.

His hands made fists, the knuckles white.

Why doesn't she shut up? he thought. Why the hell doesn't she?

As if in answer to his thought, the singing stopped. And the silence after its going rose up to the canyon's rim and beyond, filling all the sky. He was conscious that his knuckles ached from the tight balling of his fists. He opened his hands, staring at his rough hewn fingers.

"*Permisso, Señor,*" Juana said, and came into the cabin with the coffee.

She stood there holding the tray that Pepe had made of a slab of board. Bruce did not even turn to look at her.

"Put it on the table," he said, throwing the words backward over his shoulder like so many grains of sand.

"*Si, Señor,*" Juana said. She crossed the cabin behind him and put the coffee on the table. But she did not leave. She stood there, looking past him at the picture.

"*Bellissima!*" she breathed.

"Yes!" Bruce got out savagely. "She's lovely. Now will you please for God's sake go?"

"*Si, Señor,*" Juana said, and went out of the cabin.

But the thing she had given him, almost from the day that Hailey Burke had stood up tall in the midst of the icy water, two months ago in April and drawled: "To hell with this. I'm going to Sacramento and start practicing law—" was with him again, worse than ever. He could feel it running molten along all his veins. It sat in his middle and twisted his guts. It was a burning in him like thirst, an emptiness in him like hunger. It entered into him at night and broke his rest, so that dog-tired, sick from hunger, but unable to eat, he sat for cramped and endless hours on his bunk, until weariness vanquished him, forcing him down into the indignity of surrendering to the saturnalian riot of his dreams.

The kettle was singing now. He poured the scalding water into a bowl, stuck his shaving brush into it, swished it viciously against the coarse soap, lathered his face and started to shave. When he cut himself, he didn't even swear. He quite often cut himself now.

After that, he drank the coffee. It was barely warm, and tasted like mud. He swore, feelingly.

"Goddamned wench can't even make decent coffee!" he said; then he stopped. A smile stole over his face.

Easy, boy, he thought; being childish isn't going to help matters. This is not Juana's fault. Maybe not even mine. It's been near onto nine months since I been close enough to any other woman to even say "howdy;" and the last one before the time I met Juana was—Jo. Man wasn't meant to live alone. 'Male and female created He them,' the Good Book says. And Juana's just so gawddamned female . . . Funny. If she weren't Pepe's wife, I'd. . . .

He stood there, looking at the sullen trickle of blood from the gash in his chin.

No. Never in my life went down to the quarters to change my luck, as the saying goes. Fellows used to think I was crazy. But I wouldn't sleep with a woman I'd be 'shamed to be hitched with legally. Juana's damned fine; but she's mestiza. Wouldn't want no off color half breed brats—

But his imagination took the bit in its teeth, and crawfished out from under him, in a wild, oblique course. He saw a boy, tall and grave, with all the sun's warmth caught up in his golden skin. Black hair that was like a coolness. Tall, and straight and fine. Like the Indians' Sun God, the bringer of life. The pride in him hot and sweet and fierce. The dignity bone-deep, soul-deep; the voice that made dark music, speaking.

I'm crazy, he thought. I'm plumb stark raving loco. . . .

He took up his slouch hat and went out into the sun. He went up to the tail gate of the sluice, where the water poured into the hopper of the Long Tom. He started to work, hurling the shovelfuls of earth and water into the hopper, working like a man possessed under the sun. In spite of the dam, the water level had fallen dangerously low. In another month, he reckoned, there wouldn't be enough water to keep the Long Tom going.

Juana came out of the other cabin, and sat on the ledge watching him. He worked on doggedly, feeling her eyes upon him. They made a heat in him, greater than the sun.

Goddamn it! he thought again. Why doesn't Pepe come?

He stopped long enough to examine the black sand caught by the riffle bars fixed to the bottom of the Long Tom, and the riffle box beneath the perforated iron bottom (called the 'Tom' iron, thus giving the whole rig its name) of the long box's tail gate. He stirred the dirt with a fork, making it fall through. The water ran freer now, washing. He tossed out the pebbles too big to pass through the holes, keeping it up until nothing was left but the black sand caught behind the riffle bars. As he expected, it showed color, pinpoints of golden light, winking at him from the sand. He scooped it all out carefully, and spread it out on a sheet of canvas to dry. After that he could blow away the sand, leaving the gold.

He went back to the murderous labor of feeding earth and water into the hopper. Above him, on the ledge, Juana hadn't moved. She sat there, like that, watching him.

The sweat dripped from his face. He could smell the sour stench of his overdriven body. He worked on in a fury, under the pitiless blaze of the sun.

He had, he reckoned, enough for three cows and a bull, maybe enough for a boar and brood sow. No need to worry about planting. By the time he could get to it, it would be too damned late, anyhow. He was sick of placer mining—sick to the bottom-most pit of his soul. He had a hankering after his acres, after a life that was at least kind of reasonable.

His back ached. There was a giddiness before his eyes. Part of this came, he knew, from the fact that he hadn't eaten. But he wasn't hungry—at least not with that kind of hunger.

He was conscious suddenly, that Juana had cried out: a shrill and formless sound. He straightened up, jerking against the aching knot of his back muscles, and saw Pepe riding toward them up the gulch.

Thank God, he thought; thank God. . . .

Juana was flying towards her husband. He swung down from the saddle and kissed her. Then he was telling her something, his hands making arabesques in the sun-filled, dusty air. Bruce moved toward them. When he was close enough, he saw that Juana was clinging to Pepe and crying.

"What passes, Pepe?" he growled.

"Nothing," Pepe whispered; then he looked at Juana. "Ay-yee," he sighed. "It is better that I tell our patron, no?"

Juana nodded silently.

"It is of this dirty Mercedes—" Pepe began painfully.

"This dirty Mercedes?" Bruce said. "Why do you speak thus, Pepe?"

"Because it is so!" Pepe said angrily. "For all these months since we sent the money, we have wondered why she did not come. So at the post office, finally, I have found this letter from my uncle in response to the one I sent him. In it, my uncle declares that Mercedes departed at once the hour that she received it. . . ."

"So?" Bruce said. "Then she should have been here by the first of March. . . ."

"She has been," Pepe said.

"What?" Bruce said; "then what the devil . . . ?"

"I am coming to that, *Señor.* I made inquiries in Sacramento. I had small difficulty in finding that *mi cuñada bella*—my so beautiful sister-in-law, had verily arrived. She has been living almost since the day of her arrival in the cabin of one very dirty pig of a gringo whose name I cannot remember except that it signifies in Spanish, the son of Peter. . . ."

"Get on with it, Pepe," Bruce said.

"He was not at his cabin, unfortunately, so I could not make a nice little hole in his belly with a bullet. The cabin is an hour's ride north of Sacramento towards Ophir City. When I reached it only this whore of a Mercedes was there. She consigned me to hell, and slammed the door in my face. . . ."

"Too bad," Bruce said slowly. "Still, Pepe, since she is clearly there of her own free will, you're not called upon to get yourself hanged by avenging the family honor. . . ."

"But your money, *Señor?*" Pepe said.

"The money of *Señor* Burke," Bruce said, "which I owed him for a service. As for the rest, he gambled and lost. Do not preoccupy yourself with it, Pepe."

"What a disgrace!" Juana wept.

"Nor you, little dove," Bruce said. "This man, Pepe—Is he a miner?"

"The son of Peter? No, *Señor.* He is, I think, a bandit—the leader, it is said, of a ring of claim jumpers who—"

"The son of Peter," Bruce whispered. "The son of Peter! Peterson—that was it, wasn't it, Pepe? Ted Peterson?"

"*Si, Señor* that was it, *preciso!* He is a big man and of enormous strength. He has already gained many enemies; but since men are afraid of him, that makes nothing. Additionally, he is very *amigo* with this *gran bruto*, Terry Casey, who tried to hang me. They are of the same band. . . ."

"Did you see *Señor* Burke?" Bruce said.

"Si! What an idiot I am! He sent a letter to you. Wait, I will find it . . . Ah, here it is . . . I had fear. . . ."

Bruce took the letter, tore it open.

"There are," Pepe said quickly, "other letters for you at the post office. I asked for them, but they said I needed a note from you. . . ."

"We'll go to Sacramento tomorrow," Bruce said; "and after that —home. This of the mining is finished. Whether or not I have enough, it is time we commenced to live like human beings. I'll join you at dinner. . . ."

He went up to the cabin with the letter. It was racy, exultant in tone. In two weeks, Hailey had made more money than he could reasonably expect to clear in five years in the gold fields. His good fortune, by no means rare in the explosive growth of California cities, had grown directly out of Bruce and Pepe's translation of the Alvarez-Sutter grant.

"Two of our local tycoons," Hailey wrote, "were on the point of reaching for their shooting irons over a hundred foot gap the new surveys showed between their holdings. I suggested the only reasonable solution, a fifty-fifty division; but neither of those polecats would have any part of that. Both of them wanted it all. Took me exactly a week to find out it was personal animosity at the root of the whole thing. Both of them had more business frontage than they'll ever be able to use. . . .

"So," Bruce read on, "the judgment of Solomon having failed, a new settlement was indicated. I borrowed five thousand dollars from Nate Johnson, and bought the lot with the blessing of them both. That should have been the end of it, but it wasn't. The day after the deed was registered, one of the men involved, talking over his cups in King's Blue Diamond, let slip that I was the new owner. So the next thing I knew, there was King, himself, seated in my office, willing to offer me any reasonable price for my hundred feet of mud and water. As you might expect, I wasn't inclined to be reasonable with Rufus King. So I stuck him for fifty thousand dollars, which isn't as outrageous as it sounds, because lots downtown commonly go for forty these days, no matter how small they are. He balked at that; and, after a powerful sight of bourbon, we compromised at thirty! So, even after paying Nate back, I'm twenty-five thousand dollars richer by doing almost nothing at all. Bruce, boy, throw away that pick and shovel and hop into town! This real estate business is really something!

"About the man you asked me to investigate, I've found out very little. His name is Peterson, and he does come from Carolina. He sailed by steamer, crossed over the Nicaragua route, was lucky enough to get a Northbound steamer right away, and beat us here —even though, if he's the same Peterson you think he is, he left the East coast after us. Beyond that, nothing. Occupation—none; but he's always flush. Rufus King—and some dirty doings? I wouldn't doubt it. Oh yes, he's currently the envy of everybody in the district because he's got a Chileno woman installed in his cabin, who, the boys say, is really something! I'll continue to keep track of him, boy; don't worry. . . .

"Send me a power of attorney by Pepe, so I can get your mail. Seems you have a couple of real fat letters; but the Postmaster, here, is real strict. Anyhow, here's hoping I see you soon. Luck, Hailey."

Bruce sat there, holding the letter in his work-thickened hands. There was, he knew, a pattern in this, whose outlines were already coming clear. Ted Peterson was here, having left Carolina, having left Jo. More, he had left so shortly after Bruce's own departure, that by taking advantage of the combined services of the United States Mail Steamship Company to reach Juan del Norte, Nicaragua, then by river steamer across the Isthmus—except for the three places where it was necessary to portage around the rapids, taking new steamers above them—and finally embarking on one of the Pacific Mail Lines huge sidewheelers, he had been able to reach California before the *Flying Fish*, despite her ninety-nine day record voyage around the Horn. But that, Bruce knew, wasn't too difficult a thing to have done; because the steamship service had been organized early in 'forty-eight, and by the closing months of 'forty-nine, was so well co-ordinated that a man could easily make the voyage from New York to San Francisco in a little over a month, including changing steamers at Havana, three changes on the Nicaragua river route, or the train, keelboat, mule-back trip

across the Isthmus at Panama, and the wait for the Pacific Mail
Steamer on the Pacific side, while the Clipper voyage for all its
speed had taken three months and nine days.

Now that the problem of how Ted Peterson could have done it
had been solved by Hailey's investigation, there remained only the
"why". Why, Bruce pondered, would any man in his right mind,
married to Jo, leave her for any reason whatsoever? It came to
him finally, that the answer to that one lay in the character of Ted
Peterson, himself.

Funny, Bruce thought. Ted's a big, good-looking man; but ever
since I've known him, he's had something eating at his insides.
Reckon he's always felt a mite too sorry for himself. Had his share
of bad luck, I'll grant him that. Quite a comedown when your
old man dies a suicide and leaves you not a penny, when all your
life you've been rich. What was left of their plantation was too
small and the land was plumb played out. But another man who
would put his hand to the plough and stop worrying over things
and envying other people, could have made a go of it. Borrowed
the money, put in marl, switched to truck crops. Could of pulled
himself up that way. But not Ted. . . .

Strange. In a curious way, I reckon Ted Peterson's a coward.
Not physically. He was too all-fired brave in the war. That's it. Too
brave. A man who's got this other kind of fear gnawing at his guts
has to be too brave to make up for it. I could fight, and I could
run; and I wasn't 'shamed to do whichever one the situation called
for. But Ted couldn't run; and only the Lord God who looks after
fools and children saved him. . . .

That was one time when his luck was good—when he got fur-
loughed back home while I was lying there in the hospital not
knowing whether I'd make it or not. Home, the conquering hero,
to marry my girl, who'd turned me down for going to the same
war that he went to, too!

Reckon it wasn't all luck, at that. 'Cause being himself, a whiner
and a coward, when he had to face up to the thing that calls for
the only kind of courage that counts: the holding on, the taking it,
and standing up to the slow grind of living, he showed her what
he was, and the bloom was off that rose mighty damned quick.
Jo could be a witch to live with, if she didn't love a man. Patience
has never been one of her virtues; and her tongue sure Lord ain't

gentle. But, far as I could see, Ted worshipped Jo. Then why? Why in the name of tarnation did he leave her?

He dug into that. A man twisted with envy. Scarred with the feel of defeat. A man, whose size and physical strength had prevented his ever really being tested in the arena of natural, human combativeness, because other men gave way to him too easily. But, such a man, accustomed to the ease and comfort of living and then losing them. Accustomed to the respect of the crowd and losing that, too—when his banker father died a branded embezzler and suicide . . . He must have known the gratification of physical lust easily enough from the complaisant women to whom his bulk and good looks would appeal; but when he had come to love finally for the first time, with his spirit, as well as his body—and he had, Bruce was sure of that—he had found the object of his idolatry turned from him, in chill anger, in disgust, coming to despise him, through his own fault for some obscure reason he could not divine, as though a secret putrescence within him was revealed only to her eyes.

Such a man, then, hearing, being told that his wife had stood on a quay and ripped her handkerchief to shreds as she watched another preparing to embark; that she, in sight of friends, acquaintances, strangers, had gone into the arms of this man and kissed him in grief and anguish and tenderness and desire, the voyager being known, a former suitor. What could a man, any man, read from such an act?

Only, Bruce thought bleakly, that their kiss sure Lord wasn't the first; and that there'd been more than kissing between them. . . .

California, then—to hunt for gold? Or to hunt down the man you believe had hung the horns on you, and put a bullet through his guts? But Ted had had his chance, and he hadn't acted. Afraid? No. That wasn't the kind of thing Ted Peterson would have been afraid of. This thing was getting more and more twisted all the time.

Mercedes. Plain lust compounded with the desire to get even with Jo, perhaps. And the westward voyage a sick mixture of flight from the unbearable, the desire to start again, to rise again to wealth, to power, to respect. And also vengeance. But not perhaps the frontiersman's direct vengeance of bullet or knife. The kind of revenge a sick soul might conceive of: the hounding of the hated one slowly down to death, burying him finally under the mountainous heap of humiliations piled upon him.

That. Perhaps, that. Almost certainly—that.

Bruce sighed, and crumpling the letter into a ball, hurled it into the fireplace. The grey-pink embers reddened; a wisp of smoke stole up. The paper browned about the edges, flared. Bruce watched it burn. Then he got up and went to join Pepe and Juana.

Outside the post office, at Sacramento, he stood holding the two letters, debating with himself which one he should open first, David's or Jo's. He had no eagerness, only a faint far-off feeling of sadness, mingled with a certain reluctance to subject himself to any more disturbance of his already weary spirit. Jo was far away. It would be years, if ever, before he saw her again. He hoped that her letter would not cry out to him, reawakening old and slumbering pain.

He opened the letter from his brother first. That was easier.

"You sure Lord started something," he read, "with this California business. Heard that eight or ten boys from this county alone are going, some of them have already gone.

"Reckon I'd better warn you. Damn it, boy, that was a tomfool trick kissing Jo Peterson on the wharf! Biggest scandal since the Minister ran away with Prof. Evan's wife. Everybody's certain sure you been putting in a crop where the ground's already fenced. You told me you didn't, and I believe you; but that don't take away from the fact that you've split the Petersons completely apart.

"Ted's left home—California bound, some say. And if they're right, you'd better be careful. Lots of chance to get a bullet or a knife betwixt your ribs in that wild country without anybody's being the wiser. . . ."

Lord God, Bruce thought tiredly, how things can build up from something that wasn't anything much sure beats me. . . .

He turned again to his letter. The rest of it wasn't important, inquiries as to whether or not he had found gold, questions about the climate, the life in the territory, information about David's wife and sons, complaints over the difficulty of running the plantation, a plea for news. . . .

Bruce folded the letter and put it back into the envelope. Slowly he slit the edge of the other one with his penknife. A faint wisp of perfume stole up, persisting through all those months since Jo had written it.

"My Dearest," he read. "If it seems strange to you that I, the wife of another, call you dearest, I'm sorry. I can't help it. You are my dearest, the only man I have ever loved or ever will love. I am writing this with great joy, for soon I shall see you again!

"It is all Ted's doing. As you know, our plantation is a total failure. Your departure gave him the idea of imitating you, of going west to seek his fortune. And, after he is established he will send for me.

"I know that your brother has probably written you of the scandal I caused by my unwifely behavior the day you sailed. But I am not Ted's wife. I am not! I can never be. I am and always will be yours.

"Ted was wild with rage, but I calmed him. I convinced him that while it was true that I loved you, there never has been anything between us. I even told him the bitter truth that it was your fault, not mine. All right, I am a bold baggage, an unprincipled female; but being without you has made me so. I was a fool to quarrel with you over that Mexican business; but for that we would have been, I fondly believe, long since man and wife.

"So, when I come, I shall ask Ted for a divorce. In a new country like California, where nobody knows any of us or our histories, it will make little or no scandal. Here, it would have been impossible—as terrible as that business of our late President Jackson and his poor Rachel. I was only a child at the time, but I remember the talk. But even if it does make scandal, I will accept it. I do not care what shame, what disgrace I have to submit to in order to be free of him. Anything at all would be but a small price to pay for the joy of being yours. . . .

"I understand why you have not written me. But, as you see, there is no danger now that your letter might fall into his hands. Please, please write! Tell me everything: what you are doing, what you are thinking; anything at all except that you have ceased to love me. Tell me that, and I shall surely die.

"I am awaiting Ted's letter, sending me the funds to come to California. It has become increasingly easy to make the voyage. There are steamers every week from Charleston and Savannah, and only a little stretch of land to cross at the Isthmus of Panama. It takes only a month now. I will write you the date of my arrival as soon as I know it, so that you can meet me. You—not Ted.

"I am consumed with impatience. I hold your picture, the one you gave me in exchange for mine, the summer we were together—and weep. Oh, Bruce, Bruce—soon, my love, soon!"

Bruce's hands, moving, folding the letter, were things apart from him, working mechanically, without conscious command. The sadness inside of him was very deep and quiet and still.

And then, at that moment, he saw Juana coming toward him on a plank sidewalk. As she walked she seemed caught up in a special blaze of sun. She moved toward him, willow slender, her burnished copper skin glowing in the sunwash, the blackness of her hair haloed, her lips forming her slow and secret smile.

He knew quite suddenly and completely that he would have to send for Jo. Ted Peterson would scarcely do so, now. But against this Goddess of the Maize, this pagan child of sun and thunder, he needed stronger bulwarks than his fondness for Pepe, than even his honor, and his pride.

He stood there, waiting, wondering whether even Jo would be enough; whether even after the immediate hunger in the flesh had been appeased, he would not stretch out his hand to Juana out of older, deeper hungers; that the thing he sensed in her, the warmth of sun, the peace as deep as time, would not call out to the pain and confusion within him with an appeal beyond the resistance of mere reason.

It's only lust I feel for her, he told himself; but even as he shaped the thought, he knew he lied.

"Pepe awaits you at the Blue Diamond, Señor," she said.

Bruce looked at her a long, slow time. Then he passed a hand across his face, as if to clear away the thoughts that plagued him.

"Tell him to take you on to the farm," he said. "I'll join you as soon as I can, Chicita. I have a thing to do. . . ."

The thing he had to do was to visit Ted Peterson. Whatever lay between them, must be settled now, and finally.

8

HE RODE INTO the little clearing before the cabin, and got down from the bony nag he had rented from the livery stable in Sacramento. It was the first time he had ridden a horse since he had come to California, and bad as the animal was, it beat walking a thousand times. He'd have to swallow his pride and ask Hailey to include enough money in the loan he had already asked for, to buy a decent mount. Considering the amount of wandering about a man did in the territory, a good horse was an absolute necessity.

He knocked on the door and the girl answered it. He stood there, staring at her. Pepe was right. She was prettier than Juana. Her beauty, in the afternoon light, was like a cry in the darkness of a man's heart. She was different from what he had expected. She had no look of—viciousness, of venery. Her face was innocence, itself. She could have served as a model for a Madonna for some Spanish master.

She returned his gaze, her great dark eyes like those of a faun, deep and frightened and shy.

"Pardon me," Bruce said, "but is the *Señor* Peterson here?"

Astonishment leaped in her eyes at the Spanish; then she smiled. Her smile was something to see.

"*Si, Señor*," she said. "He is here. I will call him for you. . . ."

She disappeared into the darkness of the cabin. After a moment, Ted Peterson came to the door, yawning and scratching himself.

He saw Bruce and stopped dead.

"Howdy, Ted," Bruce said quietly, and put out his hand.

Ted hesitated barely a second, then he took Bruce's hand in a bone-crushing grip.

"Howdy, Bruce," he grinned; "never thought I'd be glad to see you; but damn it, I am!"

"You saw me once before," Bruce reminded him.

"I know. But that was before Mercedes. I feel different about the whole thing now. C'mon in. No—don't. The place is a mess. House-keeping ain't one of li'l' Mercedes' virtues. Besides I keep her so busy doing what she is good at, that she just don't have the time. Set here on the stoop. Mercedes'll bring us a drink. Won't you, honey?"

"*Si, mi amor,*" Mercedes said; and her voice, speaking, was filled with love and pride.

Bruce stared at Ted Peterson. The man had changed. The brist-ling hostility that had been so much a part of him before was gone. He seemed peaceful, almost friendly. Bruce reckoned that a girl like Mercedes could do that much for a man. That much, maybe more.

She came back with three fingers of bourbon in the glasses. Bruce sipped his. The bourbon was excellent, the best. Knowing what bourbon cost in California—from a dollar to a dollar and a half an ounce-shot glass in most bars, Bruce could see what Hailey meant when he said Ted was flush.

"Well, boy," Ted said. "What's on your mind? Know damn well you weren't suddenly overcome with friendly feelings toward ol' Ted Peterson . . . Jo, again, I reckon?"

"Yes," Bruce said flatly, "Jo."

"Well," Ted said. "What about her?"

"You promised to send for her, when you got set. 'Pears to me you're damned well set now. . . ."

Ted Peterson grinned at him, slowly, insolently.

"Now ain't you the limit?" he said. "You're not satisfied with having whored around with my wife all these years; you want me to pay her transportation out here so you all can whore some more. . . ."

Bruce put the glass down, and stood up.

"I'm not listening to talk like that, Ted," he said quietly. " 'Spe-cially not in reference to Jo. . . ."

Ted stood up, too; the motion easy, lazy, confident.

"Why not?" he drawled. "Since you know damned well it's so?"

Bruce didn't answer him. That wasn't the kind of a thing a man gave dignity to by answering.

"Why don't you send for her?" Ted mocked. "That tender little goodbye kiss she gave you ought to be worth that much to you— not to mention the other li'l' thing she's been giving you right along. . . ."

Bruce hit him, then, pivoting off the ball of his left foot, leaning with the blow; one hundred sixty-five pounds of solid bone and muscle behind the punch. Ted Peterson didn't move. He shook his head, and stood there, still grinning. A thin trickle of blood came out of the corner of his mouth and ran down into his beard.

"I won't fight you, boy," he drawled. "That would be too damned easy. You know, and I know, that I could break you in half with one hand tied behind my back. . . ."

"Try it!" Bruce spat.

Ted shook his head.

"Naw. Start fighting, and I'll get mad. Get mad, I'll kill you. And I don't want to do that. I want to keep you around a long, long time and watch you squirm. Killing's much too good for a rat bastard like you. . . ."

Bruce hit him again, the rage inside him like a sickness. But this time, Mercedes flew from the cabin, her fingers curved into talons, raking for his eyes. Her face was not the same face any more. The angel-innocence was gone; she was twisted, daemonic.

Ted caught her by the waist, and pulled her away from Bruce; but not before she had furrowed one whole side of his face with her raking nails.

Ted hung onto her while she writhed in his big arms, spitting out a stream of staccato Spanish profanity.

"Now, now, Baby doll," Ted chuckled. "Mustn't hurt him. Look what a puny li'l' feller he is. Leave him be. He's gonna send for that dirty li'l' whore I left behind, and they're going to be real happy together, raising bastards. . . ."

Bruce let his hands fall to his sides. The rage went out of him, leaving him cold and sick. He walked slowly to where he had left the horse, and mounted.

As he turned the nag's head away from the clearing, Mercedes drew herself up, and with icy formality, pronounced the Spanish language's ultimate insult:

"I spit," she said, "into the milk of thy mother!"

Little Mercedes, Bruce thought wearily, is quite a girl. Then he rode away from there, hearing until he was beyond the reach of it, Ted Peterson's bass laughter, echoing among the trees.

As he turned the horse over to the Mexican stableboy, he felt dirtied, permeated with filth down to the core of his being. Ted Peterson had won that encounter, and by a display of precisely that kind of forbearance, that mastery of self that Bruce prided himself upon. He, Bruce Harkness, had for the moment, descended out of manhood, and given way to childish anger, acting with the same violence that he had come to recognize as a mere symptom of a malaise in the spirit, a sickness of the soul. He wouldn't forget that afternoon in a long, long time.

He was aware suddenly, that the stableboy was staring with undisguised curiosity at his face. He felt a sudden surge of renewed wrath.

"What the devil are you looking at?" he growled.

"Nothing, *Señor*," the boy said.

"You better get that attended to, Hoss," Hailey said; "women are just like cats. Got poison in their claws . . ." He sat there, trying to keep the questioning out of his gaze.

"All right," Bruce said; "I'll tell you about it. Got to, anyhow, because you're kind of responsible for it in a way. . . ."

"Me? Lord God, Bruce—how?"

"Mercedes. You gave Pepe the money to send for her."

"She did—that?"

"Yep. Remember writing me that Ted Peterson is living with a Chileno woman? That Chilena, Hail, is little Mercedes. . . ."

"Well, I'll be damned!" Hailey whispered.

"She got the money and arrived right on schedule. Seems that Ted met her. By pure accident, most likely. I don't know the details. I'd sort of gathered from Juana, anyhow, that Mercedes is no lily of the valley. . . ."

"But your face? You have a fight with her?"

"Not exactly. With Ted. She cat protecting her mate. I made a jackass of myself."

"You? That's hard to believe, old Hoss—"

"Did though. Lost my temper and hit him. He wouldn't fight. He acted bigger than I did. Told me to run along. Laughed at me. So I did, finally. After a lesson in Spanish profanity from little Merciful. And these stripes. . . ."

"It's all right, boy," Hailey said gently. "Just proves you're human. As for the money, I knew it was a gamble. 'Pears to me I won though, not lost. If Mercedes is like you say, Ted Peterson can have her—with my compliments. Speaking of Ted, though, I got an idea where he gets his money. . . ."

"Where?" Bruce growled.

"Prettiest dodge you ever heard of. You know that Mex bandit you told me about?"

"Joaquin Murieta? But he hates gringos worse than poison. He'd never—"

"Hold on there, old Hoss! I never said Murieta had anything to do with it. What I do know is a hell of a lot of miners have been robbed here of late, and some of 'em killed. Every one of 'em has been a white man, a Chink, or a Nigger. No Mex. Naturally that points to Murieta. All of them happened in territory he's known to operate in—"

"Damned if I see what you're driving at—"

"I'll get to it, you give me time. Mind you, it's just a theory. But I got something to go on, now. Every surviving victim has sworn that the bandits spoke Spanish among themselves. Couldn't see their faces, 'cause they were masked to the eyes. But they all agreed on one thing: the two leaders are great big men. Now I've seen a lot of Chilenos, Mex, and such like. Bruce, I ask you one thing: You've been in Mexico. You ever seen a *big* Mexican?"

Bruce shook his head.

"No," he said; "not big like an American can be big, leastways. I've known some tall ones—like Pepe for instance; but they're always slender. They just don't grow like that. . . ."

"Another thing, boy. Mexicans ever wear whiskers?"

"Old men. The young ones, never. Got too much Indian in 'em to grow much hair. . . ."

"That's it then. Ted Peterson and Terry Casey. Damn fools didn't

have sense enough to shave off their whiskers. Stick out from under their masks. . . ."

"Got any more proof?" Bruce said.

"Yes. But it ain't worth a damn in court. Here's the real pay
dirt, to my way of thinking; but all it proves is that they ain't
Mex, that they are Americans—not who they are. They robbed a
Spaniard—a real one from Spain. Left him for dead. Only he didn't
die. He's in the hospital, getting along nicely. Bless you, old Hoss,
for teaching me the lingo so good. . . ."

"Damn it, Hail—you drag a thing out until you get a man wild."

"Bruce, did you know that some Spaniards are blond with honest to God blue eyes?"

"No," Bruce said. "Always thought they were dark."

"Not all of them. According to this fellow, two provinces, Astu-
rias and Galicia, were overrun by Germanic tribes hundreds of
years ago. And those Teutons didn't leave. They stayed right there
and mingled with the natives. And there were so many of them
that they made the Nordic type fairly common, not only there, but
all through the north of Spain. Well, this Manuel Avila looks like
that. . . ."

"And Ted and Terry mistook him for an American?"

"Right. Went on with the old dodge of speaking Spanish in front
of him. Only this boy *is* Spanish. What they spoke was gibberish.
A few words of Spik here and there—the rest of it just sounds.
They do it damn well, he says; they got the tune and the accent
down pat, only they can't speak the lingo at all!"

"I'll be damned," Bruce said softly.

"There's more to it than that. I think they're mixed up in this
business of claim jumping. We're having an epidemic of that, too.
Here of late, every living time somebody strikes it rich, a crowd
of roughs jump his claim. All strangers; nobody's ever seen 'em
before. They just appear out of nowhere, armed to the eyes. Ain't
enough law enforcement bodies to take care of 'em. They're always
stronger than any posse we can muster. . . ."

"And Casey and Peterson—?"

"Recruit 'em. Can't prove it, but I'm almost sure. The real point
is this: Bruce, you know both those big bastards. Either one of
them got brains enough to plan a thing, organize it, and carry it
out so damned neat?"

"No," Bruce said flatly.

"You know what that adds up to, then?"

"Yes," Bruce said. "Rufus King."

Slowly Hailey nodded.

"They never come near him. Neither one of 'em has been in the Blue Diamond since it opened for business, which, considering the fact that every other man in the whole district has been at one time or another, is downright odd. King rallies around at all hours, taking care of business. Not an ounce of proof. Not a jot, an iota. But all the same, I'm sure. . . ."

"Like you were sure about Mead," Bruce said.

"Yes, like that. Bruce, boy, I been practicing law a good part of my adult life. Developed a kind of instinct about these things. I can smell a crook nine miles to windward. And of all the crooked sonsofbitches I ever met, Rufus King's got the worst smell. . . ."

"What do you aim to do, Hailey?"

"Nothing. Just wait. I got another bad habit: respect for the law. And this territory's going to become a state before this year is out. I'll admit I have ambitions. Aim to be big in this state. . . ."

"You're big now," Bruce said.

"Not enough. I'm chairman of the levee committee—we've already started building so as to be ready for next winter's floods. The Judge won't make a move without consulting me; nor the Mayor. We got eighty-three lawyers in town, and I'm president of the Legal Association, treasurer of the Real Estate Development Board. I'm worth close to an hundred thousand dollars inside of six months. Fine. Sounds like bragging, doesn't it?"

"No. Truth ain't brag," Bruce said.

"Only—I'm a poor lonesome cuss who doesn't know what to do with himself. I'm 'shamed of being stupid enough to let a bastard like King prey on the whole damn countryside, and I can't find out how he does it straight enough to convict him. But I will. Damn it, boy, I will! This is going to be a great state, and I want to help make it so. And the first thing to do is to make it safe for ordinary, decent folks, so they don't get robbed, rolled in pretty waitress saloons, and occasionally murdered. There's a strong movement afoot for reform. I'm riding along with that. We're going to clean up this town, and afterwards the whole territory. And you can help. All I want from you, boy, is a promise that when I yell for you, you'll drop everything and come arunning. . . ."

"You've got it," Bruce said. "Look, Hailey—about that money—"

"You pay me back when you can. And don't strain yourself. I need money like I need an extra head. What I really need is a Missus. Been wracking my brains to see if I can think of some filly of good family in Augusta I could correspond with in view towards matrimony. But the only one I can think of is that black-haired l'il' Ruth Martin, and, like I told you, she's already married. And I was so damned happily wed so long, I lost touch. . . ."

Bruce stood up.

"It won't always be like this," he said. "Women will be coming along in a year or two—'Bye now, Hail. . . ."

"Hope so," Hailey said. "So long, ol' Hoss. . . ."

It had been on the tip of Bruce's tongue to ask for an additional loan so that he could send for Jo. But now he knew he couldn't do it—not ever. It wasn't the kind of a thing you asked men like Hailey, or even Nate; lost lonesome like himself, with their male hungers endlessly driving them in this Eveless paradise. Borrow their hard-earned money to send for a woman to ease and comfort him, with them there to watch it—their need, their desire, their hunger augmented by the sight of Jo beside him, her hand in his, her blue eyes smiling as she looked at him? It would be, Bruce thought, a damned sight too thick. Nope, have to earn the money myself. Pay Hailey back first. Jo's waited this long she can wait 'til the end of summer. . . .

Got to put in a crop. It's damned late, and there's the risk the snow might catch me. But it's a risk I'll have to take. Those boys in Nevada City and Grass Valley will pay me any price I ask for my stuff, just to break the monotony of their miserable rations . . . I'll take the chance.

Got to write Jo. But what can I say? Ted'll never give her a divorce. And even if she lived with me out of wedlock, he'd find some way to make things damned tough. She'll have to divorce him—for adultery, which won't be any great shakes to prove. The one thing that's certain is sooner or later it's going to come to killing. My life, or his. I can't. I purely can't. Maybe Hailey will get the whole band, and the law can take him out of my way. . . .

Buy myself a horse now. Then on to Marysville to stock up at Nate's. Then—

The farm. Where Juana was, sheathed forever in sunlight, with her dark eyes following his every move, and unknown things hidden behind her slow and secret smile.

Damn, he thought miserably, can't a man ever arrange his life so he'll have peace?

But once he started it, it was good. Pepe appeared in flapping white pants and a straw sombrero like a peon, and put his hand to the plough. The sweet, black earth turned up in smooth furrows. Pepe laughed delightedly at how the American plough cut the earth.

"We use a curved stick yoked to oxen," he said. "Sometimes tipped with iron—when we have iron, *Señor*. Ai-yee, but it is immense!"

They worked from dawn to dark, ploughing, with Juana walking behind them sowing the seed. They watered the stock, driving them down to the far creek. Juana had to walk all the way down there, too, two pails slung on a wooden bar across her shoulders to bring water to the house.

Have to dig a well, Bruce thought again. Next summer, though. This year, there's no time.

In the evenings they helped Juana clean and varnish the woodwork in the house, and in Pepe's and her quarters above the barn. Like all unoccupied dwellings, both the house and the barn had suffered. There were enough repairs to occupy a man for months after the farming was done.

The Preacher came to visit and saw the haste and extent of their labors. He looked at the green shoots peeping through the earth. His own were already up and a yard high.

"Risky business," he said, "late planting. Have an early winter, and you're done, boy. . . ."

"Know that," Bruce said. "It was the chance I had to take. . . ."

"I'm kind of handy with tools," the old man said. "I'll give you a hand with the repairs, nights. . . ."

The next night, he was back, a carpenter's box under his arm. Handy, Bruce soon found, was an understatement. The Preacher was one of those men born with craft in his hands. On Sunday, Nate Johnson came with him. The two of them worked all day, getting the barn, which in the present state of affairs was far more important than the house, shipshape and tight.

" 'Remember the Sabbath Day to keep it holy!' " Nate chaffed the old man. " 'Six days shalt thou labor—' "

" 'Is it lawful to do good, or to do evil on the Sabbath?' " the Preacher quoted, mildly, in his turn.

They were working like that when Pepe and Bruce came in from the fields from their weeding, from the hillside, where they had been cutting back the brush from around the young apple and pear trees. The two of them picked up their tools and began working too, waiting for Juana to bang on the iron triangle summoning them to eat.

And it was there that the young Mexican found them. He rode into the barnyard on a black stallion. As he dismounted, Bruce could see that his clothing, though entirely black and simple, was, nevertheless, very fine. Fire leaped in Pepe's eyes at the sight of him; but for once he held his tongue.

The boy, for he was no more than that, eighteen or nineteen, Bruce guessed, looked from one to the other of them.

"The *Señor* Harkness?" he asked politely.

"I'm Harkness," Bruce said. "What can I do for you, son?"

The boy put out his hand.

"Please to shake my hand, *Señor,*" he said. "That is all. I have come to thank you, in the name of my people, for what you have done for Pepe—"

Bruce took his hand. Slender as it was, looking more like the hand of a girl than that of a man, it had, surprisingly, a grip like steel.

"It wasn't anything," Bruce said.

"The life of Pepe, *Señor,*" the boy said firmly, "is, if you will pardon the contradiction, indeed of value. The life of any man is —but Pepe is beloved of many. A thousand thanks, *Señor!* If you ever have need of help in time of trouble, say but a word to Pepe, and he will come to me. And I will ride to your aid. For though men call me cruel, the life of *un Americano,* of this gran' decency enough to befriend a Mexican is to me as my own. . . ."

He bowed to the others.

"*Adios, Señores,*" he said. "Go with God all your days!"

Then he was in the saddle in an effortless, floating leap. The stallion pawed the earth, his hooves biting clods out of it, and they were gone, horse and horseman, in a rising dust cloud.

"Beats me!" Nate said helplessly. "Nice young feller, but Lord God, he do talk big! Pretty li'l' boy, kind of girlish looking—what the thunderation kind of help could he give you?"

Bruce looked at Pepe, seeing the enormous grin on his dust stained face.

"Pepe," Bruce said. "Was that who I think it was?"

"*Si, Señor!*" Pepe laughed.

"Then who the devil was it?" Nate growled.

"Joaquin Murieta," Bruce Harkness said.

Now there was August in the land, and the work slowed. The corn and wheat were up, but not nearly high enough yet. Bruce prayed that the killing frosts would hold off until the end of October. But there was nothing he could do. Nate and the Preacher had finished the repairs. The sow had a fine litter. Some of the cows were already big with calf. The weather was mild, slumberous, lovely.

Bruce rode herd on the cattle, driving them to water. His roan mustang was a joy and a delight to ride. A trained cowpony, the animal seemed to know what was going on in a cow's dim brain before she did. By giving him his head, Bruce learned to ride herd like a master. Pepe had taught him the use of the lasso; but they would have no real need of that until branding season.

At night, Bruce sat in a chair, reading by an oil lamp for hours, until it came to him how few of the words had penetrated his consciousness. He found himself staring out of the window at the barn. That was bad, very bad, so he undressed in haste and got into bed. But it would be hours, he knew, before he could sleep.

He had written Jo, telling her of his intention to send for her, and explaining why he had delayed. So far, no answer had come from her; but it was time for one now, for the mail steamer had already arrived in San Francisco, and the river boat had also, almost surely, brought the letters up to Sacramento.

He wanted to ride to Sacramento and look for mail; but he was afraid to. The last time he had visited Hailey, that rising young statesman had pointed out to him three of the girls from King's Annex, sitting at a table in the Blue Diamond. And Bruce had known with terrible conviction he had been in California too long.

He was a young man, not yet thirty. He was strong, and healthy and alone. He had within him all those curious things that make up a code of living: the pride that scorns to stoop to outright purchase; a curious fastidiousness, even a sense of cleanliness, which, on one level, made him bathe far more frequently than was the custom in 1850, and on another, made him reject with loathing the very idea of dirtying his body with the used and soiled purveyors to public lust; more, he had even a conception of decency above and beyond that ordinary variety, accidentally resulting from his pride of self that held many things done without thought by most men as entirely beneath a Harkness, abysmally below him, Bruce Harkness, a man proud and unique upon the face of earth.

He had all these things. And now, in that very nearly womanless desert that was California in 1850, every single one of them was crumbling fast.

Go to Sacramento, he thought angrily, I'll get drunk with Hailey again. . . . I won't, because I can't. . . . So, damn it, I'll stay out of Sacramento. I'll wait on Jo. I owe her that much respect. . . .

It came to him suddenly, bitterly, that Jo hadn't waited for him. If she had, everything would have been different. The tangled, tortured skein of his life would have been easy by now, easy and smooth. Still, he wouldn't go to Sacramento; he would hold on, endure. And he did not go. He sent Pepe in his stead.

He knew, within four hours after Pepe's departure, that he had made a mistake. Juana's voice, singing an ancient Spanish love song, coming to him from the kitchen where she prepared his dinner, convinced him of that. He crossed to the kitchen, threw the door open.

"Juana!" he grated. "For the love of God, stop that singing!"

"Si, Señor," Juana said serenely. "I have much sorrow that my poor voice gives the Señor no pleasure. . . ."

"Sorry," Bruce said. "Your voice is lovely, Juana. It's just that— I—"

"That the *Señor* is too much alone," Juana said. "And has this bad sadness that come from loneliness. It is a pity, *Señor;* for you are *muy simpatico,* very nice. Will not the so lovely *rubia* come to you?"

"I don't know," Bruce said dully. "I hope so."

"And I also," Juana said. "Will you eat now, *Señor?*"

But he couldn't. He tried, but the food choked him.

"It is bad about Mercedes," Juana said. "She would have been very nice for the *Señor*. . . ."

"Juana, shut up!" Bruce shouted.

"*Si, Señor*—as the *Señor* wishes," Juana said.

Pepe reached Sacramento on the morning of August fourteenth. He went dutifully to the post office and got Bruce's mail. There were three letters, one from David, and two from Jo. Without even glancing at them, Pepe stuck them inside his shirt, next to his sweaty hide.

He had other things on his mind beside letters. He had a sack of gold dust and an enormous desire to try his luck against the first monte dealer he came across, in his heart. He also had a long-nurtured thirst for some fiery *aguardiente.* Juana was becoming much too strict with him. She was forever comparing his behavior, to his discredit, with that of *el Patrón. El Patrón* does not come home reeling with drunkenness. *El Patrón* does not consort with filthy *putas* in a fandango dive. *El Patrón* does not gamble. *El Patrón*—Pepe stopped, his handsome young face alight with laughter. *El Patrón* truly does not know how to live!

He went happily along the street toward the gambling houses. But when he got to the first one, it was shut tight. So was the second. The third. Even the Blue Diamond was closed.

Pepe frowned. He approached a bearded American, who had a rifle over his shoulder, two holstered revolvers slung about his hips, and a bowie knife stuck in his belt. Pepe paused. Even in California, that degree of armament was unusual. And the man looked angry. Pepe shrugged eloquently, and went on. The next man he met was similarly armed, except that he had only one revolver.

Five more men came up the plank sidewalk. They all had guns.

Pepe wrinkled his nose. Sacramento, he thought, is today a little unhealthy. I will depart from it. Still, there is this enormous thirst that I have—

He saw a Mexican slinking along, keeping himself as nearly invisible as was humanly possible, and called out to him:

"Ai—Chico, what's happening?"

"A sufficiency of trouble," the other whispered. "The gringos fight among themselves. There are these little gringos who have no money and who squat upon the land of the big ones who have it all. They claim that the grant made by our government to *el Señor* Alvarez, and by him to *el Patrón* Sutter, is worthless. They refuse to pay for the land. The big ones have the intention to put the little ones off. And the little ones have an immense envy to kill the big ones if they try it. As for me, I have this desire *grande, enorme, fantastica, formidable* to be somewhere else!"

"And I, also!" Pepe laughed. "Get up behind me. *Vamanos!*"

They went out of Sacramento at a gallop. Pepe let the other Mexican down in front of a saloon, outside the city limits. The saloon was open. Pepe entered it. But inside, his conscience smote him. *Señor* Bruce, he thought, has been waiting for these letters of the pale *rubia* for a long time. Still, one might combine pleasure with business. . . .

He bought a bottle of *aguardiente* and stuck it inside his shirt with the letters. Then he rode away, singing happily to himself. Ever so often, he took out the bottle, and drank. The world became a finer place. In the tree tops, a million little birds sang. The sky and the river and the distant mountains danced together in slow and stately rhythm.

"Ai-yee!" Pepe laughed. "Already I am drunk!"

He pulled out the bottle again. A trickle of brandy ran down his chin. His hand shook. He spilled brandy down the side of the bottle. No more now, he thought, until I am further along. . . .

But Pepe and temptation were old friends. The bouts between them were brief and amicable. Temptation always won.

Pepe drew the *aguardiente* out again, not noticing the letter stuck to it by the thick drops of the brandy he had spilled. As he shifted his hand downward from the neck to the middle of the bottle, his fingers brushed the letter off. A gust of wind took it, sent it flying. Pepe saw the white flash of it, rising on the wind.

He jerked the bottle down and felt for the letters. There were only two now.

He gazed at the handwriting. One of them was from a woman.

"I have luck," he said to his horse. "The Patrón will have this so great happiness with this one letter of the *rubia* that he will never think to ask if there were others. And I, *tal vez*, will be able to keep my hide in one piece. . . ."

He rode on, singing.

Two weeks later, a miner, plodding up the trail towards Marysville, saw something white caught on a thorn bush. He went and got it. It was, he saw, a letter, the ink faded entirely off the envelope by the dew, and the envelope itself torn by the winds.

The miner opened it, gazed at it, curiously.

"Mighty pretty writing," he said. "Sometimes it do seem a pity that a body can't read. . . ."

He crumpled the pages, threw them from him. They lay in a little ball in a depression near the trail. The top part of the crumpled sheet showed clearly, a single line. It read, if there had been anyone to read it:

"I will arrive the last week in November. Oh, my love, I—"

But there was no one. And, after a time, the first rains came and reduced it to a sodden mass, ink stained, and useless.

Bruce Harkness, sitting with Nate in a Marysville saloon, put down his glass, and shook his head, stubbornly.

"Nope, Nate," he said. "Don't agree with you. Nothing much ever happens to a man, he doesn't let happen. A man, a real man is always master of his fate. . . ."

A miner, leaving, pushed open the swinging doors, and they heard for a moment, the noise of the rising wind.

It had, curiously enough, a sound like laughter.

9

BRUCE SAT ON the mustang, looking out over his fields. The corn was still green, and the wheat wasn't high enough. He looked up, uneasily at the mountains. Already the clouds were forming at their peaks and the snow line was lower, much lower. He turned back to Pepe.

The young Mexican shrugged.

"If we have two weeks, *Señor*," he said, "it will be enough. But that we will have so long, God alone knows. The mountains are very white, no?"

"Yes," Bruce said. His fingers moved, buttoning the topmost button of his buckskin jacket. The air had a nip to it. He had a feeling that the frost would come soon. But he didn't know. In that part of South Carolina where the Harkness plantation was, he could remember but two hard frosts in all his life. He had never developed the feeling for bad weather that Northern farmers had. There had been so little bad weather in Carolina.

His eyes rested on Pepe's face, speculatively. Again the Mexican shrugged.

"We should harvest now, *Señor*," Pepe said. "But if we do, we lose half the value of the crops. Do not ask me to advise you. I am at heart a gambler. People with this crazy love of risks that I have always prefer to lose it all than to play safe and take the half. . . ."

Bruce put his hand in his jacket pocket, and the pages of the letter rattled. He did not take it out; he had no need to. By now, he knew it all by heart—every word of it.

"I cannot allow you," Jo had written, "to send me the money to come to California. That is, after all, Ted's duty as my husband. As long as he remains my husband, he must do what he should. But I read between the lines of your letter that you doubt that he will, or that he can. He has not written me. Has something happened to him?

"If he tarries overlong, I shall obtain the money from my Uncle Ronald in Savannah. Uncle Ronald is very rich; though, I must admit, he is terribly stingy. Still, after all his preaching about the sanctity of the home, and the sacredness of marriage, I shall have some strong arguments to confront him with. . . .

"Your letter was strange. So—so distant. Bruce, dearest, have you changed toward me? If you have, you must tell me. I am quite certain that I would die of a broken heart if you have; but perhaps that is the folly of a silly girl who has dreamed only of you all these years.

"I shall write you again in a couple of weeks, whether I have news for you, or not. Oh, my Love, it is so hard to wait—so hard—"

But there had been no other letters. Not one. He had written to her three times, before another letter from his brother David informed him that Jo had gone to Savannah early in July, and had not come back. He had written David for her uncle's address, but his brother hadn't answered him.

He sat there, staring at the wheat. A crop, one good crop would establish him. At the prices he could get, he'd be able to pay Hailey back, and start next year on a sound basis. But half wasn't enough. To pay Hailey—yes. But the next year he would have to borrow again. He sat there for a long time without moving. Then he shrugged, duplicating Pepe's gesture.

"I'll gamble on it," he said.

"Good!" Pepe laughed; "and now, Señor, let us take the guns and go up into the mountains. The bighorns will be very fat still, and their flesh verily something to the taste. Juana can water the stock, which is the one thing that remains to be done."

Bruce considered the idea. He hated idleness. It gave a man too much time for thinking. And his dislike of killing did not extend to wild animals—so long as it was done sparingly and the animals used for food. Besides, it would take him out of sight and sound of Juana for at least a week. That was inducement enough, in itself.

"All right," he said; "but we won't kill more than we can use, Pepe. . . ."

"*Seguro, Señor.* We will take a mule along to carry enough supplies to keep us if we are snowed in, which is possible this time of year. And he will be of use to bring down the sheep, if we have luck. Ai-yee, but it will be good to hunt again!"

"All right," Bruce said. "Go and arrange things, Pepe. . . ."

The trail up to the cave had to be seen to be believed. It wound upward around a series of hairpin turns so steeply that they had to stop every half hour to rest the animals. They had to ride single file, leading the mule. And the trail's outside edge looked down on sheer walls of rock Bruce doubted a fly could climb. He moved his horse cautiously to the edge and looked down. Then he jerked the beast away from there, his stomach knotted and the sick dizziness blurring his sight.

"You will accustom yourself to it, *Señor*," Pepe said. "This of the vertigo always comes the first time in the mountains. It is nothing. Do not think of it—"

"I shall not think," Bruce said dryly, "nor look, Pepe. Is there much more of this?"

"We shall be there at nightfall," Pepe said.

But there was snow on the trail now, and that slowed them. Time and again the horses slipped, sickeningly. Still, by not even stopping to rest the animals, they reached the cave while there was still light enough to see by.

The cave was big. There was enough room inside for the animals as well. Pepe made a fire. After it was burning well, he draped a buffalo skin robe over the entrance. Then he busied himself with the frying pan and the coffee pot. He was skilled at camp cooking. While he worked, he told Bruce stories of his youth in Mexico. Bruce stopped trying, after a while, to separate the exaggerations from the truth. He was very tired, and his troubled mind kept restlessly flying back between the crops and Jo—and Juana. He hoped that he would find a solution somewhere, somehow, that would not be worse than the problem.

He realized suddenly, that he was more than half hoping Jo would stay where she was. He needed her, and he wanted her;

but the choices her coming would bring would be hard choices, between evils, with no good in them anywhere. The whole thing was pregnant with violence. He wanted Jo, wanted to marry her and settle down to a normal way of living; but there was Ted. He had no idea what Ted Peterson would do when, and if, Jo arrived; but he knew with bedrock certainty it wouldn't be good.

He doubted that Ted would give up Mercedes, but he doubted even more that Ted would consent to a divorce. In this game, Ted Peterson held a royal flush; he didn't have to do anything and the very circumstances implicit in the situation would wreck Jo's life and Bruce's as well. Bruce thought over what he could do to change things: He could kill Ted Peterson in a duel, or by murder, neither one of which had more than the slightest risk of being punished by law in a California where, Hailey sadly told him, there had been last year more than a thousand killings and not one conviction. He could arrange for Jo to see with her own eyes, accompanied by witnesses, the flagrant adultery her husband was guilty of, and thus have means for a divorce. But Ted's reply to that would surely be gunplay. He could live with her in concubinage, in adultery as flagrant as her husband's. And to that, Ted Peterson, he was certain sure, would answer with a challenge, not a court summons. At bottom, every road open to him led only to violence. And they were all shameful. He had to break his own code to follow any of them.

There was one more choice—a sad one, but having a saving measure more of decency than any of the others: He could sell the farm, pay Hailey back what he owed him, and go north to Oregon. There, in the Columbia River Valley, there were good lands—and immigrant families settled there since 'forty-three. Families who had come out of land hunger, which was a thing that had health in it. They, the riders of the Oregon trail, had brought their wives and goods and cattle. Presumably, there must be among them girls of marriageable age. It would be a different world, not this gold-fever-ridden madhouse. A world of health, of sanity, of peace.

But—it was flight. And, if Jo came, abandonment of her to whatever awaited her. Less shameful than the rest, but shameful still.

He saw that Pepe was looking at him, curiously.

"Do not preoccupy yourself with it, *Amigo*," Pepe said. "She will come. . . ."

"Reckon so," Bruce said. "Lord God, but I'm tired. . . ."

In the morning they got up and started climbing, leaving the horses and the mule in the cave. They were lashed together with a length of lasso rope. Pepe carried a pole and a mountaineer's pick along with his carbine. By then, it was snowing so hard that Bruce couldn't see below him; but his imagination made up for his lack of vision. There were still the rudiments of a trail that led upward to a high pass. Only hunters, trappers and Indians had ever used it, because it was too much for either wagons or pack animals. But it wasn't, all things considered, really very bad. A man could walk it with a degree of safety, even carrying a heavy pack.

What the rope was for, Pepe explained, was the possibility they would have to leave the trail and climb the rock surfaces to get near enough for a shot. Toward noon, the snow stopped, and they left the trail, climbing amid the blinding whiteness under a deep blue sky.

Bruce didn't see the mountain sheep until Pepe had unslung his carbine and taken aim. Then he saw them, patches of white a little darker than the sunwashed glare of the snow. They were pawing with their hooves, searching for fodder. He unslung his own carbine and took aim. Pepe grinned.

"After you, *Señor!*" he whispered.

Bruce centered the notched vee of the sight on the back of a magnificent ram. He drew the hammer back into full cock, held his breath, and squeezed the trigger slowly. The gun crash echoed from wall to wall of the pass. The ram went straight up, and came down, running. Pepe's gun leaped to his shoulder, spat a tongue of orange flame. The ram went down, head over heels, and lay there. The rest of the flock vanished, their whiteness blending with the snow. When they got to the ram, they found only one ball in him. Bruce had missed him, clean.

"Patience, *Señor*," Pepe said gently. "This of the mountain sheep takes practice. . . ."

"It doesn't matter," Bruce said. "This old fellow will supply us with meat for a good long time."

He stood there watching while Pepe gutted and rough-dressed the ram. Then he tied the animal's feet to the pole. When they picked him up, slinging him between them, he was damnably heavy. Bruce doubted that they could pack him down the trail.

But they did it, watching over their shoulders as the clouds came scudding down the pass and blotted out the sun. In a matter of minutes, the blue was gone, the world ghost grey—a crying note sounding in the wind. Bruce could feel the cold creeping in upon him. He seemed to be plunging deeper into an arctic subworld with every step he took. A stinging drop of sleet struck his face. It felt red hot, with that curious reversal of the senses that comes from extreme cold.

Then, without any warning at all, the sleet was whining down, biting into their unprotected faces. Their lashes and brows whitened. They stumbled along under their burden.

Dozens of times Bruce was on the point of suggesting that they drop the sheep and get to the cave. But his pride held him in check. He stumbled on, swearing under his breath. Then he saw it, the buffalo curtain flapping in the rising wind.

It was still warm inside the cave though the fire had gone out. Pepe started another one, the ruddy glow splashing their shadows, black and gigantic against the walls and ceiling. It was peaceful there beside the fire. They roasted huge hunks of the ram over the fire and ate them, hungrily. Then they lay down, smoking the cigars that Bruce had brought. Neither of them said anything. They gazed into the fire and were silent.

Pepe got up and pushed the curtain aside. The wind howled into the cave, driving a wall of snow before it. Quickly, Pepe let the curtain fall. It flapped and billowed.

"Kind of bad, eh?" Bruce said.

"Very," Pepe said. "The worst, Señor. When it blows like that. . . ."

"What, Pepe?" Bruce said.

"A week, Señor. Maybe more. And even after that, the going down will be very bad also. The trail will be covered with this vileness of snow to a man's waist. We will have to walk, feeling for the trail with the poles, and leading the beasts. It will be, additionally, very slippery. . . ."

"But we will be all right, here," Bruce said. "I see you have plenty of wood, Pepe. . . ."

"And also a good ax to cut some more should we exhaust this. And food enough, since we have the bighorn. Snow to melt for water. But it will be bad for the horses, Señor. . . ."

"Well," Bruce said; "no use worrying about it, Pepe."

Four days later, they started down the trail, leading the starving beasts. It took them two days more, which afterwards Bruce never liked to remember. They floundered, slipped, fell, dug each other out of the drifts. They went down like sleepwalkers fighting the drowsiness they both knew it would be death to succumb to. And all the way down, they kept looking for the end of the snow. There had to be a snow line; they knew that. The last of October was far too soon for snow all the way down to the valley.

But when the trail began to level out, and the snow was still there, knee deep, they knew what they were going to find. Still, realizing it and seeing it were two different things. The wheat bent over, blasted by the wind, the stubble blasted by the wind, the stubble poking through the drifts, the corn stripped and shredded, all of it lost in the peaceful white wilderness.

A man, Bruce had said, was master of his fate. A man could make decisions and abide by them. He was not the plaything of ribald gods who puffed their cheeks and blew his life into the tattered shreds of mindless destruction. From the upended, jagged bowl rim of the Sierra Nevadas to the Coast Range, dim and blue in the distance, the world was a blanket of white under leaden skies from which from time to time a sullen flake still fell. And it was all gone, all gone, the money he needed to bring Jo Peterson to California, back into his life, the little sacks of yellow dust he owed Hailey Burke, the seed for the spring planting. . . .

"I have much sorrow," Pepe whispered. "We should have stayed behind and harvested. . . ."

Bruce looked at him. Then he smiled, crookedly.

"A good gambler," he said, "doesn't whine—or welch, Pepe. Come, let's go see after Juana . . ."

He sat before the fireplace in the Preacher's farmhouse, listening to the old man's measured words. But already he knew what he must do. Go south, in another week or so—towards the end of November, when even the southern streams were full. Work the rainy season through, panning gold; but stopping in time—getting back to the farm the end of March, have the ploughing finished and the seed in by mid April. That way, it wouldn't be a gamble any more. He had a fair sum of money, realized from the sale of the pigs and those of his beef animals that he could spare. But not enough. He would have to borrow again. And from Hailey. To go to some one else—to Nate even—was to show mistrust in his own ability to pay, doubt of Hailey's generosity. He hoped he would make it this time. Failure could get to be a habit.

"Son," the Preacher said, "it's a hard thing to answer. Men have been asking that question since the time of the Prophets. There've been many attempts to explain it, but not one that really does. 'Whom God loveth, He chastiseth.' That was one. Funny. I'm a religious man, but I don't believe the Lord dotted every i and crossed every t in the Bible. That was a try, by a man the same as us, to answer a thing that bothered him, like it's bothering you; that bothers me a little sometimes, even yet. . . ."

Bruce stared into the fire. He didn't say anything.

"Accidentality," the Preacher mused, talking as much to himself as to Bruce, "blind chance. Sometimes I even get the feeling there isn't anything else . . . Study Greek in college, son?"

"Yes," Bruce said. "Why?"

"In a way, they explained it better. They had a host of gods, all of 'em immoral or maybe unmoral. It's real hard to justify our concept of a Father God Who is just, and Who cares. But the Greek's answer was the easy answer: Man, the helpless plaything of the Fates, tormented like Prometheus or Tantalus, Fury pursued like Orestes. Simple. Obvious. Everything in life bears it out. But I suspect the easy answer. There's always something wrong with it. . . ."

"Doesn't seem much wrong with that," Bruce said dryly.

"Don't be bitter, son. You've had a run of hard luck lasting several years. Another thing I don't believe in: luck. I'll show you what's wrong with the Greeks' idea of fate in a minute. It's what they leave out. The main thing: choice."

"Choice?" Bruce said. "I don't get that, Reverend."

"You've always had choices, boy. It's the paths you chose that made what you call bad luck. You could have stayed out of Mexico. Nobody forced you to go. But you had to be a hero—dog-goned useless things, heroes. Give me an intelligent coward every time, so long as his cowardice is only physical, not moral. And that cost you your girl. You had the choice of staying in Carolina and seeing her married to another man, or running off to California. You ran. You could have stuck to mining instead of turning to farming. You could have harvested a poor crop instead of waiting, stayed home instead of going hunting. Accidents, Bruce? Chance? It has been known to snow early here. . . ."

"I see what you mean," Bruce said quietly. "I got the bad habit of making the wrong decision. That's it, isn't it?"

"Weren't all bad. Some things that look like mistakes now may turn out to have been the right choices after all. What I like about you, boy; is that you seem always to choose to do the decent thing —no matter how it hurts. Fits in with another idea of mine: the time of testing. . . ."

"I'm being tested?" Bruce smiled. "For what?"

"God knows. And He ain't saying. But over a period of years, Bruce, a certain amount of misfortune, and good fortune, happens to every man living. I use those words because I don't know any other way to say those things. But I don't believe in either of them. For in the long run, it's not what happens that counts but how a man faces up to it. From that standpoint, you've done fine. You don't whimper, and you don't quit. You run away sometimes, but it's always from the fear of doing wrong—like your spending all the time you can away from where Juana is. . . ."

"You noticed that?" Bruce said. "You're mighty shrewd, Reverend."

"Nope. Just know folks. I think, Bruce, that God tests every man living to see if he's worthy of some task for the good of humanity, and his own soul. 'Why do the wicked prosper?' Because God ain't interested in them. And they don't prosper really, unless you're fool enough to confuse material wealth with either happiness or peace of soul. And wealth is not that; most often it's a burden, and a curse. When you look at it close, son, there ain't a thing, a natural living thing that's really worth anything that money can buy. Can buy a whole lot of hurtful things like soft living, hard liquor, and easy women. But it can't buy health, it can't buy happiness, and it can't buy peace. And without those things, what do you have?"

"God tests mighty hard, sometimes," Bruce said. "He's let an awful lot of his people die—and in right smart ugly ways, too."

"So that by their dying, they served Him and man," the Preacher said serenely, "giving grace and courage and hope to those who came after. If there are any things worth dying for, those are the things. . . ."

"Grace and courage and hope," Bruce said, and stood up. "You give them to me, a little, just talking, Reverend. Thank you for that. Reckon I'll be going, now . . ."

"That's my work, son. And it's good to work with things that really matter. I get a sight of comfort out of that. Good night, son. . . ."

Riding home, that moonlit November night, he was surprised at the feeling of peace he had. Nothing had changed; nothing had been solved; but he felt better about things. The Preacher had done that. He felt better able to face up to things—to face up, even to writing his long delayed letter to Jo.

Jo, now, Jo—I wonder what she's doing now? Thinking? Funny she hasn't written me even one more time . . .

Jo sat by the window of her hotel room, looking out into the street. It was raining, a slow, sullen drizzle. It had been raining ever since she had got to the town of Aspinwall in Panama, three days ago. Aspinwall was what the American steamship owners and business promoters called it—after, she had heard, a New York banker; the natives stubbornly clung to its ancient name of Colón.

Jo doubted that either Mr. Aspinwall or Christopher Columbus would have considered themselves honored by having the town named after them. The street outside her window was a river of mud, winding between thatched huts and adobe houses. People went by, looking like walking haystacks, because they wore ponchos of dried cornshucks, one end of each shuck being sewn into a burlap bag lining, and the other being allowed to hang loose. In wet weather, José Mendez, the fat little man who was to guide the travelers across the Isthmus, told her, they always wore that kind. In fact, he was busily engaged in buying up cornshuck ponchos for the travelers. They were, he swore, light, comfortable, and absolutely waterproof.

Jo didn't like José Mendez. For all his smiling politeness there was something—reptilian about him. She didn't like the way he looked at her as if—as if, she thought suddenly, bitterly, he has taken my measure, and is mighty sure what kind of a woman I am. . . . But what kind of a woman am I? Not the kind he thinks, leastways. The way he talks to me, so polite that it's nigh onto being insulting; and every time he sees me with Mister Wilkins he just grins that oily grin of his, as though he was sure something underhand is going on. . . .

Which there isn't, she added, and stopped suddenly, brought up hard against the fact that the thought had in it both the coloring and the texture—of regret. He was very nice, this Mr. Wilkins. He was the only thing that had made the terrible voyage down the Atlantic coast to the town of Aspinwall bearable. During all those days when she was wracked with seasickness, he had come into her cabin, brought her iced drinks that she couldn't keep down, bathed her forehead, and talked to her, comfortingly.

She smiled, suddenly, mischievously. If Uncle Ronnie knew she had had a man in her cabin! It had been his fear for her reputation that had made him buy her a first class ticket with a private cabin all the way to California. He had even delayed her for weeks, searching for an elderly woman to accompany her. The dear old fogy! This was 1850, modern times. The old rules for feminine behavior were beginning to change. It had been very nice to have Lucas in her cabin. She had had nothing to fear from him. He had been very gentle and considerate, even leaving the door hooked open so that no one could get the wrong idea. Never by word or deed had he—

She felt, suddenly, a perverse feminine disappointment that he hadn't attempted—anything. Of course she would have been icily indignant; and reduced him to a properly apologetic state. Then she would have forgiven him, displaying a noble compassion and a pitying womanly comprehension of the terrible desires that drove men. But he hadn't given her the chance. She thought wryly that a woman green with seasickness and wrenched with nausea is hardly an attractive object.

She narrowed her pale blue eyes.

Why am I thinking like this? she thought. I love Bruce. I'm going to him. I shall be his wife, after I divorce Ted. I love him so much that I—

That she had danced away the whole summer on the arm of one or another gay young blade without having written him a line. Properly chaperoned, of course. Taken to the balls by her Aunt and Uncle. Still, she had danced, rejoicing in her beauty, in her effect upon men after having been for so long a prisoner in her husband's house. Fending off their clumsy attempts to kiss her. Laughing, cool and remote, sure of her mastery over them, over herself.

There wasn't anything to write. I told him I was coming, and he hasn't mentioned it since! His letters sound as though he were avoiding the subject. Still, I could have written. There is always something to say to the man one loves. . . .

She did not know exactly what it was that jerked her out of her revery, but then, looking out of the window, she saw that the rain had stopped. What had caught her attention was the sudden, oppressive silence after days of roof drumming, window whispering. There was a wind now, sweeping down from the Culebra Mountains, driving the clouds seaward. In a matter of minutes, the sun broke through. It hung high above the jungle and blazed. Wherever it touched, steam rose.

The heat, all at once, with no period of transition, being born out of nowhere the instant the sun appeared, was like a blanket dropped over her head. I'll have to go out, she decided; I can't stand this. . . .

She picked up her bonnet and her parasol. Like her dress, they were both white, and had ruffles about the edges. She looked at herself in the cracked, faded mirror over the washstand. Her face was pale and tired, but other than that, she looked nice, she thought.

She went down the tiled stairs and came out on the street. And, immediately, as she had hoped, and more than half expected, she saw Lucas Wilkins coming toward her.

His eyes lighted at the sight of her.

"Jo!" he laughed. "Good news! We start tomorrow. José says—"

"I," Jo said flatly, "wouldn't give a copper continental for anything that greasy little monster says. . . ."

"Nor I, ordinarily," Lucas smiled, "but it is a fact that the rains have stopped. From what I've heard, the jungle is all but impassable when it's raining. And the Chagres River is pretty wild. That's all José was waiting for: the rains to stop. . . ."

"And to get as big a cut possible from these pirates of hotel keepers," Jo said.

"I say, you are in a mood, aren't you? Is there anything I can do to cheer you up?"

Jo laid a hand upon his arm.

"You've already done that, by coming," she said gently. "Reckon I was just plain lonesome, Lucas. Come on, let's walk. . . ."

He took her arm firmly, and guided her among the vast puddles that steamed skyward under the blazing sun.

"In an hour," he said, "they'll all be gone, and the mud will be as hard as stone. Funny country, this. I'd hate like the dickens to have to live here. . . ."

He felt her stiffen, and turning, followed the direction of her gaze.

A buzzard stood in the middle of the street, in a mud puddle, eating a drowned cat. His black feathers glistened and there were drops of water on his bald, scaly head. He tore at the small furry creature with obscene gravity, leaving tendrils of red threading the yellow-green water.

"Oh no!" Jo whispered. "Oh, Lucas, no!"

"Ugly beasts, aren't they?" Lucas said. "Stay here and I'll chase him away. . . ."

He advanced toward the vulture, lifting his cane. The bird raised his head and looked at him with yellow, lidless eyes. Lucas struck at him, swinging out and downward. The buzzard took two short, bandy legged steps backward, and sat there on the puddle's edge. There was no fear in the yellow eyes; nothing at all in them, but a kind of patience that was as old as death itself.

Lucas struck at the great bird in a fury of anger and of fear. Not fear of the physical entity, but of something else: of that patience, of that surety. The buzzard evaded the blow with clumsy ease.

Lucas turned back to Jo.

"I can't," he got out, his voice taut, strangling. "He just won't, Jo. . . . We—we'll have to walk around him, that's all. . . ."

He took her arm, and the two of them edged past the buzzard. Close, the death stench caught them full in the nostrils, so that Lucas retched audibly, and Jo clung to him, half fainting. They eased by, and the buzzard watched them for a long moment, speculatively. Then he waddled back into the pool, and went on eating the cat.

"I hate them!" Jo burst out. "They're so ugly—and so sure. . . ."

"Sure?" Lucas said, but he had already divined her thought.

"That we'll all come to that," Jo said, "no matter how young we are—how pretty—or how fine and strong. That in the end we'll be like that cat, mere food for their hungry gullets. They outlast us, Lucas. They always win. Like death always wins over life—doesn't it?"

"Good Lord!" Lucas said. "This place is making you morbid. I'm certainly glad we're leaving. . . ."

"Take me back to the Hotel," she said quietly.

"Look, Jo," he began; "I'm awfully sorry. I'm aware that I didn't measure up to your expectations in this case, but—"

"I," Jo said flatly, "hadn't any expectations as far as you're concerned, Lucas. Take me home. And don't talk any more. Don't talk, please!"

She saw, as she turned, that the buzzard had finished his repast. He rose now, heavily, on ominous wings, shaking drops of water downward from his flight. Behind her, the crowd had begun to drift away. In two minutes, the street was empty.

As empty, she thought with sudden bitterness, as my heart. . . .

First in the morning, they moved out of the town in the rattle-trap train that ran the magnificent total of seven miles, and took all of two hours to do that. Then they stopped at the end of the line, and their baggage was transferred to the edge of the Chagres River. Negro boatmen, naked except for loin clothes, and, in a few cases, ragged trousers, loaded it aboard the boats. The boatmen had the most magnificent bodies Jo had ever seen. Their muscles coiled like pythons beneath the ebony of their skins. They were like—Jo's mind sought the comparison—something out of Egyptian mythology: the faces of jungle apes, joined to the bodies of young gods.

Lucas helped her aboard, and the boatmen pushed off, grunting. They planted long bamboo poles in the river bottom, and walked aft along the gunwales, pushing on the poles. The boats crept along through the brimming river, under the trees. Crocodiles peered at them from the banks. She could see them swimming in the river. They looked like rusty logs.

She saw, to her horror, that absolutely no provisions had been made for privacy. As the hours wore on, one of the older men, a Mister Miller, began to look at her with growing embarrassment. Finally he could not stand it any longer, and walked aft, casting an imploring glance at her as he passed. She stared straight ahead, her face hot. When Mr. Miller came sheepishly back to his seat, Jo leaned over and touched Lucas' arm.

"Lucas," she whispered. "What on earth am I going to do?"

"Don't worry," he said, amusement sounding in his tone, "I'll arrange with José to have this boat land for a few minutes."

He did so, and the jungle brush made a screen as private as her own boudoir. But she was terribly frightened. The ground was alive with crawling things.

By midday, the heat was all but insupportable. José had canvas covers fitted over the bamboo rigging put there for that purpose, making a canopy. The canopy helped; but not very much.

The boatmen were covered with sweat. The leader lifted his hand, and the boat stopped, drifting a little with the current. The boatmen calmly took off their trousers and loin clothes. Jo gave a gasp, and buried her face against Lucas' coat.

"I say there, José!" he protested. "This is a bit thick! Can't you do something about those beggars?"

"No, Señor," José said honestly. "If they do not cool off in the river once in a while, they will die of sunstroke. And, unfortunately, our liner of great luxury seems to be somewhat wanting in private dressing rooms. The only solution for the Señorita is to do what she is doing—to hide her face. . . ."

Jo counted the splashes. When they were all over the side, she looked up again. The Negroes were swimming in the river paying no attention whatsoever to the crocodiles.

"They rarely attack," José explained. "Of course, if some one were to hurt himself and they smelled blood. . . ."

Jo shuddered, thinking of it.

They came at nightfall to their first stop, a clearing in the jungle which had not even existed before the discovery of gold in California, but which now boasted no less than seven hotels, all of them oversized thatched bamboo huts, bearing such grandiose names as the Silver Dollar, El Yanqui, and Grand Hotel. They were, as far as Jo could see, totally lacking in the first rudiments of either sanitation or comfort, but their prices ranged from five to ten dollars a night.

José came up to them, his fat little face twisted into a caricature of a smile.

"I have found habitations for you at the Grand," he said smoothly, "which is the best of the hotels here. That is, of course, to say that it is merely the least bad. I regret, Señores, that our accommodations for the trip are so poor. But then, the need for accommodations at all sprang up rather suddenly. . . ."

He led them to a two story bamboo and palm thatched structure set further back into the jungle than the others. It had, Jo thought, a certain picturesque attractiveness to it.

"It is kind of romantic," she said to Lucas. Then, seeing his eyes, she added quickly, cruelly: "Too bad my Bruce isn't here. . . ."

Lucas didn't answer her. They followed the innkeeper, who looked enough like José to have been his twin, up the stairs. José came along to serve as interpreter. The innkeeper's English left a good bit to be desired.

He threw open the door to a large room, and stood aside, beaming. Jo came into the room, and looked around, seeing that it really wasn't bad, better in fact, than the room she had had in Colón. But then, something in the innkeeper's attitude caught her attention. He was quite literally beaming, bursting with pride—over what? Jo followed the direction of his gaze, and her eyes, too, came to rest on the enormous brass bed, polished until it shone like gold. She was aware that José was convulsed with silent laughter, and had been for quite some time. Under her sternly questioning gaze, he choked back his laughter, and said something very fast in Spanish to the innkeeper.

"What did you say?" Jo demanded.

"I said that you were not marrieds but only engageds," José grinned. "Juan is disappointed. This is his bridal suite and he is very proud of his gran bed of matrimonios. . . ."

"I will take it," Jo said flatly, "if Juan will be so kind as to give Mr. Wilkins a room somewhere else. . . ."

Juan said something else, also very fast, and the two fat villains laughed again. Jo didn't like the sound of their laughter.

"He says," José explained with bland innocence, "that he will give to the Señor Wilkins the room next door which communicates with this one. It is possible that during the night the young Señores Engageds might wish to speak with one another. When one is young and in love, there is much to say. Juan is a good host who wishes to place every convenience at the disposal of his distinguished clients. . . ."

Jo's blue eyes darkened with fury, but Lucas laid a restraining hand on her arm.

"Play along with them," he whispered. "Can't you see they're only doing this to plague us?"

Slowly Jo smiled.

"Very well," she said. "I'm sure Mr. Wilkins will be happy to bring me a glass of water in the night, should I require one."

José and Juan nudged each other, grinning.

Jo turned to Lucas and said in a flat monotone, almost without moving her lips: "That connecting door will be locked; you understand that, don't you, Lucas? I hope I shan't be forced to pile the furniture up against it as well. . . ."

Lucas looked at her, his eyes filled with mockery.

"Why, Jo," he drawled, "don't you trust anybody?"

"No," she said; "leastways not as long as they're men."

"Very well," he mocked, "but if you do get thirsty, don't forget to call me. . . ." Then he was gone through the connecting door before she had had time to think of a suitable reply.

Jo stood there in the middle of the room, looking around her. Then she walked over to the connecting door. As she more than half expected, it hadn't any lock on it. It was a mere screen of bamboo, hinged so that it swung both ways. She stood there, staring at it. Then she shrugged, and came back to the big bed.

She wasn't afraid of Lucas Wilkins that way. What she had been afraid of was herself, of her own sudden response to him. And now she didn't have to be afraid of even that any more. Not since yesterday, not since he had proven himself to be something less than a man. As she slipped into her thin nightdress, she tried to analyze her feeling about the whole thing. It was, curiously enough, strangely akin to disappointment.

She blew out the candle, seeing just before she did so that the box of sulphur matches was close at hand if she needed it. She was unutterably weary. She was sure that by drawing the covers over her head, she would be able to sleep in spite of the mosquitos. She was right; she sank instantly into slumber.

Sometime during the night, Lucas Wilkins came awake to the sound of a woman screaming. He was on his feet at once, groping for the matches. He couldn't find them, so he went through the door into Jo's room. Somehow she had managed to light the candle, and she was standing there in the middle of the room holding the candle and screaming. Afterwards, Lucas was to remember her slim form in that thin nightdress with considerable relish. But now, there was no time. He came up to her, and then he saw it, dark against the sheets in her bed, like a thick rope, coiled and ready.

"Don't move," he whispered. "I'll be right back. . . ."

It took him aching, clumsy ages to get his own candle lit and find his double-barrelled derringer. When he got back, Jo had stopped screaming. She hung there, staring at the culebra with horrified fascination.

"Hold the candle higher, Jo," he grated. He took aim, but his hand shook so that he had to steady it with the other. The first shot missed, cleanly; but the second smashed the snake's head. It thrashed about, wildly, dying the sheets red with its blood.

Jo fell against him then, clinging to him and crying. Her flesh was like ice. At another time, under other circumstances, Lucas Wilkins would have been entirely capable of enjoying the multiple sensations of having a lovely woman in an all but transparent nightdress clinging to him. But now the reaction had him hard in its grip. He had the sickening feeling that he was going to retch, or faint, or do something equally unmanly. He wasn't a very brave man, and he knew it.

"I—I'll take you into my room," he croaked, and it was then that they heard the footsteps on the stairs.

José and Juan burst into the room carrying lamps and revolvers.

José saw the dead serpent and grinned.

"My felicitations, Señor!" he said. "Most excellent shooting. They often do that. It is the—eh—warmth they are seeking. In this, they are not unlike men, no?"

His eyes, probing through the thin nightdress, were hot with ill-concealed lust.

"Juan will change your bed, Señorita," he said. "It is most unlikely that you will be disturbed again. . . ."

"No," Jo whispered; "just get that thing out of here. I'll never sleep in that bed again!"

"As the Señorita wishes," José said.

"Come, Jo," Lucas said; "you can take mine. . . ."

"But," she protested; "where will you sleep, Lucas?"

"In the chair," he said, "though to tell the truth about it, Jo, I scarcely expect I could sleep even on a feather mattress now. . . ."

"Me, either," Jo said. Then she glanced down at herself. "Oh, my God!" she whispered. "Lucas, you must let me get my robe. . . ."

"Of course," he said smoothly; "though I must confess you're extraordinarily fetching in this garb. . . ."

"I don't doubt it," Jo said dryly, "which is exactly why I'm going to put on a robe. . . ."

But she was not troubled the rest of that night either by snakes or Lucas or anything else. She was saved from any further disturbance by Lucas' recognition that this was neither the time nor the place, and that most of all the mood was wrong. Lucas Wilkins had always been remarkably successful with women, and not the least of the reasons for his success was a certain softness in his own makeup, a kind of quasi-feminine sensitivity to the nuances of a situation. He preferred to wait until he could stage the conditions to suit his convenience: clouds of roses, champagne frosting in the ice, music being played softly from a discreet distance. At such details, he was very good indeed.

And, in the morning, as he helped her aboard the boat, he was glad of his forbearance. One glance at the soft warmth of her smile showed him exactly how much distance he had regained since that business of the buzzard.

I'll have to play my cards right, now, he thought. Can't make any more mistakes like that one. . . .

But he had not considered that factor that intelligent men, far more than stupid ones, ordinarily disregard: luck, chance, accident, and it came very near to ruining his chances forever. The trouble came about through Mr. Miller—a man far too old to be making the crippling journey across the Isthmus. They had left the last of the navigable stretches of the Chagres River, and were traveling through the jungle valleys and over the tortuous trails of the Culebra Mountains on muleback. The first day showed them how bad it was going to be.

Lucas had put out his cane to push aside a heavy vine, when one of the Negro mule skinners yelled at him. Lucas drew back, glaring at the black man, but the Negro ignored the look, and came dashing past him, machete swinging. He slashed the vine in half with one clean blow and it writhed, spurting blood.

"Anaconda," José explained. "Not so very big, Señor; but big enough. These snakes squeeze one to death. . . ."

Jo and Lucas looked at one another. It was a toss-up which of their faces was whiter.

And, after that, it started to rain.

José kept them plodding doggedly onward. There really wasn't very much jungle left, and he wanted them out of it, and into the mountains before the rains became too heavy. In the jungle, rain could mean death in any number of unpleasant varieties: no fires to keep the snakes and wild beasts at bay; sicknesses of a dozen exceedingly ugly kinds; and the swarms of crawling insects attracted to the warmth of their bodies if they halted even for a moment.

But, by the time they had mounted upward into the cool mists of the Culebras, old Mr. Miller was reeling in the saddle from fatigue. No one paid him any attention except Jo. She kept looking at the old man, wondering if she dared ask José to halt the mule train so that he could rest.

Only, there wasn't any place to stop. The trail wound upward, so narrow that they had to ride single file. In the gorges below them, they could hear the angry roar of the river. Jo had the feeling that the old man was riding too close to the edge. A moment later, she was sure of it.

Mr. Miller reeled sidewise, hung grotesquely from the saddle at an oblique angle, then ever so slowly, while Jo, her voice frozen

deep in her throat, kicked her mule forward towards him, he slid
gently and peacefully down and out of the saddle, taking a thousand aching years to do it, until he went crashing over the edge,
rolling down the steep slope, bouncing like a doll of rags, not even
crying out.

Jo found her voice.

"Lucas!" she commanded sternly.

Lucas came up beside her, and sat there looking down. He was
a city dweller, a man who all his life had been accustomed to
ease and comfort. Even to look down that gorge made him giddy
and sick.

"Go after him," Jo said.

"Jo!" he whispered. "Lord, Jo—I couldn't! For the love of God,
Jo, darling, you don't expect me to—"

Jo sat there, looking at him. Her eyes were blue ice, filled with
contempt. Then the sight of the naked, pitiful self-reproach in
his face moved her. Whatever else she was, Jo Peterson was not
really unkind. She put out her hand and touched his face, and
once again her eyes were soft and warm.

"It's all right, Lucas," she said gently. "A body can't be brave all
the time. And you were brave—for me. Reckon that's the nicest
compliment I've ever had. You aren't naturally, are you? But I
mattered enough for you to be. . . ."

"Yes," Lucas got out. "God, yes! If that were you down there,
I wouldn't have to think about going. I'd be down there now. . . ."

And seeing his eyes, Jo knew he spoke the truth.

An hour later, the Negroes brought the broken body of Mr.
Miller up onto the trail. He very probably had been dead before
he left the saddle. His heart had not been able to stand the strain.

It was soon over, after that. They came down into the sunbaked
city of Panama, fought their way through the hordes of would-be
porters and beggars who besieged them; bought back from the
very thieves who had stolen it the baggage that had gotten "lost"
in Panama City; found a hotel somewhat better than the ones on
the Atlantic coast. Because of the strange twists of the Isthmus
of Panama they were considerably further east in Panama City
than they had been in Colón from whence they had started. But
they didn't know that, then. There were a great many things they
still didn't know.

Two days later, stalwart Negroes lifted them into their arms and waded out through the surf to where the boats of the S.S. *California* waited. The last leg of the voyage was at hand now; all the worst was behind them.

Jo leaned over the rail of the steamship *California* and watched the coast of Panama slipping by. At her side, Lucas Wilkins smiled down at her, his eyes confident, sure. She seldom mentioned Bruce Harkness any more, and that was a good sign. He was beginning to make progress. Thank God for those bloody snakes! he thought.

It was very warm. Jo felt the perspiration gathering on her skin, under the light cotton clothes she wore. It made her conscious of her body. The beautiful body she had cared for so tenderly, bathing it, perfuming it, attending to its needs.

Its needs. Did a woman have—those kinds of needs? The kind that men had—that turned them so slack-mouthed and horrible, their eyes glaring, their breath panting out? She was a married woman, but she didn't know. Good women, everybody seemed to think, didn't have any feeling about—that. They submitted to their husbands' incomprehensible desires because it was their wifely duty, and that was how you got children. But they didn't like it. Still, there had been times, even with Ted—when I was very close to liking it, she admitted to herself with a sudden, fierce spasm of honesty. And that time when I kissed Bruce on the quay, things happened to me. Inside I wanted him. I wanted him like that. I always have. And with him, I will like it; I will! If that makes me a bad woman, then I'll be bad!

Funny. Ted always stopped in time—before it got to the point that, that—Oh, God, I don't know! What does happen? What can?

She turned and looked at Lucas, her blue eyes filled with speculation. She didn't know how she looked at him, but Lucas did. Joy bubbled and sang along his veins. Now! he exulted; now—tonight!

"I've arranged for us to dine together," he said smoothly, "at the same table, across from one another. Of course there will be other passengers; but we won't mind that. We'll just ignore them, won't we, Jo?"

"Yes, dear," Jo said absently. She was unaware she used the

word, saying it, in fact, out of the long habit of marriage. But the blood rushed to Lucas' ears, and beat in a delirious tide.

She dressed very carefully for dinner. When she came into the dining saloon, she saw men's eyes sparkle and women frown. She didn't know which pleased her most: the sparkles or the frowns.

Lucas stood up, his dark eyes glowing. He was magnificently clad in dinner clothes. His studs were diamonds. He was, Jo was sure, quite the finest gentleman she had ever seen.

He bent over her hand, kissed it. This gesture, usually so false in an American, was in him easy, perfect, sure.

"My dear," he said. "You are ravishing!"

"Thank you, my Lord," she laughed. "And you are my very *parfait gentil* knight!"

"What more could a man ask for?" he sighed. "I've ordered champagne. You like it, of course?"

"Of course," Jo said. How could she admit to such a man that she had never tasted champagne in her life? Not even wine. Her parents had been very strict.

The champagne was good. It was pink and had bubbles in it that tickled her nose. She found that she laughed, gaily, easily. The dinner was wonderful. But she didn't eat very much. She listened in a marvelous glowing haze to the compliments that Lucas showered upon her. There was an inexhaustible supply of champagne. She felt that if she released her hold on the chair, she would float up to the ceiling. What a wonderful, wonderful feeling to be able to float!

After the coffee, there was brandy. She didn't like the brandy very much and said so.

"I prefer champagne," she said.

"I'll see that you're well supplied," Lucas said, smiling. He leaned close. "There'll be a moon tonight," he said. "Come up on deck with me? I want to show you the moon. . . ."

"But I've seen the moon," Jo said.

"You've never had *me* show it to you," Lucas said.

"That's true," Jo said gravely.

"Then you will? Oh, please, Jo—say you will!"

"Why, of course, silly," Jo laughed. "Of course I will. . . ."

After dinner, she went down to her cabin, took off her dress, so as not to wrinkle it, and lay down in her petticoats. Champagne was wonderful, but it was awfully strong. The cabin revolved in a slow and stately dance before her eyes. She closed them, tight. In a matter of minutes, she was asleep.

The knocking on the door awakened her. She leaped up, seized her robe. She was still dizzy. And she didn't feel good any more. She opened the door a crack. It was the cabin boy.

He held, on a tray, a huge silver bucket frosted over with cold. In it a bottle stood, with a napkin wrapped about its neck. There was one glass, with a piece of ice in it to keep it cold.

"Compliments of Mr. Wilkins, Ma'am," the cabin boy said. "Shall I open it now, Ma'am?"

"Why—ah—yes!" Jo said. She couldn't feel any worse, she decided.

The boy shot the cork ceilingward. He fanned the neck of the bottle with a napkin. He swirled the ice around in the glass, until it, too, was frosted. The champagne was so cold that it didn't even foam when he poured it.

It was very warm in the cabin. Jo discovered that she was, after all, very thirsty. She took the glass and drank it down, all at once. Almost immediately, she felt better. She danced around the cabin, humming to herself. She poured herself another glass. . . .

She could see her face in the mirror. Her cheeks glowed. She was usually very pale, but now she had color. Champagne was wonderful. She resolved to drink it every day of her life.

Outside, it was already dark. She'd have to dress again soon. Lucas Wilkins. Such a nice man, and a gentleman. He'd respected her privacy ever since she'd gotten over the seasickness. She wondered, suddenly, what effect it would have on him, if he could see her waltzing around like this in her petticoats. She hoped it would have an effect on him. That was one way she liked to make men suffer.

She put her dress back on. She felt wonderfully cool. She wasn't wearing any stays. It was too hot for stays, and truly with her slim body, she had never needed them. Nor anything to support her there—in front. She arched her body, feeling with a curious warmth, her thrusting, pointed roundness.

I am beautiful, she told herself. No wonder men—want me. I am, I am!

She laughed gaily, downed the rest of the champagne in the glass, and started for the door. Then she remembered something: the locket she always wore about her neck. Her amulet, her talisman. Gravely she crossed to the bureau, and put it on. It had a picture of Bruce in it—a daguerreotype he had given her that magic summer long ago, in exchange for hers. But she didn't think about that. She gave her silvery blonde curls a final pat, and went out of the cabin.

The moon was magnificent. It hung low over the sea, filling half the sky. The waters blazed with it. The *California* ploughed through the moontrack and all the night silvered.

She was having a hard time keeping Lucas' face in focus. Her eyes didn't behave properly any more. He was close to her. Much too close. She blinked at him, her eyes star sapphires in the moonlight.

Then his mouth was on hers, burning. She brought her hands to push him away. But Lucas Wilkins was a man of experience. His mouth moved on hers, slowly, caressingly, expertly. Her mouth parted under his, seeking air; then he was kissing her in a way she had never been kissed before, in a way that, but for the moon and the champagne, would have horrified her. Her palms, against his shirt front, slid upward. Her hands locked about his neck. She was kissing him back—in the same way.

She was aware, with a part of her mind, that she was doing these things, but she didn't recognize the "she" who did them. That was somebody else, a woman she didn't know, had never met. He went on kissing her, endlessly.

There was a flame at the core of her. She felt that inside herself, she was melting, running liquid and molten, losing form and substance, dissolving.

He released her. Stepped back.

"Come," he said, taking her arm. They went down the stairs, came to a door. He pushed it open. Only one oil lamp held back the dark. On the table, still another bucket stood. Two glasses this time. She watched him from a thousand miles away as he poured.

"To—us," he said.

"To—us," she echoed.

He stood up after a time, and took her glass from her hand. He drew her upright. He was kissing her again, that special way.

He stopped, lifting something in his hand.

"I'm afraid I can't get this off," he said ruefully.

She opened her eyes. The locket lay heavy and dull golden in the palm of his hand. She took it from him, to shift it so that the catch of the chain would pull around to the front of her throat where he could reach it; but her fingers touched the hidden spring. The locket flew open, and Bruce Harkness stared up at her with grave, accusing eyes.

She stared at the picture. Then she let it fall. Her hands came up, pushing wildly. She doubled her knees, bringing one of them up into the pit of his stomach. He rolled away from her in pain and astonishment, and she was up, running across the cabin, leaving the slippers she had kicked off, hurling herself through the door, down the passageway, toward the stairs.

Two women came towards her. She saw, in their horrified eyes, that she was all but naked, her dress unbuttoned down half the front; only the thin, almost transparent chemise covering her breasts. But she didn't care. I'll never see them again, she thought viciously. The old bitches!

Then she had her own door open, and was inside the refuge of her own cabin. She slammed the door, locked it. She stood in the middle of the stateroom, trembling. In the mirror, she saw her reflection. Her face was awful, her lips puffy and swollen, her eyes wild.

I look, she thought, like one of those awful creatures that men—pay. . . .

She crossed to the bunk and lay down upon it, crushing her lovely dress beyond any hope of wearing it again on this voyage. The tears stung her eyelids, ran scaldingly down her face.

"Oh, Bruce!" she wept. "Bruce, Bruce, Bruce! I'm not good enough for you, now! I'm not. I'm not. I'm not!"

She sat up, staring out of the dark porthole. Words shaped themselves in her mind, formed with the crushing weight of conviction.

I'm a bad woman, she thought. I was going to. With him—a
stranger. A man I met on a voyage. With a face, a name, an unknown person who'd been kind to me. . . .

She shook her head, but she couldn't stop her thoughts. They
bore down upon her, heavier than death.

With him. With anybody. I'm that kind of a woman. Oh God,
Oh God, I—

Then she buried her face in her hands, and surrendered to her
tears.

He sent her slippers back to her, carefully wrapped, accompanied by a note in which he humbly begged her forgiveness,
promising never again by word or deed to repeat his offense if
only she would grant him the continued pleasure of her company.

She sat there, in the flood of morning sun coming through the
porthole, hearing the creak and thunder of the walking beam, the
heavy splash of the side wheels. She held the letter in her hand,
and her thoughts were bitterly honest:

Poor thing. Apologizing for what was as much my fault as his.
For trying to do what I wanted him to. Oh God, how I wanted
him to! Begging my pardon because a cheap woman of easy virtue
was shamed into changing her mind. . . .

She got up, bathed, and dressed herself with some care. Then
she went up on deck, and searched until she found him.

His eyes lighted with mingled joy and fear at the sight of her.
She went straight to him.

"Jo," he said. "God, Jo, I was a beast! Can you forgive me? I
was such a fool. . . ."

"No," she said flatly. "You weren't a fool, Lucas. Whatever you
were, you weren't—that. You guessed right. And your tactics were
—effective. You took one look at me and decided: that one there—
that little blonde filly. Easy mark. One good hard shove and
she'll—"

"Jo!" His voice was stricken.

"But you were so right, Lucas. Only I didn't know it. I thought
I was a decent woman. I didn't know I had the makings of a—a
tart in me. Thank you, Lucas—dear, dear Lucas, for opening my
eyes."

"Jo, dearest," he groaned, "I didn't mean . . . I swear I never—"

"All right," she said brusquely. "You didn't know. Neither did I. Now we both do. So we'll have to arrange things on that basis. I'm in love with Bruce Harkness. I mean to marry him. And I want to come to him—as—as clean as I can, Lucas. I'm asking you to help me. It's quite simple, really—"

"How?" he whispered. "How can I help you, Jo?"

"Don't kiss me. Don't offer me champagne. Be gentle with me— if you can. Can you, Lucas? Even knowing that if you don't, I'll do what you want me to—what I want to—in five minutes flat, with no resistance? Maybe even without champagne. . . ."

He stared at her.

"Only, it wouldn't be—nice. I don't mean nice in the moral sense. What I mean, I think, is that it would be ugly. Two animals, without sentiment or tenderness or love, seeking together to satisfy a bestial appetite—"

"Jo, for God's Love!"

"If my indelicate language shocks you, I'm sorry. You made me indelicate, Lucas. You would have taken me without love. And love is the only thing that justifies—that. That transforms it, exalts it, makes it fine. . . ."

"But I do love you, Jo!" he said. "I swear it!"

"You think you do now. This morning, if Bruce's picture hadn't stopped me, you'd have looked at the thing, the female thing I would have become, and felt like vomiting. So would I. You'd have ended by hating me."

"No, no," he said. "I love you, Jo—nothing can change that. . . ."

She looked at him, her eyes bleak.

"Well, I don't love you," she said. "Have I your promise you'll behave?"

"Yes," he choked. "God, Jo, I never heard a woman talk like you before. . . ."

"You've never met an honest woman—up 'til now," she said. She smiled wickedly, remembering. "Come walk me about the deck, Lucas. There were some nosy old women who saw me running down the corridor barefoot and all disheveled. They're dying to know where I came from. I want to give them something else to talk about—Come on!"

For the rest of the voyage, he was the soul of attentiveness. His behavior was painfully correct. He seemed frightened of her. Her brutal candor, even in an age that had produced women like Angelina Bloomer, Tennessee Claflin, and Virginia Woodhull, shocked him. He had the feeling that if she ever changed her mind and said: "I'll come to your cabin tonight," he wouldn't be able to accomplish it, so chillingly had she affected his nerve.

He helped her ashore at San Francisco, found her lodgings for the night, took her to dinner, met her for breakfast, got her safely aboard the steamer for Sacramento. He stood on the wharf, holding her hand across the rail. She leaned forward suddenly, out of pure malice, and kissed him goodbye. He stiffened, fell back.

When the little sternwheeler butted its way around the first bend, out of sight, he loosed a vast sigh of relief. He felt as if he had been saved, by a miracle, from nameless terrors.

The minute Jo stepped ashore in Sacramento, she was surrounded. There were, by November 1850, a few women in Sacramento; but every new one who arrived could be sure of getting married within hours if she could make up her mind that fast among her hundreds of new suitors. Even the girls in King's Annex and the other brothels were not immune.

"Some of our best families in years to come," Hailey often said, "are going to have to keep padlocks on their closets to keep the skeletons still!"

The men crowded around Jo, hat in hand, staring with awed reverence.

"Lord God, she's pretty!"

"Ain't seen no blue eyes like that in so damn long. . . ."

"Howdy, Ma'am. Could a lonesome polecat like me escort you to your hotel, maybe?"

"Naw, let me! Where's your belongings, Ma'am?"

Jo looked from one to the other of them. She wasn't afraid. For all their villainous expanse of whiskers, they were like little boys, apple in hand, trying to get a smile from the teacher.

"I'm sorry, gentlemen," she said, "but I'm not sure I'm going to a hotel. My husband is here. Do any of you know Ted Peterson?"

She saw, the instant before they veiled their eyes, that many of them did. And that they were afraid to admit it. Something was wrong—terribly wrong. She searched their faces.

"Well, do you?" she said.

The silence rode in upon her. In the interval, she heard hoof-beats, as a rider crossed the street, blocks away from her. The horseman was leading a pack mule. She thought for a moment that there was something familiar about him; but she dismissed the thought as clearly impossible. He pulled up his horse, staring at the crowd down at the wharf. He was too far away for her to make out what he really looked like.

"Well," she said again, "aren't you going to answer me?"

"I do," a crisp voice cut through the silence, its accents clear, cultivated, faintly mocking, "I shall be glad to take you to him, Madam. . . ."

The crowd opened, let him through. Looking at him, Jo felt a queer tingle of excitement. He was almost too handsome to be a man. Better looking by far than Lucas Wilkins. Better looking than anybody. His clothes were very fine, sober and tasteful. Every inch of those imported fabrics had cost him a fortune, she knew. In all that mud, he had managed to keep his boots spotless.

"Permit me to introduce myself, Mrs. Peterson," he said. "I'm Rufus King. Your husband lives an hour's ride north of here. I'd suggest that you leave your valises at my place, and I'll take you up in my buckboard."

"Thank you, Mr. King," Jo said. "You're very kind. But I don't understand about my valises. Why can't I just take them with me?"

"Your husband," again that note of mockery—or did she imagine it?—was in his voice, "is not prepared for your arrival. His cabin is hardly the place for a lady. Surely he will want to come back into town and join you at the hotel. . . ."

"You mean it's too small?" Jo said.

"I mean it's too—crude. Will some of you boys be kind enough to bring the lady's things to my place?"

"Yessir," some of the miners growled; but there was an ugly look in their eyes, gazing at him.

At the end of the street, Bruce Harkness sat for a long moment

on his horse, gazing at the crowd. Then he kicked in against the
animal's sides and rode on.

Wonder what all the commotion was about? he thought. They
had somebody plumb surrounded down there. Looked like a
woman. But King seemed to have taken over. I know that polecat
from any distance up to a mile. No whiskers, and those clothes,
I reckon. Must be getting himself a new filly for the Annex. Oh
well, it's none of my business. Got to be hitting the trail. Long
way to those diggings. . . .

Ted Peterson stood on the steps of the cabin, gazing at Jo. He
made no move to help her down from the buckboard.

"So," he said. "Your pimp sent you the money to come after all,
eh? Said he would. What're you doing here? You ought to be off
somewheres bathing and powdering yourself so's you'll smell real
nice when he—"

"Ted!" Jo got out: "What on earth are you talking about?"

"As if you didn't know," Ted laughed. "One thing I can't figger
is why he ain't with you. Got cold feet, I reckon. Or did he already
sell her to you for the Annex, King? She's right pert good, I can
tell you that. . . ."

"Ted Peterson!" Jo spat. "Are you crazy?"

"Yep. Like a fox. Crazy enough to know I don't want no parts
of you, Jo. Not ever. Had a bellyful of your lying and your cheat-
ing. More'n a bellyful of your hoity toity ways. . . ."

He saw her eyes widening endlessly, staring past him. Without
even looking, he let his arm fall about Mercedes' shoulder.

"Got myself a good woman now. A li'l' gal what's true down to
the marrow of her bones. Don't have to worry about where she
is, and what she's doing, 'cause she's always here. You understand
that, Jo?"

"Yes," Jo whispered. "I understand perfectly, Ted."

She turned to the man beside her.

"Well, Mr. King," she said. "Shall we go?"

Once they were out of sight of the cabin, King reached out and
took her hand.

"I'm sorry, Mrs. Peterson," he said, his voice sincerity itself, "but
I truly didn't know about that. If there is anything I can do. . . ."

Jo shook her head. That hurt. She didn't love Ted. She wanted to divorce him, but it hurt. She had rehearsed over and over again in her mind, the cold and deadly words with which she was going to reject him. Only, it hadn't worked out like that. Ted had done the casting off, not she. She was wounded in her tenderest part—her pride. She hated and detested Ted Peterson; but she didn't like being rejected by him. Lord God, she thought, what a complicated mess we women have for minds!

She shot a sidelong glance at Rufus King. She wondered if she dared ask him about Bruce. He seemed kind. Maybe he really hadn't known about Ted and that—that common little Mexican tart!

"Mr. King—" she said.

"Yes?" he said. "Yes, Mrs. Peterson?"

"You seem well acquainted hereabouts. Do you happen to know a man named—Bruce Harkness?"

King looked at her, a tiny frown creasing his forehead. Her voice, speaking, saying that name, had told him all he needed to know. His mind raced with that icily precise calculation that had made him a prince of gamblers. Harkness' crop had failed. He knew that. It followed then, that Bruce would head south, back to the diggings, and spend the winter trying to recoup. It was likely that he had already gone. If so, that one last threat would be out of the way for months.

Time, King thought, that's all I need—time. With this kind whose very walk shows what's burning them, it's always just a question of time. •

He gathered his actor's face into lines of grave sadness.

"Mrs. Peterson," he said; "I'm sorry you asked me that. . . ."

"Why?" she breathed; "why, Mr. King?"

"Because, already once today I was unwittingly put in the position of having to reveal—unpleasantness to you. And now, you put me in even a worse position. . . ."

"Why?" Jo said; "oh, for God's sake, tell me!"

"Bruce Harkness is—dead," Rufus King said.

10

She would never cry again. In that first month after Rufus King had told her of Bruce's death at the hands of Murieta's outlaws, adding convincingly the one small detail that clinched the matter once and for all in her mind—"He wasn't armed. Mr. Harkness, it seemed, had a horror of violence. Everyone knew he never carried a gun . . ."—that one small detail that fitted, because she knew that about him, too, she had cried enough to dry up the wells of weeping for a lifetime. She had cried over lost love, and wasted opportunities, and the utter desolation of her chances once her pitifully small sheaf of bank notes was gone.

She could not even save herself by marrying one of the men of Sacramento. She was bound still to a husband who had cast her off and flaunted his concubine before her for all the world to see. She had not the money to arrange a divorce, despite all the evidence she had. What was left for her, then?

The Annex, she thought bitterly; certainly I have the inclinations. . . .

But Rufus King had saved her from that. He had come to visit her in her hotel room on Christmas day.

"I paid your hotel bill," he said flatly. "Up until New Year's. Tyson told me you owed for three weeks. No—don't thank me. I want to apologize for the necessity of having done it. I suppose your recent experiences have led you to doubt that men can be disinterested. . . ."

"They have," Jo said quietly; "but thank you just the same, Mr. King. . . ."

King smiled at her. His smile was something to see. "That murdering bastard," Hailey had often told Bruce, "can charm a bird off a branch. . . ."

"I'm not disinterested," he said easily; "but there aren't any strings attached to it, actually. I've been down and out myself. Rather a depressing feeling, isn't it?"

"Very," Jo said.

"Come have dinner with me at the Diamond. Turkey and all the trimmings. Christmas is no day to spend alone. . . ."

"All right," Jo said. "Give me time to get dressed properly. I am hungry. Besides," she looked him straight in the face, "I'd better find out just what kind of an ax you're beginning to grind. I have no intentions of ending up in the Annex, Mr. King. If this is your regular recruiting drive—forget it. I'll find some way to pay you back the money."

King threw back his head and laughed aloud.

"You flatter me," he said. "You're far too lovely for the Annex. I don't cast pearls before swine, Mrs. Peterson."

"Just what do you do with pearls, then?" Jo said.

King laughed again.

"Your directness is refreshing," he said. "As a matter of fact, I do have a proposition to make you. Don't look so alarmed. It's a straight business proposition. I simply want to offer you a job. . . ."

"What kind of a job?" Jo demanded.

"Simply a job—which involves nothing dishonorable or personal. Couldn't we discuss the matter after dinner?"

"Yes," Jo said; "I'll be down as soon as I change."

The dinner was perfect. There was champagne with it. Jo had one glass, and left part of that.

"What's the matter?" King said. "Don't you like it?"

"Too much. I'm afraid of it. It makes me—irresponsible."

"Then don't. In the job I'm offering you, you'll have to be eminently responsible. Look—Jo—may I call you that? It's time we became friends. . . ."

"If you like," Jo said indifferently.

"I want to clear up one point: this is neither charity nor a subtle assault upon your virtue. I want to hire you for one exceedingly practical reason: You're right for the job. Your looks, of course—

and your perfect self command. I think you'll greatly increase my take. . . ."

"Doing what?" Jo demanded.

"Spinning a roulette wheel. You'll be the first lady Croupier north of San Francisco. . . ."

"Good God!" Jo said.

"It's perfectly honest. My wheels aren't fixed. You simply cater to a normal human desire. Nobody will ever stop men from gambling. Why not accommodate them? Make the surroundings, say, more attractive . . . You will receive two hundred dollars a week and all expenses. You will not be called upon to make free with your favors to anybody—not even to me. Of course," he laughed, "if you should ever feel so inclined, I should be delighted. But you won't be pressed, lured, forced, or anything at all. You'll be a working girl—like a girl in a millinery shop. Come, Jo, what do you say?"

"Those men," Jo said slowly, "drink. And most of them haven't seen a woman in a long time. . . ."

"I shall be there. I have a revolver behind the bar. I have a couple of strong boys to keep order. You won't be molested, I promise you."

And she hadn't been. She had sat there—night after night, clad in the costumes that Rufus King had bought her: a full skirt, reaching to just above her ankles, topped by a shoulderless, skin tight bodice that left absolutely nothing at all to the imagination, to which she had added a black velvet ribbon about her slim throat, pinning to it the locket containing Bruce's picture, swearing to wear it as long as she lived—and said in her clear voice to the men who played now with wild recklessness, forgetting as they gazed at her with longing or tenderness or lust, to pay much attention to the wheel itself:

"Make your plays, gentlemen! Gentlemen, make your plays!"

Not one man had gotten seriously out of line. Invitations of course: to dinner, to go riding, to have a drink—all of which she refused with cool politeness. She was not even tempted to break her solitude. She took a certain feminine joy in her sorrow.

She neither wrote, nor received letters. She fervently prayed that no one from home, nobody she had known before, would ever enter the Blue Diamond and see her there, dressed so immodestly, doing what she was doing—or what was worse, living in a private apartment above the gambling hall, across the hall from King's own.

Still, it had its compensations: her apartment was wonderfully comfortable, even luxurious. She had a colored girl to cook for her, and to wait on her hand and foot. And she had the adoration of every man in Sacramento, not excepting the married and the old.

Thanks to her, the Diamond had doubled its business. King raised her salary to three hundred dollars a week, then to four, telling her she was worth every penny of it.

Toward her, he behaved with circumspect gallantry. He never entered her apartment without her permission; while there, his behavior left nothing to be desired. Or almost nothing. What it did leave, drove her into black moods of exasperated self-contempt. She cursed herself with the picturesque invective learned from the miners. She considered herself damned and doomed.

It was actually very simple: She was a woman, who had been married, who had known physical love. And she lived in an age, and in a society that denied the existence of female sexuality, holding it, when indisputable evidence that it did exist was presented, a deviation, a rare malady found only among the low, the base, the daughters of white trash, the born prostitutes. And by the very universality of their belief, they forced upon several generations of women, a life of rare torment. Jo had no way of knowing how many other women, that warm March night, sat and watched the moon blaze and wept because, on the very simplest possible terms, they needed a man.

But with Jo, that Spring night in 1851, the problem was more complicated: she was strongly attracted to a man whom actually she despised. She knew Rufus King for what he was: a man whose basic cynicism was so deep, whose contempt for humanity was so great, whose ego was so insufferable, that the things he did calmly, casually to people affected him no more than stepping on insects affects a child. That people like him were actually sick, she had no way of knowing. In 1851, the world had not outgrown the concept of villainy. She saw what he did and hated him: his receiving for his brothel dozens of young girls from the East, all but kidnapped into slavery, seduced by agents he employed in

the larger cities, agents, Jo guessed, not unlike himself. She saw
his use of markers, ringers, strippers in poker games, his fixed
wheels—all but hers. She had insisted upon that . . . And his
Lucky Golden Horseshoe Bar, where the horseshoe suspended
above the semicircular bar was only a common iron one dipped
in gold, and where miners who had had good luck were given
all they could drink on the house and even a free night at the
Annex, in order—Jo strongly suspected—that they could be robbed
of their claims.

Only, he was such a splendid animal. Only his manners were
so gentle, and so fine. Only he had that indefinable something
that Lucas Wilkins had also had, and in much greater measure—
the ability, if that were the word, to appeal to every base instinct
a woman had, and to call into being a few more she hadn't known
she possessed.

More, he was almost the only man who attracted her at all.
There was one other; but she had given that up as hopeless: the
tall, red-haired, freckled-faced lawyer called Hailey Burke—a man
as homely as unabashed sin, but wonderfully attractive for all
his good-humored ugliness. Burke, she felt sure, was a good man,
a kind, warm hearted, gentle man. He never gambled. He came
into the Diamond from time to time, and watched her, his blue
eyes gentle and sad. Only, she had found out, Hailey Burke was
the leader of the Sacramento reform element, pledged to cleaning
up the town, determined to shut up the gambling palace and the
whorehouses, to finishing off men like Rufus King—and women
like herself—like what she had become.

Still, there was no contempt in his eyes when he looked at her,
but something else—something more: a dark, indefinable emotion like—pity? She didn't know. What she did know was that
he would never approach her; that he would never stoop to any
sort of relationship at all with a woman who spun a roulette wheel
in a gambling hall.

She had believed that her sorrow over the death of Bruce Harkness would sustain her; but now she remembered with bitter self-
accusation her behavior in Savannah the summer before, her near
adultery with Lucas Wilkins . . . If Bruce's absence, living, had
not been enough, accompanied, as that had been, by hope, what
could she expect of the hopeless circumstance of his death?

I should simply move into the Annex, she thought. That's all I'm fitted for. . . .

There was a moon caught in the plane trees, silvering the night. She could hear the nightbirds calling, far off and sad. She sat by her window, clad only in a thin nightdress, hearing the echo of their sadness in her heart. After a time, she got up, and went to bed. She lay there for two hours, staring at the ceiling, the lamp burning on the night table at her side.

The knock on the outer door was so gentle that at first she thought she imagined it. But it came again.

"Come in!" she called. "It isn't locked . . ." She never locked her door. Why didn't she? Was it perhaps that she hoped—"Oh, God," she whispered to herself. "Oh God, Oh God, Oh God. . . ."

"I saw your light," Rufus King said gravely. "I thought you were ill, perhaps. . . ."

"No, I'm not sick. Beyond a headache, that is. I just can't sleep. . . ."

"I'll get you some laudanum," he said. "That should do the trick. . . ."

Then he was gone, before she had had time to say anything at all.

She lay there, wondering where he was going to get laudanum this hour of the night. Perhaps he already had some in his quarters. She hoped he had. Sleep would be such a blessed relief.

But he was gone so long that she began to grow drowsy after all. She turned and blew out the lamp. She didn't need it, really; the moonlight flooded the whole room. She lay there, debating whether or not to close the curtains in order to darken the room. But she didn't feel like getting out of bed. She closed her eyes, dozed and dreamed, awoke, and dreamed again.

She heard the door open very softly. Through her lashes, she could see him standing there looking at her. She pretended to be asleep, thinking: He'll go away; if he thinks I'm asleep he'll go away . . . She wanted him to go away; and she didn't want him to. Both. And at the same time.

He sat down on the chair, facing her. The thud his boot made as he took it off, let it fall, shocked her eyes open. She lay there, staring at him. He smiled at her, gravely, and took off the other boot. Then he stood up, and without any haste at all, took off the rest of his clothes.

His body was magnificent: wide-shouldered, slim hipped, well-but not over-muscled. He crossed over to the bed, and stood there, looking at her.

"Move over," he said.

She lay there the whole eternity that lay between two heart-beats. What difference does it make? she thought; What difference does anything make now? But then, with a fierce upsurge of that honesty that was the finest element in all the complicated mixture that made up her being, she rejected the thought, know-ing it for what it was: an excuse, an attempt at self-deception before her shame at what she knew she was going to do.

I wonder what he'll be like? she thought hungrily. Ah, God it's been so long. . . .

Then, very quietly, she moved to the far side of the bed, and stretched out her arms to him.

                                                                    •

And in the morning, in full daylight, he had done a curious thing: He had turned to her and began again to caress her. And then, abruptly, he had stopped. Her eyes flew open, staring up at him, seeing on his satanically handsome face, the most mocking of all smiles.

"What's wrong?" she whispered; "did I—?"

He smiled down at her.

"Nothing," he said. "I suddenly find that this bores me. . . ."

She stared at him. He moved again, and her throat tightened. He stopped.

Her face twisted; her mouth moved, forming words. But what were the words? What could she say?

He put out his hands and moved her away from him. Calmly he got out of bed and started to dress. When he was clothed, he turned to her.

"It would be nice," he drawled, "if it were true—that myth you women believe in: that no man can understand you. You see, Jo, darling, I do understand you. So very damned well."

His smile held all the confident mockery in the world.

"This way," he said, "you'll always be here waiting, when I want you. . . ."

Then he opened the door and went out very quietly, leaving her there like that.

Jo lay there, staring at the blank surface of the door. And for the first time in her life, she had a deep and pure and unmixed desire—to kill a man.

She lifted the cup and drank the coffee down all at once. Then she leaped from the bed, calling to Tildy: "Get my bath ready. I'm going out!"

Sitting in the tub, she calculated wildly. I have enough money: I'll take the first steamer and—But she wouldn't. She knew that. Scoundrel or not, one touch from this man could set all her body screaming. She had needed that all her life. Well, she had it now. And for it, she had to pay—with her freedom.

She bent down her head, and cried.

I won't go back through Sacramento, Bruce decided. Head straight for Marysville. Better that way. When I visit Hailey again, I want to do it right—with the money I owe him in my hand. . . .

He thought idly of the possibility of there being letters for him at the post office; but he dismissed it with a shrug. David had stopped writing him, largely from a lack of anything to say. And Jo—

No hope of that. It's been too long. Something's happened. Another man, maybe. Out East, more'n a few wives have had husbands who've been gone too long, and who don't write, declared dead so they can marry again—Not too hard, if you know the right people. And Jo's well acquainted in Carolina. . . .

He didn't care very much any more. He had had a peaceful winter. He'd left Pepe and Juana behind to take care of the livestock. Without Juana there to torment him visibly, he'd been able to manage. When you drove yourself past exhaustion every day, sleep came easily enough at night.

His leather bags were fat and bulging with the dust. He wouldn't have to borrow again. Thank God for that. And once the crop, to be planted as soon as he got home, before even April had come, was in, he'd be free of debt and on his way.

But lonely still. He'd be able to do something about even that, now. Spend some money on decent clothes, ride up to Oregon, find himself a wife. Even the prospect comforted him.

The summer was perfect. It was warm, but not too warm. By August, his fields were a joy to see. But Bruce sat on his horse looking at them, making a litany of curses in his heart. This tension between Pepe and Juana—was he, perhaps the cause of that? Just yesterday, he had heard Pepe's voice rising in a staccato volley of Spanish profanity in the barn, then, clear and sharp as a pistol shot, the sound of a slap. He had jerked open the small door, gone inside.

Juana stood there, her eyes closed, a trace of tears about her lashes, and, angry red upon her coppery face, the print of Pepe's hand.

"God damn it, Pepe!" Bruce growled; "that wasn't necessary! I don't hold with beating on women. . . ."

"Ah, but it was, *Señor!*" Pepe said mockingly. "Women are such stupid beasts, that this of the blows is from time to time required."

"What did she do?" Bruce demanded.

Pepe smiled at him, coolly.

"*Mi Juana,*" he said; "has greatly augmented her ambitions, *Amigo.* And, under the circumstances, it is necessary that they be curtailed. . . ."

Bruce hadn't gone into it any further. He knew that he'd get no further information out of Pepe. Besides, it was not his business, anyhow. He didn't like it, though. None of it—especially not the cool and insolent look in Pepe's eyes.

The August days shimmered by on a wash of sun. By the middle of the month, Bruce saw that he would be able to harvest by the first two weeks of September, long before any danger from the cold. The last weeks of August were the easy time, when there was nothing much to do but a little weeding, watering the stock, and household repairs.

He saw Juana going to the spring for water, the pails slung on poles across her shoulders. He thought again about digging the well, but he didn't feel up to it. Indolence possessed him. He lay back against his chair, gazing up at the mountains.

He felt thirsty suddenly, and went out back to get a drink of water from the earthen jug. But there was no water in the jug, not a drop. It came to him then that Juana had been gone a hell of a long time.

I'll just mosey down to the creek, myself, he thought, and have a drink. That water's always cool. See what's keeping Juana. Ought to stay away from her; but still, scarce as women are, it pays to keep an eye on her. Some of those miners just might wander through and—

He quickened his steps, thinking of that.

There was a clump of birches near the water's edge. He came up to them, walking quietly, not with any conscious intention, but from habit; for in that wild country a man's life depended often enough on not making any noise, and he had learned to walk like that.

He was almost to the stream's edge before he saw her. She was bathing in the little stream, splashing about like a child.

He knew he should go away from there, that he should not look; but he could not turn away his eyes.

She stood up suddenly, a golden statue of a tribal goddess in that wash of sun and water, the droplets glistening on her skin, and threw her hair back, night-black and heavy, streaming silver, raising her arms to push it out of her face, her pale coppery breasts rising with the movement.

He backed away from the stream's edge, not daring to stay. When he was far enough, he turned and ran. He ran all the way to the barn, tore down his saddle, flung it upon the mustang. He went out of the yard at a gallop.

He didn't stop until he reached the first saloon in Marysville. He went in and proceeded to get blind drunk. Then he meandered down to the wharf and bought a ticket on the downriver steamer to San Francisco. He might as well have stopped in Sacramento; but he didn't want Hailey to see him like this. More, in his present mood, he did not want to risk an encounter with Rufus King. He had the feeling that he might violate his own hard held code against violence.

That it is always upon such accidental circumstances that a man's life is made or broken never even occurred to him. For, had he decided to stop in Sacramento, he almost certainly would have entered the Blue Diamond and found Jo there. The consequence of such a meeting would have been unimaginable. But he did not. And, as a result of this simple omission, nothing in his brief, eventful history would ever be the same again.

His behavior, after he had gone ashore on the Barbary Coast, surprised even him. Nothing about him was simple any more: he suffered love, never lust. He did not want a woman; he wanted the woman, this woman who could be all things to him: angel and lover, companion and comforter. He did not, could not, desire with his body what awoke no response in his mind and heart and spirit.

He found that out in Big Tim's, a "pretty waitress" saloon in the middle of that roaring gulch of humanity, even subhumanity, that had already achieved immortal infamy under the name of the Barbary Coast. Big Tim, with a stroke of imaginative genius, had managed to gain fame by an innovation unusual even in the San Francisco of the early 'fifties. The innovation was the costume of his waitresses. In front, it was reasonably demure, consisting of the usual skin-tight bodice, which emphasized whatever charms with which they had been endowed by nature—charms that, due to Tim's careful selection of his girls, were usually ample; and a full, ruffled skirt falling below the knees. But the back of this costume was something else again: the skirt, seen from the rear, was merely an apron, cut well above the hips, so that, since the girls were also required to wear black silk stockings held up by a garter belt, and absolutely nothing else, the effect when they wheeled smartly about and marched away after taking an order was a trifle startling.

Bruce sat there peering owlishly at the sudden flash of white and dimpled flesh as the waitress walked away from him. Other men were roaring with uncontrolled laughter at this same spectacle, but he sat there, groping through his thick alcoholic fog for the reason why he found the whole thing singularly unpleasant. He couldn't find the reason. The nearest he could come to it was:

Hadn't ought to. They're folks—human beings. Not right to shame 'em like this. . . .

When the waitress came back, he saw her eyes. They were big with a thousand nights of terror. He saw, drunk as he was, that the girl bent over his table from as far away as possible; seeking to avoid being jerked into his arms, a thing that, judging from the shrieks and laughter coming from all over the place, was already happening to most of the others.

"Don't worry, li'l' girl," he said gruffly. "Won't bother you. Why don't you just—quit?"

"And end up in the cribs and cowyards?" the girl said bitterly. "There are worse things than this, Mister. Besides, you don't quit this job. Try it and what gets done to your face, you can't even work in the worst crib on Telegraph Hill. Only when a girl gets too old and ugly can she get outa here. Then she gets thrown out—to starve. . . ."

"Sit down," Bruce said. "Have a drink with me. Sitting down, you'll at least be covered. . . ."

"You—you're nice," the girl said, and the tears were there, bright and sudden in her eyes. Then she said, in a hoarse whisper: "It'll only be cold tea—and you'll be charged for it like it was whiskey. . . ."

"Don't care. Sit down. Long as I'm here, you won't be bothered. Talk to me. Lord God, it's been so damn long since I had a woman to talk to. . . ."

The girl eased down into the chair.

"That's hard, ain't it?" she said. "No trick at all to find a girl to sleep with; but talk's another matter. Dear Lord, I wish more fellers like you'd come into this place. . . ."

"Talk," Bruce said. "Tell me about yourself. . . ."

She did. It was the usual, pitifully sordid story. It came to Bruce that if anyone back East had ever started an organization to send decent girls out to California as wives for the miners—an organization that had one half the efficiency of the vice rings which enslaved the innocent and stupid and shipped them West like so many cattle—the whole problem of the state's future would have been solved overnight. But no one had, because it was both slower and less profitable.

His attention was caught by another group of waitresses who had come into the saloon. These girls were modestly, even voluminously dressed. Under their ankle length skirts were many petticoats.

"Oh, Lord!" the girl said. "Now I gotta go change. . . ."

"Into that?" Bruce said.

"Yes," the girl said acidly. " 'Nother one of Tim's bright ideas. You take it all off—at fifty cents the piece. After that, for two dollars more, you—"

She got up and fled, the print of the cane bottom chair showing pink on her flesh.

All over the saloon, the hilarity was at its height. There was the ring of coins on the table tops, and the rustle of feminine garments being shed. Some of the girls had beautiful bodies. Many of the tables were set in alcoves with curtains that could be drawn. Instead of the cane bottom chairs of the center tables, they had benches that were quite long enough. Some of the men didn't even bother to draw the curtains.

Bruce got up and flung down a few bills, more than enough to pay for his drinks, he reckoned. Then he blundered out of there, sick to his soul with abysmal disgust.

There were, he was to find, places on the Barbary Coast which made Big Tim's look like a paragon of gentility. He stumbled into one of them three nights later, in which an exhibition was being held of such a nature as to sober him temporarily by making him reel outside and heave up all the very nearly poisonous whiskey that remained in his stomach. He almost went home that same night, as he should have, but the memory of what he had seen remained with him so strongly that he got drunk again in a vain attempt to forget it.

That he got home at all, somewhat damaged in body and spirit, but alive, was due to Brother Nate. The saloon keeper in Marysville where Bruce had begun his titanic binge was a friend of Nate's. And he knew Bruce, knew, moreover, how completely unusual such behavior was in him. So he led Bruce's mustang over to Nate's store and told Nate the story. Brother Nate set off almost at once for Sacramento. From Hailey, he learned that Bruce hadn't even stopped there.

"Then he's in Frisco, by God!" Nate said. "And if I don't find him right away, the Good Lord alone knows what'll happen to him. . . ."

Finding one man on the Barbary Coast was not an easy task; but Nate did it—exactly five minutes after Bruce had been sapped with a black jack and rolled in an alley for all that remained of his money, after having rejected the attentions of two little Mexican girls in a fandango dive whose proudest boast was that they could prove their virginity by medical examination. And they were indeed virginal, for no man in the history of their murderous establishment had ever escaped being knifed or bludgeoned long before he got what he had paid for.

Nate took Bruce back to Marysville, and nursed him through the healing of his broken head, and one of the most monumental hangovers in human history, with bluff kindness.

At fifty-five, Brother Nate still understood how it felt to be young.

Bruce got back to the farm in time to help Pepe with the harvest. Work had always been his refuge and his strength. He drove himself, falling in bed each night too tired to even undress. He slept like a dead man, too weary to dream.

By the fifteenth of September, the crop was in and sold. He had realized forty thousand dollars from the sale of his wheat, his corn, his apples, pears, beef animals and pork. He could have gotten more, but his basic honesty prevented him from charging all the traffic would bear. Being human, he felt a momentary twinge of regret when he heard a farmer from the high Sierra Valley to the east boasting of having gotten the same sum of money for sixteen acres of potatoes; compared to that, his earnings from his hundred and forty acre farm were moderate enough. But he couldn't repress his feeling that to charge one dollar per apple or forty dollars the bushel of wheat was pure thievery.

But with the money in his hands, he felt better. He bathed and dressed himself in his one remaining good suit. I'll go down to Frisco after, he decided, and have some decent clothes made. Heard tell they've got some pretty fair tailors down there now . . . Then he mounted and rode down to Sacramento to pay his debt to Hailey.

"Lord God, boy!" Hailey growled, "but you're a sight for sore eyes! Where in hellfire have you been? Ain't seen you in so damn' long—"

"Didn't want to come before I had the money to pay you with, Hail," Bruce said.

"And you stayed away on account of that? Damn it, boy. I ought to kick your tailbone up past your tonsils! I didn't give a damn if you ever paid me. Our friendship's worth a damnsight more to me than seven thousand lousy dollars. . . ."

"I cared," Bruce said. "Here it is, Hail—"

"Sure you don't need it? You strap yourself to pay me, I'm going to be mighty damned mad. . . ."

"No," Bruce said. "I did fine. Made forty thousand this year. . . ."

"Great! Does my old heart good to hear it. Come on, let's go over to King's and have a drink. . . ."

"No," Bruce said. "Later, Hailey. Let's just sit and talk a spell. Why do you always go to King's? Thought you didn't like him. . . ."

"Funny, but I do. That sidewinding cuss who strikes without even rattling is my chief interest in life. I'm going to be sorry when I finally do get the goods on him. He's so damned slick it's a joy to watch him operate. Him and me are right pert friendly; that is, we respect each other. He knows I'm the chief danger to his existence, but he doesn't lift a hand against me. Gets too big a kick out of outsmarting me, I reckon. And damn if he doesn't win out every time. . . ."

"Found out about his connection with the fake Mex bandits and the claim jumpers yet?" Bruce said.

"No. I know how it works, though. King's got one special bar in the Blue Diamond, called the Lucky Golden Horseshoe. Any man who can show enough dust to prove he's made a good strike, can have all the drinks he wants for free, and a filly at the Annex to keep his toes warm—also for free, if he feels so inclined. . . ."

"Quite an institution," Bruce said dryly.

"Yep. That's how he finds out. But what I ain't been able to figure yet is how the devil he gets the word to Ted Peterson and Terry Casey. Never seen either one of 'em in the Diamond. Not even once. I'm certain sure he's got a go-between, but with all the

men who come in and out of that place, it's damn near impossible
to find out who it is. . . ."

"Don't let it fret you, boy," Bruce said. "He'll make a slip and
you'll get him."

"If I don't die of old age, first," Hailey said.

"You don't look so pert," Bruce said. "Anything wrong, Hail?"

"Yes," Hailey said slowly. "There is. I'm in love, Hoss."

"You are! Congratulations. Who's the lucky woman, Hailey?"

"Rufus King's mistress," Hailey said.

"Good Lord! Didn't know he had one. When did all this happen?"

"She came here last November—same day you stopped by—
'bout a month and a half after the Squatters' Riot. She's been here
ever since, running a wheel in the Diamond. First off, she had her
own apartment above the place, 'cross the hall from King's. But her
colored maid let slip that King moved her into his in March. Broke
my heart. She's the prettiest li'l' ice water blonde you ever did
see. Hotter'n a firecracker for all her paleness. You can tell that by
just watching her walk. . . ."

"Forget her," Bruce said. "Cheap little whore like that ain't
worth troubling yourself about. . . ."

"I love her, Bruce," Hailey said doggedly. "Know it doesn't make
sense, but I do."

"What else do you know about her?" Bruce said.

"Little or nothing. Not even her name. Boys all call her Honey—
or Hon. Seems she doesn't want her real name known. Oh yes—
there's one other thing. I did hear talk that there was some con-
nection between her'n Ted Peterson. . . ."

"Ted? What's the matter with Mercedes?"

"Nothing. They're still together. This was before this new filly
came here, I mean."

Bruce stood up.

"Before," he whispered; "before—You mean back East?"

"Yep. What's the matter with you, boy? You look like living
hell!"

"Come on!" Bruce said; "Goddamnit, Hail, come on!"

"Where you going, boy?" Hailey said.

"To the Blue Diamond. She's there, isn't she?"

"Yes—but I don't understand—"

"You will," Bruce said. "Get a move on, Hailey!"

They stood in the doorway, looking at her. She didn't look up.

"Make your plays, gentlemen," she intoned. "Gentlemen, make your plays!"

Hailey could see Bruce sag.

"What's the matter, ol' Hoss?" he said. "You sick or something?"

"Yes," Bruce said. "To the pit of my stomach, Hailey. . . ."

He groped in his breast pocket, came out with the daguerreotype. Wordlessly, he passed it over.

He heard the sharp intake of Hailey's breath.

"Why—it's the same girl! The one you was talking about sending for, only there was some catch to it. . . ."

"Ted Peterson," Bruce said. "She's his wife. Catch enough, Hailey?"

"I'm mightily sorry, Bruce," Hailey said gently. "I didn't know. . . ."

"Ted's wife, and King's mistress," Bruce said dryly. "I call that a real, double barrelled catch. . . ."

He turned to leave the hall.

"Aren't you even going to talk to her?" Hailey said.

"No," Bruce said flatly. "What's there to talk about—now?"

But Jo raised her eyes and saw them. Even from where he stood, Hailey could see her face paling, her eyes widening endlessly until they threatened to eclipse her face. Then she was off her stool and running toward them; they could see her mouth moving, shaping the word, and when she was close enough they heard it: "Bruce! Oh my God, Bruce, Bruce, Bruce!"

She flew toward him, her arms outstretched. But when she was still a yard away, she stopped dead. Slowly her arms came down to her sides. It was, Hailey thought, the most pathetic gesture in the world.

"No," she whispered, "I cannot touch you—can I, Bruce? I'm not fit to, any more. It would be like being touched—in public—by one of the girls from the Annex, wouldn't it, Bruce?"

Bruce didn't answer. He just stood there, looking at her.

She was crying now, crying in such an absolutely hopeless agony

of shame and grief, that Hailey half turned to get away from the
sound of it.

"Don't, Jo," Bruce said. "Please don't cry. . . ."

"Don't cry! This is nothing! You should have seen me, heard
me the night King told me you were dead! I was insane, out of
my mind . . . The woman at the hotel had to tie my hands . . .
Don't cry—oh my God, Bruce, don't tell me that. Not you. When
all you had to do was to meet me—you had the date and the hour
and we came in right on time. . . ."

"I had the date and the hour?" Bruce growled. "Lord God, Jo—
I never had a line from you! I haunted the post office. I kept waiting, hoping. . . ."

"You didn't get a letter from me," Jo whispered, "saying I was
arriving the twenty-ninth of November on the *California?*"

"I did not." Bruce said; and hearing the pain in his voice, seeing
his eyes, Jo knew he did not lie.

"Lost," she said. "That one letter out of all I wrote you . . . Oh
God, why did it have to be that one? I didn't write after. I wanted
to save it all, I reckon, all the millions of things I had to say to
you. . . ."

"Jo," Bruce said gently, and put out his arms.

"No, no!" she wept. "Don't touch me! You'll dirty your hands!
You didn't understand about women like me, Bruce. It's very simple, really. Rufus understands it perfectly. All you have to do is
stretch out your hand—and push. . . ."

Hailey stood there, looking at the two of them, the tears bright
in his own eyes. They were compounded in equal measure of pity
and of rage.

"That sonofabitch!" he said. "Told her you were dead! You
heard that, didn't you?"

"I heard," Bruce said grimly.

"It doesn't matter now," Jo said quickly. "You mustn't fight him,
Bruce. Not over me. Men don't fight over cheap tarts—do they,
Bruce? Tell me, do they?"

"No," Bruce said. "But you aren't—"

"Oh yes I am. Worse than that. Oh, Bruce—Bruce darling, please
go! And promise me you won't fight him. Promise me!"

"All right," Bruce said; "I promise. . . ."

Then he and Hailey turned and walked out of there.

Jo stood there, watching them. When, finally, she got back to her table, Rufus King was standing beside it.

"Those two," he said mockingly, "they were not molesting you, were they, Jo?"

She looked at him very slowly, from head to heel.

"You bastard!" she said quietly, and sat back on the stool. Her voice, speaking, was utterly without emotion.

"Make your plays, Gentlemen! Gentlemen, make your plays!"

11

"Somebody," Hailey grated; "should kill that son of a bitch!"

"Me, for instance?" Bruce said mildly.

"Well—" Hailey said, and stopped.

"On what grounds, Hailey," Bruce said. "Tell me that—on what grounds?"

"She was your girl," Hailey said doggedly, "and she loves you— Lord God, boy—it's written all over her. . . ."

"Does she?" Bruce said, and there was ice and iron in his voice. "Look, Hailey, as lawyer for the defense, would you take the case of a man who killed another one over the wife of a third party?"

"No," Hailey said honestly. "I wouldn't. I wouldn't have a hope nor a prayer of getting him off. You're right, Bruce. Lord God, but your head works cool!"

"Not cool, Hail. I'd strangle that bastard in a minute, but for one thing: Little Jo doesn't want me to. And for his sake, not mine. Maybe even for her own. . . ."

Hailey stared at him. He knew by now how Bruce used the diminutive in speaking of a woman—nearly always as a term of contempt.

"Somewhere along the line, Hailey, boy," Bruce went on quietly, "I lost my sentimentality. A man mostly figures that the woman he loves has to be a lily white angel, just because he loves her. Doesn't matter: she can be like Jo—plenty white, but no damn lily. . . ."

"That's mighty ugly talk, Bruce," Hailey growled.

"Ugly as truth. Look, Hailey: how much does King pay her for spinning that roulette wheel? Guess—how much?"

"Don't have to guess; he told me. Four hundred a week. Says she's worth every penny of it. . . ."

"And how long has she been at it?"

"Since right after New Year's. I begin to see what you're driving at, boy. . . ."

"She became his mistress in March. Women, like men, do a lot of things to escape hunger, poverty. But by March she had two months' salary behind her—over three thousand dollars. She wasn't hungry, Hail. She was already eating mighty high on the hog to my way of thinking."

"Goddamnit, Bruce, I don't like your way of thinking! I been fighting all my life to keep from admitting that folks are as rotten as they show themselves up to be. I don't want to live in a world that's so blamed ugly. I truly don't."

"You're a good old cuss, aren't you?" Bruce said fondly. "Not everybody's rotten—only about ninety-five per cent. Look, Hailey, Jo Peterson has by now, I'm certain sure, enough evidence to divorce Ted ten times over. What's more, in two weeks she earns enough to pay the cost of the court and a battery of high-powered lawyers. So tell me another thing: has she divorced him?"

"No," Hailey said miserably. "If she had, I'd know."

"No divorce then—not even to become Mrs. Rufus King. No, Little Jo compounds the felony and makes a divorce from Ted an absolute impossibility under California law, and that of most other states, by committing adultery herself. She can't divorce Ted now—Or am I wrong about the law?"

"You aren't wrong. I helped write the laws myself when we became a state last September. Both parties guilty—no divorce. Lord God, what a lawyer you would have made!"

"Been times I've had to think straight to stay alive. Sort of formed the habit. Jo moved in with Rufus in March; in two weeks it will be October, Hail. She could have bought a steamer ticket any old time, gone back home. She stays there, old Hoss, and will stay for the simplest of all reasons: she likes what she is doing. . . ."

"There're extenuating circumstances," Hailey said slowly. "She thought you were dead, remember. And I reckon she'd already been confronted with little Mercedes. . . ."

"She mourned one hell of a long time, didn't she?" Bruce said dryly. "All of four months. That is, if they hadn't commenced their parlor games before moving day, which, naturally, they had. . . ."

"You're sure taking this mighty cool-headed, boy," Hailey said. "If I were in your place—"

"But you are," Bruce mocked. "You told me yourself you love her. . . ."

"I do," Hailey said. "And if there were any legal or ethical way to get her out of this mess, I'd do it. And I'd marry her—no matter what she's done. . . ."

"Then," Bruce said, "you're in a worse spot than I am, Hailey. I'm sorry you feel that way, because you're going to get hurt. Forget her, Hail. She's not worth it. Reckon she never was, but I didn't know it, then. Tell you what. Jo knows that King deceived her, lied about my being dead. She's got grounds to be mighty mad at him, hasn't she? Well, the day you hear she has moved out of his apartment, send me a letter to the General Post Office in Frisco, and I'll send you five hundred dollars, no—a thousand. And you don't even have to cover the bet."

"Thank God I ain't got a mind like yours," Hailey said. "I wouldn't want to live with thoughts like that. . . ."

"Nor I," Bruce said softly. "Tell you the truth, Hailey, it hurts like hell. . . ."

"Knew you weren't so blamed hard," Hailey said. "Why're you going to Frisco, boy?"

"Get some clothes, mainly. Then I'm heading for Oregon. Heard tell they've got some mighty pretty fillies in the Columbia Valley. Want me to bring back an extra one for you?"

Hailey shook his head.

"No, boy," he said sadly. "I still want—her. . . ."

Rufus King came up the stairs and into the apartment. Jo was not in the bedroom. He walked through all the rooms. She wasn't in any of them. He crossed the hall, and tried the handle of the door to the other apartment. As he expected, it was locked.

Thoughtfully, he took a key out of his pocket and opened it. He moved calmly, with no perceptible haste, into the bedroom. Jo was sitting on the floor, with her face crushed against the bed.

She had on her thin nightdress. He could see her shoulders shaking. He thought she looked very fetching.

"Oh, come now, Jo," he said. "You hardly have occasion for tears. . . ."

She whirled, her eyes venomous.

"How did you get in here?" she said. "Walk under the door? You could you know, and with your hat on!"

Rufus King threw back his head and laughed aloud.

"Your invective," he said, "is refreshing. You have an imaginative mind, Jo."

"You bastard!" she said.

"Bastard?" King mocked. "That's much less clever. You disappoint me. Try again, Jo. . . ."

"Bastard!" Jo wept. "Dirty rat bastard!"

"This," King said, "grows monotonous. All right, I'm a bastard. But that's hardly a distinction. All men are, just as all women are whores at heart. . . ."

"Get out of here!" Jo screamed at him. "You hear me, Rufe—go!"

"Oh, for heaven's sake, Jo," he drawled with exaggerated weariness, "come off of it. Don't tell me you let that sawed-off dirt farmer with the good earth under his nails upset you so. I said he was dead. And he is—in the sense that he's never really been alive. . . ."

She came up from the floor in a wild rush. King watched her come. At the last possible moment, he stepped aside, and smashed his open hand across her face with deliberation and care and icy ferocity; but without anger—with absolutely no anger at all.

She lay there in a crumpled heap at his feet, sobbing.

"Get up," he said. His voice was flat, calm, emotionless.

She lifted her bruised, tear-stained face, and stared at him.

"I said get up, Jo," he said quietly.

She scrambled to her feet like a frightened child.

"Now put your arms around my neck and kiss me."

She hesitated.

"Jo—" he said, his voice endlessly deep.

She went very quietly into his arms. He kissed her a long time and very thoroughly, with care, and precision and mock tenderness and simulated passion. He had never felt any real tenderness, nor its twin, that true passion born of love, in all his life. He was, perhaps, incapable of them, as he was incapable of even comprehending love beyond its sexual manifestations. But those he comprehended very well indeed. His hands moved on her body like a master violinist's upon the singing strings. He kissed her eyes, her throat, found her mouth again, tormenting it with his own until he had the note he sought: the muted shuddering in the flesh, the ragged beat, breaking the rhythm of her breathing.

Jo heard, incredulously, somewhere near at hand, a curious sound—as though a woman moaned in passion. Then she realized that the sound came from her own throat.

I'm damned, she thought, as Rufus King picked her up, and crossed the hall with her as though she were a puppet or a doll. But by then, she was past really caring.

But, later, listening to her hopeless sobbing that went on and on in such abysmal self-contempt, such utter despair, Rufus King came to a decision.

Troublesome fellow, this Harkness, he thought. Perhaps I've underestimated him. Better if he were eliminated for good and all. Ted, now—this is the sort of job he'd relish. . . .

Night long, Bruce Harkness walked the streets of San Francisco. He had still another week to wait until the suits he had ordered could be finished. That was bad, because it meant he would have to cross the mountains into Oregon in late October; and late October was no time to be crossing mountains. He decided finally, to buy a round trip ticket on a coastal steamer north to Oregon.

The trip to Sacramento was a waste of time. He knew that. He was sure he'd find the situation entirely unchanged. But he kept hoping he was wrong. When he had delivered his cool and bitter denunciation of Jo to Hailey, he had been arguing against himself as well. He realized now that if she herself had not held him back, he would have taken her in his arms and back into his life. He also knew that he would have been a fool to have done so; but among the many things he accepted about himself was the fact that he was often a fool.

He had no intention of going back to the farm before his departure to seek an unknown bride. The further he stayed away from Juana, the better. He remembered, suddenly, the old Preacher's words: "Would it shock you if I told you that neither you nor Hailey as men is fit to tie Juana's shoe laces as a woman?"

Bruce stopped, the shame knotting inside of him, thinking: I am not fit—even to touch her hand . . . And I had the nerve to condemn Jo. . . .

What it was, the thing that held him there, rooted by the tendrils of memory was his first night in San Francisco. He had arrived in the morning, visited the tailor, stood for his measurements and come back to his hotel. And there he had sat with two weeks in front of him and nothing to do in those two weeks but think.

He had, in his months of solitude, done a good deal of reading; in college, he had been a better than average student. His mind, with its endless questing after the why of things had led him naturally enough into history, philosophy, and the great dramatists; but none of them provided any answer to his problems: Jo, whom he had given his young life to, his first youthful Spring of love, turned harlot, lying, even as he sat here in this dingy hotel room alone, in Rufus King's arms. And Juana who—he could admit it now, he had grown enough for that—surmounted the irrational prejudices of his youth, realizing in his heart the irrelevancy of whether or not her grandmother had been red, or black, or even green, he had come to love Juana with mature judgment, with considered reflection, for more than her beauty, or rather for that very special beauty shining through the transient loveliness of her flesh; Juana, married to Pepe, his friend, his gay and laughing companion, for whom he felt, truly, a brother's love. . . .

His two problems, that were in essence one problem: the emptiness of his life; his loneliness made bitter by contrast. Nothing he had read or seen or heard provided any answers; what they did give him were comparisons for how it felt: The Inquisition with its rack, thumbscrew, iron maiden; the Roman Circus, with its beasts that dragged and tore; the Aztec Priest, with the still pulsating heart of the victim, dripping in his hand. . . .

And these were nothing, being physical; for no device of man's invention, in the long, sick history of human cruelty can approach the pain that one man alone, sitting in an empty room alone, can create for himself in the darkness of his mind.

He had gotten out of there finally, fled into the familiar refuge of drunkenness, and driven by his needs, his desires, his painfully acute moral sense submerged under the roaring tide of alcohol, he had gone down the line in the red light district around Telegraph Hill. Or, more truly, tried to. But one look at the pitiful creatures in the cribs, cowyards, shanties of the Hill, their hard, rouged faces, blasted out of femininity, even out of humanity by terror, by disgust born of their nightly knowledge of what man is capable of, by disease, had all but sobered him.

He had gone into another saloon, and renewed his sorry state. And from there, after making inquiries, to a brothel on Portsmouth Square. A very luxurious brothel, all velvet and plush, where the girls were young, and in the dim lights, if a man were drunk enough, pretty. He had gone upstairs with one, a plump brunette selected with drunken craft to be as different as possible from either Jo or Juana.

But he had tarried too long; the fog of drink was clearing. And he could not. A lifetime of training, and his natural decency were too strong for him, stronger even than his need, his lust. He had fled from there to the sound of the harlot's mocking laughter. He never tried that avenue of escape again.

Instead, the night long wanderings, to weary himself into sleep. Instead, the hours of stillness, gazing out of his window, staring out upon nothingness, upon the black and formless shape of his despair. So, and in such a fashion, did Bruce Harkness pass his final week in San Francisco. As he climbed aboard the steamer for Oregon, he had the feeling he never wanted to see that town again.

The Columbia Valley, even in October, was misty and warm. It was, one of the other travelers told him, never really very cold there—something about a current that swung eastward from the coasts of Japan, bringing the mist laden tropic winds with it. And the valley was lovely beyond anything he had imagined.

On both sides of the river the farmlands spread out, incredibly black and rich. The farmhouses had that look of snugness, of comfort, the lands themselves the singing beauty of fields tilled by men who loved the soil with total passion. The men of 'forty-three had been solid men, good citizens, driven West by land hunger, which was a thing Bruce could understand. Gold fever was a sickness; but the love of land was a deep and profound and healthy thing, having in it not only the stalk and the foliage but the very roots of life itself.

But Bruce did not continue eastward up the Columbia. That he did not, was, like so many things in his life, due to a chance encounter. He was standing on the deck of the river steamer, watching the broad farmlands drift backwards, when a man, obviously a farmer by his dress came up and stood beside him.

"Planning to settle?" the man asked.

"No," Bruce said. Then seeing the open, friendly, completely honest face, he decided to risk it: "To tell the truth," he said, "I came up here looking for a wife. . . ."

"You've come to the right place, partner," the man said. "Lots of sweet little fillies in Oregon. 'Specially down my way in the Willamette Valley. More'n there's boys to husband 'em. Though, from the looks of you, I ain't rightly sure as how the Oregon girls would please you. . . ."

"Why not?" Bruce asked.

"They're country girls. Broad beamed, sturdy. Good complexions though. Damned pretty. But a city feller like you is apt to cotton to something slimmer and more delicate-like. . . ."

Bruce threw back his head and laughed aloud.

"City fellow!" he said, and spread out his broad, thick fingered, work hardened hands. "Ever see a city fellow with paws like these?"

"Bless my soul!" the man chuckled. "Had me fooled, boy. The way you're dressed and all. . . ."

"Bought these duds in Frisco," Bruce said. "Though where I come from, South Carolina, a planter is apt to dress kind of fine. By the way, the name's Bruce Harkness. . . ."

"Clifton Rayburn. But you call me Clift, boy. Tell you what— why don't you come and visit with me a spell? Got a farm down near Woodburn on the Willamette River. My girls is already married, but I'm certain sure they'd be happy to introduce you around. Ain't a thing on earth womenfolks love better than match-making, and that's a natural living fact. . . ."

"But," Bruce protested, "you don't know a thing about me. For all you know, Clift, I could be a swindler or a confidence man. . . ."

"Could be, but you ain't. Countryman lives too close to God and nature to be fooled by a face. And you got a good one: square and clean and honest. What do you say, boy?"

"I say fine and thank you mighty kindly," Bruce laughed. "I've been in California a long time. Got a little place up in Pleasant Valley that's a sight to see. But a farm ain't a farm without a woman on it. And if there's anything scarce in California it's women."

"Decent ones, leastways," Clift said dryly. "Plenty of the other kind. Gather you don't cotton to that. . . ."

"What I want, Clift," Bruce said quietly, "is a wife. There's a difference. . . ."

"Now I know you'll do," Clift Rayburn said. "The Missus'll be mighty proud to have you visit with us. She's been pining for company since the girls moved away. And we never did have no boys. . . ."

So it was done. Afterwards, Bruce was to look back on those two weeks with the Rayburns as among the happiest in his entire life. He was entertained in farmhouses up and down the valley. He went to an even dozen square dances. He was introduced to twenty-five or thirty buxom, uncomplicated farm girls, any one of whom would have made him a good wife and a fine mother for whatever children they might have had.

There was one in particular, a plain, pleasant girl with warm brown eyes and a delicate spray of freckles across a saucy, up-turned nose. Her mouth was wide and always smiling. She had hair the color of molasses, and a plump, pretty figure. Moreover, she liked him. Most of the girls did, but Sally made no bones about it. She was very nearly perfect for him and he knew it.

He drove her home from the last square dance in Clift Rayburn's buckboard. There was a moon silvering the Willamette, and the nightbirds were calling.

He ached to ask her, but he couldn't. He wanted to, knew it was the right thing for him, but he simply could not. Then, suddenly, he was aware that she was crying.

"Sally," he croaked. "Sally, honey, what's the matter?"

"You," she said. "You're going away, and I won't ever see you

again. I know you don't love me—that maybe you can't. But anyhow, it hurts. Right now, it hurts a little too doggoned much!"

Then she whirled and kissed his mouth. She hadn't had much
practice, but she had imagination. He settled back, staring at her.

"Sally," he got out, "I—"

"Don't talk," she said, and kissed him again. She sat there in
the moonlight, looking at him, the unashamed tears bright on her
cheeks.

"There's somebody else," she said. It was a statement, not a
question.

"Yes," Bruce said honestly, "but it's no good, Sally. She's already
married. And to one of my best friends at that. . . ."

"Then go back to California," Sally said calmly. "Go get yourself shut of her. Get her out of your system. Then come back to
me. I'll be waiting, Bruce. . . ."

Juana's face rose unbidden in his mind. He knew exactly when
he would be free of her—when he was dead and in his grave. It
wasn't fair to ask Sally to wait.

"Come back with me now," he said suddenly, hoarsely. "Sally, I
need you. I'll never be able to—without—"

"No," she said flatly. "I won't share you with her even in thought.
I can't marry a man who has a divided mind. When you don't
even think about her any more, when the sight of her don't plague
you—come back. Not before. . . ."

"All right," Bruce said. But he knew when that would be.

Never.

It was night when he reached Hailey's lodgings in Sacramento.
He found his friend busy arraying himself in full evening attire.

"Got a soup'n fish?" Hailey demanded gaily.

"Yes," Bruce said. "Had one made in Frisco. Don't know why,
except maybe to get married in, or buried in, more likely. Why?"

"We're going to a ball. This, old Hoss, is our night to howl!"

"A ball?" Bruce said; "with the number of women there are in
Sacramento? Who're we going to dance with—each other?"

"Nope. The fillies at the Annex. Got an engraved invitation from
the Madam, herself."

"No," Bruce said. "No more whorehouses, boy."

"You mean you been in one?"

"Yes," Bruce said honestly. "Only it was no good. The only thing I felt like doing was puking. . . ."

"Ol' Holy Ghost Harkness!" Hailey laughed. "C'mon, boy, get dressed in your new monkey suit. This is different. This here's a social evening. . . ."

"And what the devil is a social evening?"

"A Sacramento Institution. Frisco, too, I've been told. One night a month, the gals are given a heavy dose of respectability. Flowers, champagne, place cards, evening dress *de rigeur;* no rough stuff, no tiptoeing up the backstairs. Everybody comes: the Alcalde, the councilmen, everybody. Boy, it's a howl! It's so damned correct you want to bust out laughing; yet it's kind of pitiful, too. . . ."

"I can see how it would be," Bruce said.

"Those poor creatures get so much pleasure out of it. I've seen 'em cry, because it reminds them of their lives before. You know, Bruce, some of them kids is pretty decent. They were forced into that life by some of those smooth city boys that King hires to recruit 'em. Thought it was love, the real thing, you understand. A woman in love is capable of anything. Throws judgment, sense, morality right out of the window, and ends up in the Annexes of this world, weeping over what a fool she's been. So, put on your duds, boy; your virtue ain't in any danger tonight. . . ."

"Haven't any," Bruce grinned; "just got bad nerves, and a weak stomach. All right, Hail, I'll come. . . ."

The ballroom of the Annex was splendid. There were flowers everywhere, brought up from southern California, packed in damp straw, at fantastic expense. The girls were beautifully gowned, and very pretty, until Bruce saw their eyes. What was man, what was the nature of him that he could put a look like that into the eyes of these gentle creatures, born to soothe and comfort him? Bruce didn't know. He had the feeling that he shouldn't have come. Five minutes later, he was sure of it.

For Jo swept in on Rufus King's arm, clad in an evening dress far more daring than any worn by the Annex girls. It was orange red, almost the color of flame, falling over steel hoops, which made its skirt bell-shaped, to the floor. The bodice was a second skin, embroidered with rubies, real or false—Bruce couldn't tell. It was cut in extreme decolletage, leaving her snowy shoulders bare. Her

ostrich plume fan was dyed the same color as the dress; and the
long gloves, mounting above her elbows, were a trifle deeper red.
In her silvery hair was a fluff of plumes that matched her fan.

Bruce saw the red velvet ribbon about her throat, and the an-
tique locket pinned to it. He recognized that locket, and knowing
what it contained, felt the cold sickness rising inside him.

Rufus King saw him first, long before Jo did; and, for a moment,
strangely, the gambling master's habitual self-mastery deserted
him. He stopped dead, stared at Bruce, looking for all the world
like a man who has seen a ghost. The abrupt halt disturbed Jo.
She looked up at King, then followed the direction of his fixed
gaze.

Her glance flickered over Hailey, came to rest on Bruce's face,
held there, locked. The color drained down, out of her; and her
eyes were naked. Naked and defenseless and pitiful.

"I'm getting out of here," Bruce said.

"No," Hailey said. "Let them go. They'll leave now."

He was right. In a few minutes Bruce could see Jo talking ear-
nestly to King. She seemed to be pleading with him. King
shrugged, got up, took her arm. They went out of the door together.

"Too bad," Hailey said. "That headache must be right smart
painful. . . ."

"What headache?" Bruce growled.

"The one she got the minute she laid eyes on you. C'mon, let's
have fun!"

That, Bruce thought, is a pure Lord impossibility, now. . . .

But it wasn't as bad as he had thought it was going to be. He
selected as a partner a demure little brunette with permanently
downcast eyes. She answered his attempts to chat with her with
grave dignity, and her speech was cultivated and fine. It came to
Bruce that no woman of his acquaintance had had a command of
English of such pristine grammatical purity as this demure daughter of joy. He could talk as well as that himself when he had left
the University of South Carolina; but his friends had ridiculed him
out of it, holding it an affectation to talk better than a fieldhand.
He found himself, surprisingly, making the effort, forming his
phrases with the polish that befitted his very real culture—a culture he had concealed so well that only the Preacher had seen

through the pose, the night he had put the question to Bruce as to whether or not he had studied Greek.

Reckon I let slip before him, Bruce thought. Only man I know I can talk with about things more than two inches deep. But Lord God, this one's a sweet little thing. . . .

Hailey danced by with a big, flamboyant blonde in his arms. He paused beside Bruce, jigging in time to the music.

"The miners came in 'forty-nine," he sang, miles off key. "The whores in 'fifty-one. And when they got together, they made the native son!"

The big blonde laughed uproariously. Bruce looked at his partner. She was blushing, really blushing.

Sweet li'l' thing, Bruce thought, the champagne and the music and his years of loneliness working their alchemy in his blood. He didn't know it, but he was, at that moment, in the gravest danger he had ever faced in all his life.

The dinner was magnificent, accompanied by the incessant popping of champagne corks. Bruce toyed with his food, giving his full attention to the champagne and the little brunette. Her outlines were blurring before his sight. He peered at her owlishly, filled with a vast and overflowing tenderness.

"Nice li'l' girl like you," he said thickly, "shouldn't be in a place like this. 'S not right. Tell you what. I got a farm up in Pleasant Valley. Kind of lonely up there. . . ."

The girl looked at him, her eyes searching his face. They were very brown and clear and warm. Then they clouded. Slowly she shook her head. Bruce was already too far gone to notice that her precise grammar, her Young Ladies' Academy phrasing had deserted her.

"Look, Shorty," she said flatly. "You're a real nice feller. I'm going to tell you something. Must be drunk or I wouldn't be talking like this—spoiling my own chances . . ." She paused, peering at him with real compassion. "Most of the girls will tell you how they was dragged into this—and mostly it's a lie. They'll all tell you how they was taken advantage of by the minister's son and left in the family way—which ain't so either. . . ."

She stopped, gazing past him, her brown eyes soft with memory.

"Funny. He was the minister's son, though. Skinny little freckle-faced kid all of twelve years old with a face like an angel. I was thirteen. And it was me what took *him* up into the hayloft. Funniest thing you ever did see. There we was, hanging onto each other for dear life and crying cause we didn't know what to do . . . But after we got desperate enough, we found out—and Lord, it was fine. The roof fell in and the sky reeled around real crazy like—Lord, Lord but that li'l' skinny bastid was good. . . ."

She smiled to herself, remembering.

"Guess what I'm trying to say, Shorty, is that I was born a whore, like most whores and a mighty heap of women who're legally married, but who've got a mighty heap of charity to give out on the side. More than likely, I'll die one. You're a real sweet boy, Shorty —and you deserve something better than that. Now, Gawddamnit, get outa here before I change my mind!"

Bruce stood up, made her a huge bow, and meandered out of the door.

Hailey saw him go.

"That boy's in a bad way," he muttered. " 'Scuse me, Hon," he said to the big blonde, and getting up, went after Bruce.

He found him on the board sidewalk, leaning against a lamp post. There were tears in his eyes.

"What happened to you, Hoss?" Hailey said. "There you were, big as life and twice as ugly, having yourself one hell of a time; then all of a sudden. . . ."

"She didn't like me," Bruce said morosely. "She threw me out. . . ."

"Good thing she did," Hailey laughed. "Way you was going over there, I was scared you'd end up married to her. . . ."

"I—" Bruce began, then he stopped. The cold night air was beginning to clear his head. "Goddamnit all, anyhow!" he growled.

"Air's good, ain't it?" Hailey said.

"Yes," Bruce said. "Look, Hail—" But whatever he was about to say was never to be finished in this world; for at that moment the Mexican boy came out of the shadows and took his arm.

"*Venga, Señor!*" the boy wept. "Oh, *Señor, debe venir!*"

"I must come where?" Bruce said. Then he saw the boy was Jaime, the son of Preacher Rowe's hired hand.

The boy's answer washed over them in a flood of staccato Spanish too fast for Hailey to get more than the names.

"Pepe and Juana?" Hailey said. "The Preacher—hurt—I got that much. Lord God, Bruce, what did he say?"

"Our coats still inside?" Bruce said. By his carriage and his voice, Hailey knew he had become instantly, icily sober. "Going to be cold up there. I'll need a coat. Go get 'em, Hail. I'll wait. . . ."

"Lord God, Bruce—tell me!"

"Get the coats, Hail. I'll tell you on the way to the livery stable. Haven't got time now."

Hailey was back with the greatcoats in three minutes. They were fur-lined and warm. Gloves in the pockets, mufflers. But top hats wouldn't do, Bruce decided.

"Bruce, for God's sake!" Hailey said.

"Pepe found gold on my place. Or somebody said he did. Claim jumpers got there last night. Tied up Pepe. Didn't find any gold so there was a disturbance. The Preacher got shot. He—he's dead, Hail. . . ."

"Goddamnit!" Hailey whispered. "Goddamnit to hell!"

"Most of the boys didn't hold with killing a clergyman. There was a dispute between them and their leaders. A big man, Terry Casey, most likely—held 'em off at gunpoint. Then he and another big man—"

"Ted Peterson!" Hailey said.

"Took off with Pepe and—Juana, along with two other bastards. The house was burnt. The barn, likewise. Stock slaughtered. And me down here, dancing in a whorehouse!"

"My fault," Hailey said grimly. "C'mon boy, let's go wake up that stablekeeper."

Five minutes later, the stablekeeper was staring at them, groggy with sleep, and hopping mad.

"Damn it all!" he growled; "there's limits! A man got to have his sleep. . . ."

"Shut up," Bruce said coldly, "and trot out the fastest cayuse you got. I'll buy him. You can name your price. After I get through with him, he won't be worth shooting. . . ."

"Two nags," Hailey said.

"No, Hail," Bruce said. "You're staying here."

"The hell I am! I'm in on this, too, boy!"

"That's why you're staying. You're going to leave Rufus King free to do some more damage?"

"Damn my soul! Of course! The way he looked at you—like he'd
seen a ghost or something. . . ."

"He had," Bruce said. "I was supposed to be inside that house—
roasting, instead of at the ball."

"Got him!" Hailey exulted. "Got him! Done made his slip! Same
one most men make. A woman! He was so scared that little twitch-
tail bit o' fluff was going to get out of his hands that he tried
another little round of murder. . . ."

"The Preacher," Bruce whispered. "And, by God, if they've so
much as touched Juana, I'll—"

Hailey's hand went inside his coat pocket, and came out with
the little Colt.

"Here, boy," he said. "And don't tell me nothing stupid about
not needing no gun!"

Bruce took the little revolver, pocketed it.

"Thanks, Hail," he said.

"Here's your hoss," the stablekeeper said. "That'll be two thousand dollars. You said I could name my price. . . ."

Bruce paid him without a murmur.

"See you, Hailey," he said. "Take care of the kid. . . ."

Then he was off, down the street; the white of his stiff-bosomed
shirt front showing in flashes, as he pounded past the street lamps.

He was in the outskirts of Marysville before morning, when the
horse collapsed under him. He jumped free, and watched the
beast thrashing about, its eyes rolling drunkenly, covered all over
with foam, pawing the earth feebly, unable to rise. He walked
up to the beast, and put the muzzle of the revolver into its ear.
But he turned away his head as he pulled the trigger. It was hard
to kill a horse that had served him faithfully to the death. But
merciful. The beast was already dying, before he fired, the foam
from its nostrils flecked with red.

He made his way into the town on foot, got Brother Nate up.
The two of them rode for the Valley together, on fresh mounts.
Nate had a rifle, and a hunter's outfit, complete with coonskin
cap, for Bruce, tied up in his saddle roll. Bruce wouldn't stop to
put them on.

"Take it easy, boy," Nate growled. "We can't replace these
horses. Ride 'em to death like you did that other one, and we'll
have to walk. . . ."

"Those bastards," Bruce whispered. "You know what they do to women, Nate—'specially Mexican women . . . If they've touched Juana—"

"In love with her, ain't you, son? Really in love," he said gently.

"Yes," Bruce said. "Yes, damn it, I am!"

The farm was deserted. The house still stood because it was built of adobe, but it lacked roof and rafters and windows. The barn was a smouldering pile of embers from which a wisp of smoke rose straight up into an icy, leaden sky.

Nate sniffed the air.

"Gonna snow," he said.

"Come on, Nate!" Bruce said.

They found Josefina cowering in the kitchen of the Preacher's house. The old man lay upon the bed, looking as though he were asleep. He held the Bible against his chest. There was a little round hole through the Bible.

"Jesus brought him home this morning," Josefina whispered, crossing herself. "And now he has ridden to bear the word to Joaquin. . . ."

Bruce looked at her.

"Juana?" he croaked.

"Below. She sleeps, I think. *La Pobrecita*—she—"

But Bruce was gone, tearing down the cellar stairs.

Juana sat up, her black eyes wide with terror. She was bruised all over her face. Her clothing was in rags. There were dried clots of blood from a hundred scratches on her arms and legs.

Bruce came toward her, his lips moving, shaping her name. But he couldn't say it. He tried, but he could not.

She got up slowly, painfully. In two strides, Bruce reached her. His arms swept out, crushing her to him. He hung there holding her, and crying.

"Juana," he whispered; "oh, Juana mia, I—"

Then he felt the tears on her face mingling with his own. And then, incredibly, her mouth was on his, moving with a tenderness so great he had not dreamed such a thing existed in this world; so gentle-sweet that the pain of recognition, of knowing, was beyond belief or bearing or even hope.

He stepped back.

"*Lo siento mucho,* Juana," he said. "For this I have much sorrow —and also much shame. Forgive me, *Querísima,* for I—"

"For this," her voice caressed him, "there is neither shame nor sorrow; for when has it been needful to be ashamed of love? I— I have known how you felt a long time, *Señor.* I have had much sorrow that I could not—"

"That you could not, what, Juana?" Bruce said.

"To say that," she whispered, "remains shameful still. Both shameful, and a sin. . . ."

"Pepe!" Bruce said. "Lord God, Juana, tell me—"

"I do not know. They took him with them. Two of them Pepe recognized. He told me to tell you they were *esos brutos grandes,* Terry Casey and Ted Peterson. . . ."

"Thought as much," Bruce said. "Go on, *Lindísima.* . . ."

"You must not," Juana whispered, "call me those things, *mi Patrón.* Even though I was feeble and answered the cry of my heart, you must not. Neither *Querísima* nor *Lindísima* nor any of those so lovely words of love that your voice with its *si dulce accento Americano* makes music of in the saying. *Por favor, Señor* Bruce, you must not. . . ."

"Sorry," Bruce said. "Please go on, Juana."

"There were very many of them. They had been told that Pepe found gold in your little river which was a lie. I heard them say the name of this man *el Rey* who—"

Bruce frowned. Then he remembered Pepe's habit of translating English names into Spanish. He had probably always said it thus to Juana. El Rey—the King. Rufus King. No room for doubting now.

"They were very angry when they found no gold. They wrecked your so beautiful *rancho, Señor,* burning the house and the barn. It was the flames that brought *el* Padrecito Rowe. He talked to them, mounted on a fallen tree. They, most of them, were inclined to listen to *un Padre;* but those big ones, filled with that vileness of drunkenness and additionally with lust, shouted at him; and when he rebuked them with gravity and dignity, *el Hijo de Pedro*—Peterson, no?—shot him. . . ."

"With lust," Bruce grated. "Tell me, Juana—did they—?"

She smiled at him. Her smile put a warmth at the core of his heart; and his blood, flowing, made a singing.

"No. They tried. But they were in the midst of this *gran discusion* with the others, who were shocked and fearful over the enormity of killing a *Padre*. For this reason they sent me on toward this *rancho* with one man, smaller than the others for a guard. Then they departed with Pepe, telling the little one to meet them at the cave. . . ."

"The cave!" Bruce said. "You make riddles, Juana. . . ."

"No, *mi Patrón*. This was part of the cleverness of Pepe, who, when he needs it, has this tremendous sagacity. He told them—"

"No," Bruce snapped. "Tell me what happened to you, *Almacita*. . . ."

Her eyes rebuked him, gently.

"I'm sorry. No more endearing terms. Go on."

"They had tied my hands; but I am, as Pepe says all women are, part mule. So I kicked him, so that he fell down that deep gulch, forgetting I was tied to him. I was pulled down with him. But he was unconscious. So I worked a long time to free my hands. I got them loose finally, leaving them like this—"

She held them out to Bruce, and he saw how the lariat had taken all the skin off the back of them, stripping it off as one removes a glove. And he caught them in his own, and bent over them, kissing them in an agony of tenderness and compassion and of love, until he felt the trembling in them run like a galvanetic current up her arms, until she trembled all over like an aspen in a rising wind; and, raising his gaze to her face, he saw that her eyes were bright with a rush of tears.

"Juana," he whispered. "*Juanacita mia*—I have no right; no right. . . ."

But the tortured hands came out to him, touching his face more gently than a breath, both palms lying along the slant of his cheeks, drawing, by a pressure so nearly imperceptible, his face toward hers, that he was half sure he imagined it; but her mouth on his was a reality beyond imagination, beyond belief: that sweet sighing warm softness for which no words of comparison existed in any language spoken of men; that slow aching, unbearably poignant tenderness which stopped his heart, his breath, performed its miracle, drawing him through his agony of desire into tranquillity, past his torment into peace. . . .

"Nor I, this," she said. "But the Merciful God surely cannot deny us even so little—And now, thou knowest. . . ."

"Yes," he said; "now, I know. . . ."

They stood there, looking at each other.

"Tell me the rest of it, Juana," he said.

"Ah, *si*. This *pistolero* regained his senses as I was standing there, holding my hands and trying to dominate the pain. He caught at me, and I fought him. We tumbled over and over among the rocks until I was torn like this. I found a stone and hammered at his face until it was a face no longer. I left him there, screaming like a woman in childbirth, and came here. That is all."

His eyes held hers. He stood there, a long time, before he got it out.

"And Pepe?" he said.

"Pepe—lied to them. He told them that they had been misinformed. That truly he had found gold greater than their imagining, the motherlode that all men seek; but not upon your *rancho*. He showed them those nuggets you brought back with you, and offered to lead them to the place high in the mountains, beyond the cave, where the gold was, if they would spare his life. . . ."

"Good God!" Bruce said. "But when they don't find it, they will—"

"Kill him," Juana said gravely, "unless he has success in his intention which is clearly to lead them, unskilled as they are, over gorges and crevasses into which he may force them to fall. I think he can do this. Pepe is the finest mountaineer in all the world. I think truly that he can do it, but—"

"But what, Juana?"

"Pepe was but lightly dressed. And even down here, it is cold. If he is injured, even a little—"

She stopped, searching his face with her eyes, reading in it the black and bitter struggle that mounted in him like a storm; the temptation visible as the mark of Cain upon his forehead.

She had kissed his mouth until he was branded with her tenderness; she had called him 'thou' which in Spanish is a pledge unto the death. And now, she stood there placing this thing squarely between them, balancing his love for her against the temptation to do nothing, to let Pepe die up there in the white silences, slow drifting down the wind; balancing her husband's life against her certitude that he could not do this thing, against her knowledge of the kind of man he was, against his honor and his pride.

She saw his shoulders sag.

"I must go and change into mountain clothing," he said simply. "As thou hast said—it will be cold—"

She stood there, looking at him, and in her eyes there was something that troubled him to look at: a longing deep as earth, commingled with pure heartbreak, shattering itself against the icy pinnacles of her confusion and her grief. Then something else came—a pride in him, a glory in the kind of man he was, that grew and grew until it dominated the confusion and the grief, rose even above the longing and the pain.

"Yes," she said. "You must go."

She came to him, and kissed him, once more, very simply.

"*Vaya con Dios,* Bruce," she said. "Go with God!"

And as he went from her, she added softly, shaping the words just below the level of sound:

"With God. And with all that remains of this—my heart. . . ."

12

THEY BURIED THE Preacher that same night, not far from the house, in the midst of the rolling fields he had so loved. Brother Nate said a few words, and read a passage of Scriptures, his gruff voice choked with tears. And each of them said a prayer for him: Nate and Bruce and Jesus and Josefina and Juana. Except for Nate, no one prayed aloud.

Kind of presumptuous, Bruce thought as he knelt there; a man like me, praying for a man like you. Reckon if there ever were a Saint, you were. You told me I was in my time of testing. I still am, Preacher. And I'm sick and hurt and scared inside and I don't know what to do. When you see the Good Lord, ask Him for me. I'm too mixed up to pray directly. Besides you can put it better than I can. Ask Him if the testing extends out beyond the end of hope. Ask Him that. And tell Him—

But that, Bruce could say himself: "Father, into Thy Hands do I commend my spirit." And: "Not my will, but Thine, be done. . . ."

Then he had gone back into the house, not telling Nate what he was going to do, leaving the grief-stricken storekeeper brooding by the fire in the kitchen, secure in the belief that they would start the search for Pepe in the morning. He went directly into the Preacher's bedroom, and stripped off his ruined and dirty evening clothes, which had served him in the space of days, as the garb of worldly pleasure and the sober garments of funeral prayer; he began to dress himself in the fur-lined outfit of the mountain men. When he was fully clothed, he kicked aside his evening clothes, feeling as he did so, his boot strike something hard. He bent down and drew out the revolver. He stood there looking at it, lying in his hand, lovely with the deadly loveliness of engraved blued steel and carved ivory grips; and remembering the little hole, brown about the edges, through the tooled morocco binding of the Preacher's Bible—that same Bible that the remorseful friends of the can-can dancer had given the old man—he felt cold suddenly, cold and sick.

He lifted his eyes toward the place where the mountains were, though he could not see them through the night.

"All right," he said. "It's come to where to do the only decent thing, the only thing I can stomach doing, I've got to end my last chance. So I'll play it Your way, Lord. . . ."

He tossed the pistol onto the bed. "Into Your hands—really into Your Hands . . ." he whispered. Then, pushing open the door, he went out into the night.

And in the morning, Juana found the pistol there. She stood there, looking at it.

He—he forgot, she told herself; but even as she thought that, she knew that Bruce had not forgotten the weapon. She did not move, staring at it, probing into his mind, as she conceived of it, for his motive. Then her bandaged hands flew to her throat.

The *rubia* had come, she knew that. This milk-pale blond American had come. Pepe had seen her, had made poetry, speaking, describing her beauty. And made also blue smoke in the air with his invectives, telling of her falseness, of how she had betrayed *el Patrón*, turned harlot for the lure of gold. . . .

He—this Patrón of hers, changed now into man and lover, who could melt her living flesh into pure tenderness since the day she had seen his lust, his woman hunger for her, transformed into this miracle of love, containing still his lust, his hunger, but transmuting them into this thing that it was death itself to have to deny: this need for all of her, her body and her spirit; the mere comfort of her presence—a finger's touch, even, the smallest smile—which she must in honor deny him, asking him out of that same honor to end any chance that they could ever love—he, then, had left his weapon lying there and gone out into the night, the cold, to face three *gran pistoleros,* with the sick lust of killing festering in their hearts—unarmed. . . .

I, she wept inside her heart, I condemned him! I, not this pale
harlot of a *rubia!* He turned to her only because of the lack of my
own love . . . It would have been better to have betrayed Pepe,
and gone to God with that sin on my soul—than this, than this!

She snatched up the Colt in her stiff and painful fingers, thrust
it into the waistband of her skirt; then she turned running, going
into Josefina's room, taking the woman's coat and gloves, a shawl
for her head. Then to the barn, taking the Preacher's ancient nag,
saddling him, oblivious of the pain in her stiffened fingers, mounting, riding away from there toward the cloud shrouded mountains,
whispering:

"Thou—thou art not much, *caballo;* but this day thou must recall thy youth. Think that thou art young and strong and take me
there, oh *caballocito viejo*—for upon thine ancient bones, and
what I have left of strength rests Pepe's life—and his. . . ."

They went up the sheer face of the rocks at right angles to the
trail. Pepe was at the head of the line, each of the four of them
bound to one another with ropes.

Why does not the snow come? he thought. Oh *Padre Dios,* why
have You not sent the snow?

He went up, digging hand and toe holds with the knife they
had allowed him to keep, after he had convinced them of its absolute necessity for the work, saying: "But, *Señores,* what could
one man with a knife do against three with guns even if I were so
mad to try?"

He needed the snow. The rocks were dry and not at all slippery.
Even with this sickness of heights showing greenly in their faces,
he doubted that he could dislodge them without the snow. Each
time they crossed the narrow shelf of the trail, he grew cold with
fear that they would recognize it for what it was: a trail, even a
fairly easy trail down which he and Bruce had been able to de-
scend an enormously heavy mountain sheep without too much
danger. It wound upward in sharp spirals along the same route
which he led them by this murderously brutal climb over rock
faces sheer enough to defeat a fly.

But their gold lust dulled their senses, dominated even their
normal human fear of heights, of falling; leading them up a climb

that should have been beyond their powers, until Pepe saw despairingly that the precipices were behind them, that above this steep slope up which they could nevertheless walk almost upright instead of having to crawl, there was only one more, a little face of not more than fifty feet high, and they would have reached the mountain's top, and his end.

This one, then. A man falling from fifty feet, could not regain his feet before he rolled over the edge into a drop of half a mile. This one.

"Our Father," Pepe prayed silently, "and our Holy Mother who has compassion on sinners; and *Jesusito,* for Whose garments, gamblers like me cast lots. . . ."

Then he went up the rock face slowly, hoping he had not dulled the blade too much. And there on the edge, as though the Good God Himself had provided it, he saw what he needed at last: a projection of rock around which a man could hook one arm and hold on long enough against the shock and pull of all that weight falling to—

He reached it, hooked his left arm around it, rested.

"One moment, *Señores,*" he panted. "I am very tired—and this requires strength. . . ."

They waited, sweat-soaked despite the cold, clinging to the little holds he had dug, their eyes green and sick with terror, until Pepe, gathering the last ounce of his strength, kicked down and out with terrible force, catching Ted Peterson, who was next to him, full in the face, sending the three of them out and down until the jerk of their falling weight made the rope bite into his middle until he thought it would cut him in half; and he, hanging there with a strength greater than he had, sawed at the rope while they screamed at him, groping for their pistols, but not having enough time before the razor sharp edge he had preserved with such care parted the final strand, and he was free.

He saw them rolling down the slope, toward the edge. He watched them with satisfaction and joy and weariness and horror, seeing Ted Peterson brought up hard by a miracle against the one boulder in their path, while the others, Terry Casey and the man whose name he did not know went on over, swinging from Ted as they had swung from him.

He saw Ted's teeth show white, and heard them crying, while

Ted's hands moved, coming out with his sheaf knife, hanging there.

"Die, you bastards!" he called. "Now I'll have it all!" And then he cut them loose.

Pepe saw the big man try to rise. But his right leg doubled grotesquely under him. He slashed at his pants with the knife, and Pepe saw the white of his thigh bone, sticking raggedly, sickeningly through his flesh.

Pepe caught air into his lungs and hauled himself up onto the ledge, leaning back upright against the mountain wall, too sick-weak to move, the reaction gripping him. And below him, Ted Peterson brought his big Colt Dragoon out, sighted it with care and called:

"Come get me, you 'Greaser' bastard! Come get me off of here!"

Mutely, Pepe shook his head.

"No," he whispered. "No!"

The walls of rock reverberated with the guncrash. The sledgehammer blow smashed Pepe back against the mountain wall; and then, bending over, like a man bowing to a lovely woman, feeling in his guts, low down, the white hot stab of pain, Pepe went down upon the trail.

He lay there on the ledge, completely hidden from Ted Peterson's fire, feeling the death in him. His fingers moved feeling for the wound. It was low—very low, just above the groin. A man could live for days with a wound like that, before he died raving from the pain. He unwound his bandana from his neck, and thrust it into the wound to stop the bleeding. But he could feel it running inside him, and the weakness in his flesh was almost greater than his desperation, his hope.

He started crawling down the trail, leaving a smear of blood behind him. He got two full yards before all the light there had ever been in the world spilled abruptly out of the sky.

And it was there that Bruce Harkness found him. He knelt beside Pepe, seeing that he lived, feeling the fever already burning in his flesh. Then, as tenderly as a father with a child, he lifted Pepe's slender form onto his broad shoulders and started down. And then he heard his name.

"Bruce!" Ted Peterson called. "Bruce!"

Bruce turned and saw him there.

"Come get me," Ted said; "put that 'Greaser' bastard down and come get me. He's done—and I've got a chance. I'll make it up to you. I swear it. Pay you for the damage we done. . . ."

Bruce stood there, looking at him, his eyes as cold as death.

"I'll give Jo a divorce—fix that sonofabitch, King, so he'll never get out of jail, I'll—"

"No," Bruce said. "No choice, Ted. I can only take one now. And Pepe is my friend . . ." He stood there, looking down; then that thing in him he had always had, but which the Preacher had brought to the surface, to the level of consciousness, rose in him. That vast peace of soul too big for anger or hatred or revenge.

"Wait," he said, and eased Pepe down again. He took off his fur-lined coat and hurled it down within reach of Ted's outstretched hand. "Cover yourself with that," he said. "Soon as I get Pepe bedded down and comfortable in the cave, I'll come back for you. . . ."

Ted lay there, staring at the coat. And because at bottom men live and die by their beliefs, by what they are, he could not believe this thing. It was beyond his bone-deep knowledge of the totality of human selfishness; it shattered against his impenetrable disbelief that there was any man living who walked in honor and in grace.

He jerked the Colt out, pointed it.

"Come get me!" he screamed. "Leave me here to die, you bastard, and I'll take you with me!"

"Don't be a fool, Ted," Bruce said mildly. "Kill me, and you really don't have a chance. . . ."

Then he lifted Pepe once more to his shoulders and started down the trail.

Ted Peterson watched them go. He let Bruce get twenty yards down the trail before his rage, his terror overcame him, his disbelief in man, judged by the only standards that he had: himself. He sighted carefully on the middle of Bruce's broad back, and jerked the trigger. Jerked it, not squeezed it as he should have for accuracy, so that the heavy ball went through Bruce's left side, far out, missing his vital organs; but spinning him head over heels, falling, rolling, and Pepe rolling with him, limp as a doll of rags.

The slope took them down, down to where no gun on earth could reach them. And Bruce, lying there, felt the two wounds, where the heavy calibre ball had gone in and come out. He jerked out his kerchief and jammed it into the wound, cut off one shirt tail with his penknife and made a wad which he pressed against the wound in his back. But he could feel the strength going out of him—now, when of all times, he needed strength.

He got his arms under Pepe, wormed his way beneath the inert body of his friend. He came up to his knees, feeling the tearing inside him, the pain that knotted his guts and popped the sweat out on his forehead. But he came on up, pulled up, he was sure by the Preacher's invisible hand, seeing as he did so, the first downy flakes steal down the leaden sky. And knowing what that meant, he went down that trail, lurching like a drunken man, falling and getting up, and falling again and getting up and staggering on until the black mouth of the cave was in sight. The last twenty yards, he crawled, dragging Pepe behind him.

He lay inside in the icy dark, seeing the curtain of white blotting out all vision; remembering with bitter sorrow that he had stampeded the horses the men had left, not thinking that he would need one to take Pepe down, knowing that no horse living could take the weight of both of them down that trail in the snow, if, indeed, he could gather strength to ride.

But now, there were more immediate things: the fire and Pepe's wounds. He had no idea how hard such simple things could be to do with a hole through his guts. But he accomplished them finally, dominating by sheer force of will the agony that every movement cost him. He made Pepe as comfortable as he could, and lay down by the fire, too hurt sick to even attend to his own. He kept the fire going as long as he could, cursing the puerile pride that had made him hide his intention from Brother Nate, ignoring at the same time, the compassion that had made him unwilling to endanger the older man.

Juana will tell him, he thought. And he will come with Jesus and the others; because I cannot—I cannot—

And the night was a velvet curtain, shutting out the sky.

When Juana reached them, the fire was dead, and the two of them half frozen. She worked quickly, stifling the hysteria that rose in her, getting the fire going. She saw that Pepe's wound was already dressed; but that Bruce's bled still, in a stubborn, steady flow. Her petticoat was clean, and white. It would serve admirably. But water?

She saw the pail and seized it, racing out into the whining wilderness of snow, scooping the snow up with her aching hands, paying no attention to the ache. Then she set the pail over the fire to melt the snow. It would take time. The snow must not only melt, but the water must become hot. Then she remembered the horses. She went out and got them. Bruce's was in a bad way; but her own had still not been too long in the cold. As she tugged at the bridles, she heard far off and faint, a sound coming down the wind like someone crying. She listened, but it did not come again. She pulled the animals into the cave, past the fire, not knowing that what she had heard was Ted Peterson taking leave of his misspent, twisted life.

The water was hot now. She bathed Bruce's wounds, holding hard against her grief and pain; then Pepe's, easing them both, piling over them the blankets that Pepe had stored there long ago, pushing the saddle rolls under their heads.

She sat there, watching them. Bruce's eyes flickered open. He smiled at her; then they fluttered shut again.

Juana sat there staring at the horses and what was in her heart was a hurt greater than both their wounds. One extra horse. Enough to take one down, when the snow slackened in the morning. One—not two. She would have to ride in order to even get one down safely. And neither horse could carry the weight of two all but lifeless men through the drifts. She bathed their faces with water. She forced a few trickles down their throats. Pepe's skin was fire-hot with fever. He started talking suddenly, raving: "Joaquin will come—I sent him word—I told him—" The rest was an incomprehensible jumble, trailing off into silence.

Slowly Juana got to her knees and lifted her face toward the rocky ceiling. She folded her hands and began to pray very quietly, not even realizing that she spoke aloud.

And drifting out of his private darkness, Bruce heard her.

"Sainted Mother of God, show me the thing I must do; because the one I leave behind must die. Why have You put upon me this hard choice, tell me, *Madre mia,* why?

"Pepe is good and nearly always gentle with me, beating me only when I greatly merited it. And I have loved him all these years very truly and tenderly. But more, Little Mother of Jesus, with a mother's love for a gay and laughing boy, than with a woman's love for a man. . . .

"But, this other—*mi Bruce*—Oh, *si, si, Madrecita!* Mine! Is a man. So much man, so enormously much man, with the terrible maleness in him that is a glory, because he dominates it with courage and with honor. And him, I love—as a woman should love a man—with all my heart, with *mi espiritu,* my life, my soul. . . .

"And like that, too. I confess it. You were a woman once, *mi Madre;* you must know. Until my body cries from wanting his body; until I think his touch would stop my heart. . . .

"And Thou hast put upon me the choice between them! Between my good and gentle Pepe, for whom I have still this great fondness; and this man, *si muy macho,* so much male, that he makes of me *asi hembra,* a wild female thing, his mate, with but a look. Between even the vows I made before Our Father God, in His Own Church, and this terrible hunger in the blood. . . .

"Oh *Madrecita mia,* dear, sweet little Mother of God—have pity upon me! Have pity!"

He could not bear it. He could not support the sight of her face, tear-streaked in the firelight. He turned his face away from her, and looked straight into Pepe's eyes, wide open, cool, and sane.

But that was unbearable, too; so he closed his own, retreating easily, instantly into darkness.

Juana sat there, feeling the weariness in her flesh growing greater even than her pain and her confusion. She banked the fire, to keep it through the night. She lay down beside it; and though she did not think she could, she slept.

Sometime during the night, Pepe Córdoba woke up, raving: "I must find Joaquin! I must! He will save us—he will not let us die. . . ."

He started crawling toward the mouth of the cave, impelled by the furious heat of fever, by his faith in Joaquin, by his own still fierce pride.

But outside, he made a scant yard, before the icy blast of sleet-laden wind sobered him. He realized that he was outside, and half turned to crawl back again; then he remembered why he had come, and with that, starkly, Juana's prayer.

He lifted his face into the whining sleet and smiled.

"Mother of God," he whispered, "*Mira!* I do not take my life, for that is a sin. I merely place it in Your hands. If You do not allow me to reach the horses, I will know that You have willed it so . . . That Juana may have her happiness with this good and great and just man, who is so very truly my friend. . . ."

He crawled on, not knowing he could not find the horses, not even realizing that they were already inside, where Juana had brought them to keep them warm.

And in the morning, Juana found him. He was only five yards beyond the opening of the cave.

She was still kneeling there beside him, the tears freezing on her face, when Brother Nate and Jesus and a rescue party from Grass Valley came stumbling up the trail.

13

Jo SAT IN the private office with Rufus King, helping him count the last night's take. She was very good with figures, and he had entrusted her with all the bookkeeping. Since that night, two weeks ago, that she had seen Bruce at the Annex, dressed in finest evening wear, and looking like the Carolina gentleman she remembered, she had made no overt show of the rebellion in her heart; she waited, and watched, and was still.

"Getting better all the time!" he said exultingly. "Very soon, Jo, you and I are going to be able to retire to a life of leisurely extravagance. Back East again. New York, Boston, Saratoga . . . After that, Europe. How does that strike you, Doll?"

"Just fine, Rufe," she said.

"You don't seem overly enthusiastic," he began. "Oh, damn! Will you see who that is, Jo? Shoo them away, whoever they are. Find out what they want, and tell them I'll see them tonight. . . ."

"Yes, Rufe," Jo said, and went out through the little door that opened behind the Horseshoe Bar.

The two Mexicans stood there, cigarettes dangling from their lips. They were so small and skinny and bowlegged that Jo could hardly keep from laughing—until she saw their eyes.

"What—" she got out—"What do you want?"

"*El Señor* King, *por favor*," the taller one said pleasantly, that is, if a man an inch shorter than she was could be considered tall.

"Why do you want to see him?" she whispered.

"Business," the Mexican shrugged. "He is, *quizás*, here?"

She looked into their eyes and she knew. Slowly, she smiled.

"He's in there," she said flatly. "Go right on in—"

Then she walked around the end of the bar and let them pass. She kept on walking without haste even after she could hear King's voice, hoarse and animal-like with terror, begging:

"If it's money you want—take it! Look, there're millions here—millions! You can have it all. . . ."

Then, short, and ugly, and muffled, the shot.

Jo stood on the sidewalk. I'll go to Hailey Burke, she thought. He'll take me to Bruce—he'll—

The two Mexicans came out of the Blue Diamond, walking very slowly. The cigarettes still dangled, only a trifle shorter now. They saw her there and stopped.

"*Gracias tanto, Señorita*," the taller one said. As he pushed back his sombrero, Jo saw that he had only three fingers on his right hand. "And when you see *el Señor* Harkness, tell him this: Joaquin never deserts his friends. *Adios, Linda!*"

Then they mounted, and moved off at a slow trot, down the street.

Jo waited. She wanted to give them all the time they needed. Then she crossed the street to Hailey's office. He was not there. So she walked calmly down to the prison brig, anchored in the river, that still served Sacramento as a jail, and found the Sheriff.

"You'd better come," she said. "I think that Mr. King has been shot. . . ."

They let her go, finally, after taking down her minute description of the two men, a description as completely false as she was able to make it, giving the murderers' heights as six feet and six feet two respectively, their coloring as fair, as far as she had been able to see behind the masks they'd worn, their purpose, robbery. In this she made a serious error, for nothing had been touched. More, it gave birth to the legend that was to be told all over California with a thousand variations: Manuel Garcia, Three Fingered Jack, had stuffed a bag of gold dust into King's mouth to shut off his cries, thus giving to King unearned immortality as the man who choked to death on a million dollars' worth of dust. This wasn't true at all—both because no single sack could possibly hold more than a few hundred dollars' worth—a fact which they should have known—and because a single bullet killed him.

She got out of that one, too; because she honestly didn't know why her paramour had been killed. But she hadn't the slightest intention of helping them find and hang the men who had delivered her from her shameful servitude.

She climbed the stairs to the apartment and changed into her riding habit. Then she crossed the street again to the hotel and gave orders that all her things be moved to their best suite at once. She took only the money that King had paid her for her work, leaving in a neat pile the fortune in jewelry and clothing he had bought her; whereupon Tildy promptly stole them, to be relieved of them in her turn, when her Chileno lover decamped, leaving her to go back to work as a maidservant.

Jo rented a horse from the livery stable, and rode up to Marysville, spending the night there. In the morning, after inquiring the whereabouts of Bruce's farm, she rode up into Pleasant Valley. She saw the smoke curling from the chimney of the lovely adobe house. The roof was new and the windows back in place, though she did not know that then. Brother Nate and a crew of Bruce's friends from Marysville had restored the house in three short days of herculean labor. Even the barn was beginning to rise again.

She got down from the horse, and walked up to the house. It seemed deserted, except for the smoke, so she looked in the window. Then she saw it, the death of all her hopes: Bruce sitting blanket-wrapped in a great chair, and the tawny Mexican girl with hair like night, bending over him, kissing his mouth as though there could be no end to the joy she found there.

Jo reeled back from the window, whirled, and ran straight into Hailey Burke's arms.

"I'm sorry," he said. "But I couldn't help seeing that. I was away when you came, at the Mayor's house still trying to convince him to take some action against King. No luck. Only somebody saved me the trouble. . . ."

"Yes," Jo whispered. "Somebody did. . . ."

"Come on, let's go say howdy to Bruce and Juana. They're married, Jo. Juana feels terrible to have married again, so soon after—Pepe's death. But she had to stay with Bruce to nurse him back to health; and they were going to later, anyhow; so getting around scandal seemed wiser than respecting grief. And she is grieved, truly she is. . . ."

"Not from what I saw," Jo said tartly. "But Rufe taught me about women. Nothing they do surprises me. Incidentally, Mr. Burke, I've never even heard of these people before; either this Pepe or this Juana. I was under the flattering illusion that Bruce was up here pining—for me. . . ."

"He was," Hailey said. "It wasn't until after—that day we came into the Diamond that he turned consciously toward Juana. Though, if you'll pardon my seeming lack of gentleness with your feelings, Ma'am, I think he's been in love with her from almost the first day he met her. Only he didn't know it, or had too much respect for Pepe, or both . . . You'll come in?"

"No," Jo whispered. "I—I couldn't, Hailey—Oh, pardon me! It's just—"

"It's just what, Jo?" he asked gravely.

"That it seems I've known you all my life. You're such a comfortable person, Mr. Burke. . . ."

"Hailey, please. We're friends, aren't we?"

"Friends?" she said, the pain moving through her voice. "You could be friends with—with a woman like me, Hailey? Even knowing. . . ."

"I'm neither judge nor jury, Jo. Certainly not executioner. Will you wait for me by the gate? I must at least say hello. . . ."

"Of course. But Hailey, please don't tell them I was here— please!"

"As you like," he said, and turning, went into the house.

Jo waited the full half hour it took him to come out again. She didn't know why she waited; but she did.

They rode towards Marysville, almost without talking. But the silence between them was without tension. About halfway down, Hailey turned to her.

"I got some more news for you, Jo," he said. "And being no hypocrite, I won't pretty it up with all the polite pretensions about how sorry I am. I'm not sorry. I'm plumb, downright glad."

Then he looked straight into her eyes and said it:

"You're a widow, too, now, Jo."

"Oh!" she whispered. "How—? What happened? Tell me?"

He told her then, all of it, hiding nothing:

"When they found him, he was covered with Bruce's greatcoat— the same coat that Bruce had risked freezing to leave with him

'til he could get back and save him. But Ted didn't believe Bruce
was coming back, couldn't believe any man could be as decent
as Bruce actually is—so he shot him . . . And Bruce Harkness
went down to that cave with Pepe on his back, bleeding like a
pig all the time, when he had the best excuse in the world to drop
Pepe and make damn' sure he'd get Juana . . . Only Bruce ain't
like that. . . ."

He turned to her, his eyes filled with pride and awe.

"It is hard to believe, ain't it?" he said. "Knowing that boy, being
his friend, has been the greatest privilege I've ever had. . . ."

"And mine, too," Jo said. "Even if I did throw it away . . . Tell
me, Hailey, what became of that Mexican girl who Ted—?"

"Gone. Skipped. Loaded down with dust that your sainted husband stole. Gals like little Mercedes are like cats. They always
land on their feet."

"Don't be so hard on her," Jo whispered. "You make me afraid
of you. After all, she was as good as I am. No—better. If you're
that strict with her, I don't see how—"

"I can be nice to you? Don't aim to be—not too nice anyhow.
One of the reasons why I'm glad you didn't get to Bruce. He ain't
polecat enough to handle you. What you need, Jo, is a *hombre*
like me who'd let you stand upright just long enough to cook our
supper, and who'd beat the living daylights out of you if I ever
caught you looking sidewise at another man!"

"Cut out the supper," she mocked him—and herself, knowing
the truth lay at the heart of her jest. "Hire a cook who'd bring it in
on a tray, and you'd never need to beat me, Hailey. . . ."

"You mean you would?" Hailey whispered huskily. "Oh, Jo,
honey. My friend Nate Johnson in Marysville is a Justice of the
Peace among other things. By tonight he could have us spliced
so damned tight, legal, and proper that—"

"Hailey!" she said. "Wait—I didn't mean—Please, Hailey—no!"

"Sorry," he said abruptly. "California fair makes a man wild,
don't it?"

"And a woman," she said honestly. "Or maybe it just brings out
the wildness that's already there. . . ."

She looked at him and her eyes were very clear.

"Listen to me, Hailey," she said. "In the more than two years
since Bruce Harkness left Carolina, I haven't done a single decent

thing. But I'm going to, now. I'm going to say 'No' to you. It's hard to say it. I could learn to love you—most any woman could, I reckon. And it would be so easy to use you as a way to escape my past. . . ."

"Jo—" he said.

"No. Hear me out. Only it wouldn't really be an escape. Because there really isn't any past, or any future, Hailey. They're the same thing, and they kind of melt into one another like one wave in the ocean blends into the next. What I was, I am; what I am, I always will be. I could make you some mighty pretty promises, maybe even mean them while I was saying them. But I wouldn't keep them, because I can't. There's no escaping that, Hailey. Wherever you go, you take yourself with you. And I am," her voice, speaking, was flat, controlled, bleak, "a—a faithless wife, a loose, lustful female. I betrayed my husband, and Bruce Harkness, too, in my mind and heart, a thousand times, long before I came to California. On the boat coming over, I came within inches of betraying them in the flesh. All Rufus King did was to recognize what I was; what I am. If I married you, within a year, maybe less, I'd do the same thing to you. Not because I didn't love you, but out of curiosity, out of boredom, out of the inescapable circumstance of being what I am. . . ."

"Jo, please!" Hailey got out.

"Finally shocked you, didn't I? It's true. I find myself looking at strange men, and wondering how they'd be in that regard. I reckon I never was intended to be a wife. Jo Rogers, the eternal mistress. Only, from now on, I'm going to be my own. I'm going down to Frisco and open a gambling house—an honest house. The men that interest me, I'll take up with, on a strictly temporary basis. When I get tired of one, I'll throw him out. And he'll have to understand from the beginning that's how it'll be. So I can't marry you, Hailey. You're much too fine. You're going somewhere politically, and I'd be the worst hindrance you possibly could have. . . ."

She smiled at him, softly, warmly.

"It'll take me a month to get my affairs in order," she said, leting the husky note steal deliberately into her voice. "Rufe left a will in which I'm mentioned. If you like, I'll move in with you

for that month, with the strict understanding that it will only be
for that length of time. . . ."

Hailey's mouth was a line, bisecting his face.

"No," he said flatly. "Not like that, Jo."

"I thought not," she said calmly. "Come on now; we'd better
ride. . . ."

Six months came and went before Hailey Burke rode up to
Pleasant Valley again. He mounted that trail on an April day
white with blossoms. He knew what he had to do now; there remained only the doing of it.

Bruce was half hidden by the well he was digging when Hailey
rode into the yard. Juana couldn't walk all the way to the Spring
for water. That was quite impossible, now. He hoped the child
would be like her, as coppery as she, as lithe-limbed, perfect . . .
He heard Hailey call and straightened up, his head and shoulders
protruding above the ground.

"Hail!" he roared; "why you old son of a horse thief! Where in
hellsfire have you—"

"I've been busy, boy," Hailey said gravely. "Been putting my
affairs in shape to go away. Came up here to drag you down to
Frisco with me so's we could whoop it up a couple of days before
I sail. That is, if Juana'll let you go. . . ."

Bruce's face fell.

"Lord God, Hail," he said. "That's bad news. Never thought
you'd leave California. Sort of was depending upon you to rally
round and—"

"Oh, I'll be back," Hailey said quickly. "Just a fast trip back
East for three or four months. Been corresponding with a little
filly I used to know in Augusta. Sweet kid as I remember. Her
older brother and I were schoolmates. She's a widow, now, which
I didn't know until I started writing folks back home again out
of pure lonesomeness. It ain't gone too far yet; but I know she's
willing. Sent me this picture. . . ."

Bruce took the daguerreotype and stared at the serene little
heart-shaped face, smiling up from under great masses of black
hair.

"Nice," he said, "very nice. But why don't you just send for her like most of the fellows who're importing wives from back East do? Save yourself a might heap of trouble that way. . . ."

Hailey shook his head.

"No," he said. "Can't do it that way, Hoss. Reckon li'l' Jo plumb put the fear o' God in me far as women are concerned. I got to see this filly first—see how much she's changed. Court her. Get to know her. Slower that way, I'll vow, but a hell of a lot wiser. . . ."

"Reckon you're right," Bruce said. "Still, I was counting on you to—Heck! What am I thinking of? You'll be back by that time . . . By the way, how is Jo? Heard anything of her?"

"From her," Hailey corrected. "She writes me regularly. She's got a gambling palace of her own now, built with the money King left her. Calls it *La Rubia*. That's Spanish for The Blonde, isn't it? Only the boys have already changed that into Ruby's Place. Very popular. She's behaving, or rather misbehaving as usual. I kind of feel sorry for her. Well, old Hoss, can I drag you off to Frisco?"

Bruce frowned.

"That makes it kind of hard, Hailey," he said. "You see, I can't exactly leave Juana right now. . . ."

Hailey looked at him, and his mouth widened into a huge grin.

"No!" he said. "Why bless my soul, ol' Hoss! You got life in you yet! Who th' hell would of thought it!"

Juana came out of the house then, as slim, as glowingly lovely as ever.

"One would think, Señor Burke," she said in an English that amazed Hailey, "that this of our *niño* was to be tomorrow instead of seven months from now. I am very well except for this sickness of the mornings. But he, *Santísima!* He will not let me walk or move or do anything at all. He even stopped me from cooking until we tried to eat that which he had prepared; then, truly, we were sick!"

"Juana, honey," Hailey said. "I'm sorry, but I'm gonna kiss you. I'm so damned happy over this I could bawl like a yearling calf!"

He kissed her, and stepped back, grinning.

Juana smiled at him.

"Now," she said, "I must go and get you some wine and some little cakes that I have made. Then I will leave you two to lie and boast like the little boys all men are at heart. . . ."

"Lord, Bruce," Hailey said, after she had gone inside. "How she can talk good English! Taught her, didn't you?"

"Yep," Bruce said. "But mostly she taught herself. Worked at it every minute of the day and night. . . ."

"Every minute, Hoss?" Hailey mocked.

"Well," Bruce grinned, the peace in him very deep. "Not exactly, Hail. . . ."

"Glad I'm going back home," Hailey said. "Way you look—so all fired happy, makes me twicet as anxious. Don't reckon I can persuade you to come to Frisco with me, now. . . ."

"No, Hail," Bruce said contentedly. "Don't reckon you can. . . ."

Juana sat on the edge of the well, watching Bruce dig. When he straightened up, only his head showed above it, now. Then he climbed slowly out of the well. He was holding something in his hand. He held it out to her, and she saw what it was. She looked at him, her eyes big with remembered terror. Slowly, Bruce smiled.

Then he threw the nugget, bigger than a pigeon's egg, with no base metals or even quartz or anything at all streaking it, the gold a deep, reddish color, entirely pure—back into the well. He picked up the shovel and began to throw the dirt in again, working steadily, but without haste, filling it in.

"I will help you, *mi marido*," Juana said.

"No," Bruce said. "Think of the child, Juana. . . ."

He worked steadily until the well was filled. Then he pounded the earth flat with a post used like a ram. After that, he raked and brushed the spot with branches, leaving them there after he had finished, covering the scar in the ground. In two days, Juana knew, there would remain no sign of digging.

They went into the house, and Juana stretched out on the bed. She lay very quietly in a peace as warm as sunlight, as deep as time itself.

"*Mi Corizon*," Juana said. "My Heart—this of the gold—It was not fear with thee, was it? Tell me it was not fear?"

"No," Bruce said. "Why do you ask me that, Juana?"

"I would not like it to have been fear," she said: "For fear is a thing for women—not for the kind of man thou art. . . ."

"No," Bruce said. "Not fear. But Gold is an evil thing."

He lifted her, raising her up so that she could see out of the window into the last warm wash of sun.

"Of this I have no need, *Paloma*. I know it is a rare way of thinking, but nothing of importance can ever be bought with gold. What, Love, could it bring me that I have not already? For I have already found my treasure, *Juanacita mia*. This—" he pointed through the window, "and thee. . . ."

Juana looked out of the window, seeing the sunlight on the valley, the young corn tossing in the light, Jesus and Josefina moving down the rows, making lovely arcs with their chopping, and then she turned back to him, surging up, seeking his mouth, her own moving upon his, whispering:

"And our *niño*. Add that and thou wilt have right, my soul. . . ."

The End